ROOTS
REVEALED

ROOTS REVEALED

ROOTS RUN DEEP SERIES BOOK 2

TRACY MICHELLE SELLARS

ST JOSEPH, MISSOURI USA

For more information on Tracy Sellars, please visit — VowsToKeep.com

Editor: Debra L. Butterfield
Cover Design: Carrie Dennis Design
Printed in the United States of America.

To my firstborn, Autumn, who searches for truth with all of her heart and compels me to be more passionate for my Savior. Thank you for your undying devotion to our Savior. You make me happy.

"With my whole heart have I sought thee: O let me not wander from thy commandments. Thy word have I hid in mine heart, that I might not sin against thee." Psalm 119:10–11

PROLOGUE

Waterford Cove, Virginia
August 1890

The noise was deafening. As the thoroughbreds' hooves pounded around turn two, the smell of victory hung in front of each gambler like the proverbial carrot. Almost within reach. Almost attainable. The air felt thick with humidity, the promise of money almost as suffocating to those who would risk it all for the promised prize.

Sunshine struck the eyes of Summer Edwards as she tilted her huge straw hat in an effort to hide her face. Her hands shook as she adjusted long white gloves. For the hundredth time, Summer questioned her attire for the day. In an effort to blend in with the debutantes who frequented the track, she had selected a soft silk dress of pale purple. Now sitting among the browns and dark blues of the gamblers' wives, she felt more like a peacock among wrens.

As the horses came around turn three, her heart hammered in her throat like the animals' hooves as they strained toward the finish line. It was all Summer could do to not bring her hands to her ears. Only the stares from a man on the next bench over caused her to keep up her ruse. If she were to finish what she came here for, she must focus on the task at hand. And right now, that included making it seem like she belonged here, that there was nothing unusual about her presence.

Even amidst her jangling nerves, Summer felt a rush of adrenaline. Her parents had taught her that honesty and purity were to be valued above all, but she couldn't help but revel in this subterfuge. Her mother would surely swoon if she knew her baby girl was being ogled like this. But it wasn't her parents' disapproval or the men's stares that made her heart beat erratically. It was the adventure. It was trying to go unnoticed. It was the satisfaction of helping a friend. But if she didn't soon accomplish what she came for, all would be for naught.

A dark brown, almost black steed pushed his nose ahead of another equally impressive piece of horseflesh, bringing the crowd to its feet. Shouts of joy and groans alike mingled as the horses crossed the finish line.

"A fine day for Mr. George Wilson," intoned a small, wiry man sitting in front of Summer. "But an even finer day for me." He patted his shirt pocket as he stood and made his way over to the booths, presumably to collect his money.

Summer glanced around to see if she could spot whom she came to find. Laura, her lady's maid, had told her to look for a man with yellow hair, brown coat, and ratty bowler hat. Why, that could be any number of men here. The benches teamed with a sea of movement, causing Summer to think she may have to find a different route to discover what needed to be disclosed.

She left the bench and stood in the crowd, all the time looking right and left for Laura's brother, Landon Moore. As people jostled each other trying to get their share of the earnings, Summer's hat was nearly knocked from her head. As she wove her way through the masses to the exit gates, she admitted defeat. Summer would have to tell Laura she had failed in her mission.

"I tell you, the money is mine!"

Summer whirled toward the commotion in time to see an angry young man with bulging muscles lift a fellow up by his shirt collar. Summer recognized the man whose feet were dangling off the ground as the one who had sat in front of her.

Surprisingly strong for his size, the smaller man grabbed the other by the neck, and they both went tumbling to the ground in an angry flurry of arms and hats.

The younger man's bowler fell off, revealing shaggy blonde hair. Summer stood gaping at the scene wondering if this is what the pursuit of money did to people. She also wondered if perhaps her search for Landon may have not been in vain after all.

Both men stumbled to their feet. A flash of metal caught Summer's eye as the wiry man drew a knife. His opponent reached into his coat and Summer stifled a scream as a gunshot rang out into the stifling air.

Not wanting to see the scene that followed, but unable to tear her eyes away, Summer watched in horror as the blonde man was brought under submission by the authorities while the other lay in a pool of his own blood.

She had wanted adventure. Longed for more in life besides what was expected. Desired to live beyond herself. But Summer Edwards did not sign up for this. The crowd was in a panic and no strong arms reached out to catch her as she fell into a heap of purple silk

ONE

I am so afraid, Marvin. Just so afraid. Has it come to this? She will find out the truth and we'll be to blame. Why don't we send your brother, Dustin, with her? Someone to make sure she doesn't find out? No, that will never do. Oh, what is to be done?

The snippet of conversation she had once overheard floated vague and uneasy in Summer's mind. "Mama?" Summer thought she formed the word, but it seemed as though her tongue wouldn't cooperate. She thought she could faintly hear her parents' voices as they talked in whispered tones in the dining room. The room reeked of stale cigar smoke. Her mother would never allow such vulgarity in her stately home.

Daring to force her eyes open, Summer realized she was still at the races and someone had carried her to a bench in the track office. She must have fainted during the ruckus.

"Good to see you finally coming around," said a gruff voice. "Need a hand up?"

Summer peered through partially closed eyes at a man sitting behind a desk. "Yes," she managed to say. "Thank you."

Taking the man's rough hand, she swung her feet to the floor and stood slowly, taking a moment to get her bearings. She placed both hands on the doorframe to steady herself and gazed out to the empty area near the pay booths. The track stood deserted; the horrific scene she had witnessed seemed to have vanished into thin air.

"Seems as though you're gonna be just fine, miss. If it's all the same to you, I'll just be heading home. Been a long afternoon 'round here." He grabbed his hat from a hook, and Summer turned her head in his direction in time to catch his expectant look. Yes, he most likely did want to get home. So did she. And the sooner, the better.

With a nod of reassurance, she said, "I'm feeling much better, thank you. I'll just make my way out and take my buggy home. I do appreciate your help today."

"Think nothing of it. I was tempted to faint myself." The man took his leave out the back door of the office, muttering something under his breath.

Summer reached for her reticule that was tucked under her makeshift bench-turned-bed and was about to leave when she heard the murmuring of two voices just beyond her line of sight.

"Here's what I want to know: is this a done deal?" The nervous voice continued, "You promised me no one would know and that I would get the job."

Summer's heart rate picked up as she realized this could have to do with what happened earlier. She took a chance to peep past the doorway and saw a balding, heavyset man wiping his perspiring forehead and looking at a thin man who sported clipped brown hair. The other man's head was turned so she couldn't see his face, but she could just make out the tip of a moustache and a pair of wire-rimmed spectacles.

"Frederick, my man, have no fear. I have this entire situation under control. Moore is in jail, and I left no tracks. I let slip to Moore that Fairbanks was trying to steal his winnings. Ha! What a fool he was to believe that. But rest assured. No one will ever know it wasn't his gun that killed Nigel Fairbanks. You just give me my share, and all will be well." He clapped the heavy man on the shoulder. "In reference to your employment, I can assure you that your services will be more than welcome by George Wilson. He will be in dire straits without Nigel Fairbanks pulling the wool over his eyes." He laughed derisively.

The men's conversation began to fade as they walked away. Summer quickly pressed her back to the wall of the office and tucked her purple skirts to the side, keeping herself hidden as best she could. This would be a perfect time to have borrowed her aunt's latest acquisition, a new-fangled portable camera. If she could capture their likeness on film, she'd be able to turn the photograph into the police.

When their footsteps could no longer be heard, Summer sat down hard on the office bench. But it wasn't simply her residual lightheadedness that had her rubbing her temples. She knew without a doubt she'd have to tell her lady's maid and friend, Laura Moore, that her brother had just been framed for murder.

Elizabeth Anton reached into her reticule once again for her kerchief. She must stop crying. It would never do. Just never do. What was done, was done. But, oh, how she longed to go back in time.

Settling back on the davenport, she tried yet again to read the first paragraph in the book she had borrowed from Summer. The words blurred on the page as her mind traveled back to a time and place she longed to forget and yet cherished to remember.

"I believe her eyes will be green. Just like yours, Lizzy." Elizabeth's sister, Ruth Edwards gazed at the newborn with all the love of a new mother. "I can't wait to get her home and show her off to all our friends."

Elizabeth dropped her gaze to her shaking hands. She could bear the shame no longer. She knew what the future held for her. Pain. Memories. And enough money to drown them both out. She would trade all the banknotes in the world for time shared with her precious baby girl.

But she wasn't a fool. Had never been one, not even now at age seventeen. She knew money would not be the answer for her young daughter. Oh, she was happy that her sister and new brother-in-law would be able to shower the little one with the lavish things in life. But her true wish was for the babe to know love. The love of family. And that was the one thing she couldn't give. Could never give.

And so, she must step back. Walk away and never look back. Stuff this secret deep down where no one would ever be able to find it. Ruth motioned for her husband to grab the suitcases, then mother, father and baby headed for the door.

But there was one thing Elizabeth must know, one final question that needed to be asked. She drew in a deep breath and prayed for the courage to voice what pressed most on her heart. Her voice trembled as she resolutely stood and asked, "What will you call her?"

Marvin Edwards put his arm around his new bride and looked down into the face Elizabeth would forever have etched in her mind. A vise so strong but so sweet wrapped itself around Elizabeth's heart as he whispered one word. "Summer."

Freedom. That was what Summer sought when she came to Virginia to visit her aunt three months ago. She had no idea that when she defied her parents' wishes to travel that she would be forced to witness an ugly murder and the twisted plot that seemed to surround it.

Back in North Carolina, where she was born and raised, life was so much more complicated than it was at her aunt's quiet home. The only daughter of doting parents, she had been trained from a very young age how to be the epitome of elegance and grace. Summer knew just how to receive a caller, how to arrange her hair, and what was appropriate conversation at the dinner table.

Upon coming of age, the expectations had shifted dramatically from predictions of a little girl's future to the demand of foregone conclusions. What used to be the daily chore of welcoming the social elite to tea and attending fashionable balls had turned into the insurmountable task of finding the perfect husband and becoming the perfect wife. The thought of both made her want to run far away. And so, she had.

The seeds of what life could be like away from her parents had taken root last summer when Summer and her mother had accompanied Summer's father, Marvin Edwards, on a business trip to the east coast. The three had spent only half a day visiting Summer's mother's sister, Miss Elizabeth Anton, first going to church and then out to lunch.

The afternoon train had taken the threesome the first leg of their trek, but just as the wheels of the locomotive sped toward North Carolina, wheels of change had begun to turn in Summer's mind. There were things to be discovered in Waterford Cove, Virginia. New memories to make. Wonderful autonomy to be gained. One day, she would return.

On the southwestward journey, Summer had secretly guarded a treasure. She kept it inside her dress pocket and would bring it out to study when she was alone. It was a small, circular photograph glued onto a square piece of cardboard. A picture her aunt had taken of a sailboat heading out to stormy seas. An enormous storm looked like it would swallow the small craft, but to Summer, the scene represented dreams she held deep inside. The dream of one day having her own adventures. To sail on waters uncharted. She pledged silently to herself that someday soon, she would make a bold move and set out on the open seas of life. And even when dark clouds loomed and storms raged, she would be brazen and content, face to the wind. Just like her Aunt Elizabeth. This photograph she considered her most prized possession, for it fueled the flame that had been kindled upon her visit to Virginia.

Summer was told that at the age of five, she had met her aunt but try as she might, Summer could not conjure up any lingering memories of the beautiful woman. Once, when she was about twelve years old, her mother had shown her a picture of Aunt Elizabeth. The photograph was blurry at best. Then came the moment Elizabeth had greeted them in the vestibule at church one Sunday morning just a year ago. Summer had felt a kindred spirit with her aunt at once and the afternoon passed too quickly. Summer regrettably said goodbye to Elizabeth but was encouraged by the gift of the photograph and her aunt's promise to write. Elizabeth had been true to her word and with letters exchanged over the miles, Summer felt she was finally getting the chance to know this distant relative.

Now, as if the letters themselves had worn a path for her, she was finally in Virginia. No parents looking over her shoulder, making sure she acted just so. No butler accounting for her every hour of the day. No presumptions in anticipation of what she could bring to the family.

None of that. It was all behind her now and what lay ahead was a sea of the sweet freedom of possibilities.

To be sure, living as a daughter of one of North Carolina's most prominent businessmen had its perks, but an arranged marriage forged together for mere prestige and money held no appeal for Summer. No. She wanted love. The kind of love that wasn't planned out, that didn't make sense. The kind that set her senses reeling.

Summer knew her parents had their eye on several of the men who moved within their circles. A few of them had even been brought over for dinner in hopes of catching Summer's eye. What those overgrown boys didn't know was that they would have to capture her heart first. So, Summer had found a flaw with each of them, promising her parents she would soon make a decision. Time and her parents' patience were running out.

Elizabeth's last letter had saved the day. She had written of a young man from her church who would be an ideal candidate for a husband. Summer had come under the pretext of being courted by the man, but secretly hoped their connection would not work out. Garrett Cole had proven to be a true gentleman, but Summer was exceptionally grateful when she learned that Garrett was already in love with someone else.

When Mr. Cole had explained he could not be a participant in the nonexistent courtship, Summer wrote to her parents and explained the situation. She had also all but told them she was going to stay in Waterford Cove longer than originally planned. Anything to extend this little bit of independence she had found. That was now several months ago.

How wonderful it had been to spread her wings there in Virginia. Her aunt cared for her, she knew, but Elizabeth also treated Summer like an adult and did not watch her every move as her parents had done. Summer had a sense that Elizabeth was an explorer at heart but also observed she was afraid to venture too far from home. Most days, Elizabeth could be found drinking tea and keeping to herself in the parlor or the library of her beautiful home. But the pictures hanging on every wall and down every hall hinted at her aunt's true heart. Framed photographs of faraway places with craggy rock outcroppings or deep mountain snow. Pictures of the Wild West and its famed cowboys and horses. Hand-drawn landscapes that lured the onlooker into their unknown exploits. Pictures, pictures everywhere. They were what captured Summer's attention on entering Aunt Elizabeth's home for the first time, and Summer had commented on them at once. Her aunt had avoided answering and then noticeably changed the subject, clearly communicating that the subject was off-limits.

Summer hadn't let it bother her. In this new place, she felt free to come and go as she pleased and pursue some of the things she had always longed to do. Things her parents would never approve of. She had been jubilant when she had been able to convince Aunt Elizabeth to come along on one of her escapades.

Summer held the reins and guided the buggy absentmindedly toward Elizabeth's house as she mentally inventoried her latest feats. Learning to drive a buggy. Paying a captain to take her on a day's journey up to Cape Charles. Riding a velocipede on the streets of Waterford Cove. Taking a picnic lunch near a beautiful lake without an escort in sight. And the many, many hours she had volunteered, laying the groundwork for a fledgling orphanage.

Turning the buggy onto Lumière Square, Summer again admired her aunt's affluent neighborhood. But it was high time to stop letting her mind wander. She needed to prepare herself for the task at hand. She climbed down and handed the reins to Matthew, one of Elizabeth's trusted staff. Making her way through the back door, she knew she should let Elizabeth know she was home, but she wasn't ready to face the music just yet. She needed to get her thoughts in order before she had to break the bad news to Laura, the only other staff Aunt Elizabeth kept on hand besides a part-time cook and Matthew, who took care of all things out-of-doors. Running quickly up the back staircase of the beautiful two-story brick home, she reached her room and closed the door behind her.

Smoothing down the dress she had worn to the races, Summer noted the purple silk didn't look any worse for wear. But changing into different attire might serve her well. It did tend to draw attention. When Laura came in, Summer would ask for help undoing the buttons in the back. Laura was the only one who knew where she had been this afternoon. Summer's breath caught in her throat at a sudden thought. What if she were made to be a witness in a murder trial? Her parents would practically disown her if they knew of her presence at a horse race.

The room felt very warm all of a sudden, causing Summer to rip off her gloves and reach for a painted fan. She must do everything in her power to never let anyone but Laura know the information she had gleaned today. At all costs, she must keep this to herself.

Summer sat down on the edge of the bed and closed her eyes as the fan made circles of much-needed air around her face. Her parents would conclude she wasn't capable of making wise decisions and would keep her under tighter rules and regulations. She could see everything clearly now. Her future was on the line.

Status, opinion, and money were what mattered to her folks. And a strong-willed daughter who did not follow the rules was not what they had anticipated for their future. Or hers. A vision passed before her mind's eye in the form of a sparkling wedding dress and a loveless marriage. If her parents became privy to this information, Summer would be married off to the first available well-to-do fellow who offered his suit to her. No matter that Summer had sought to help a friend in need. No, that would not make any difference in how they felt. She would be considered a ninny without a good head on her shoulders, and all decisions from here on out would be made by her parents or future husband.

Summer shook her hair out of its pins and let the straight blonde tresses fall across her shoulders into her line of vision. Crossing the room, she perused the closet in search of another dress. This taste of freedom here in Virginia had whetted her appetite for more. More adventure. More of being on her own and making her own decisions. Now all that she sought might be thrown out the window simply because she had made a new friend and lent a hand in time of need.

A soft knock at the door and the creaking of hinges told Summer it was time to face the music. Laura entered the room, looking timid and unsure. She turned and closed the door softly behind her. "I thought I heard you come in the back."

It was a statement but Summer recognized the question in her eyes. "Oh, Laura," Summer began slowly.

But that was enough for the astute maid. She buried her face in her hands for a moment. "I knew it. I just knew it! Landon promised he wasn't going to the track. He promised he was saving our hard-earned money to buy a home, something substantial. Something that would show he was a good, honest man."

Summer's heart sank, but she prayed silently for the courage to tell Laura the truth was much worse than either of them would ever have predicted.

Sitting down on the edge of the bed, Summer looked up at sweet, innocent Laura. A girl who wouldn't hurt a flea. "Sit down for a minute. I have something to tell you." The words sounded like the pounding of a judge's gavel in a court of law. So final. No going back. Neither for her nor for Laura. Summer shook her head in distress. She could not give up her independence. She just couldn't do it. Taking a deep breath, she decided she needed a bit more time to sort this all out. "I did see Landon at the track. He was involved in an altercation, and I believe he's being held in jail as we speak."

Laura's face turned from white to red in a heartbeat. "So," she said almost to herself, "he *has* been lying to me." Her back went rigid and Summer thought she had never seen her friend look more agitated and upset. She turned eyes blazing with fire onto Summer.

"What a lowdown thing to do. When I checked our bank account last week and found there was no money left, I knew I couldn't believe a word he said. He promised me he'd take my pay and make sure it was deposited." She wrung her hands and stood to pace the room. "I was such a fool to think he had changed his ways. This is how it was after our parents passed away. Always finding some way to gamble away anything we had managed to earn. I was a fool to believe every lying word he's said to me and now he's squandered everything." She stopped in front of Summer. "What exactly did he do to get the police onto him? Or do I even want to know?"

It was the out Summer had been hoping for. She forced a small laugh. "No, you probably don't want to know."

"Then tell me tomorrow. He can just sit in that cell all night with no visitors and let his dishonesty marinate for a bit." Laura stood still for a moment, then brushed down the front of her dress, straightened her collar, and turned a placid face to Summer. All traces of her fury had been tucked away and she was once again the household staff, ready to help. "May I assist you with your dress before I tend to a matter for your aunt, Miss Summer?"

"That would be lovely. Thank you."

Summer chose a dark green dress she felt was suitable for visiting the children at the orphanage tonight. After Laura had done up the buttons and Summer was alone once again, a small but noticeable prick in her spirit gave her pause. Summer recognized it as her heavenly Father speaking to her. She vacillated briefly before bowing her head and acknowledging that although she professed she wanted her own way, when push came to shove, she would yield to the Lord. Despite her longings for freedom and the life that came with it, she would do the right thing.

Suddenly, Summer's selfishness stared her boldly in the face. How could she look into her friend's eyes tomorrow and tell her she couldn't go to the police with the information that would absolve Landon from all guilt just so she could marry whomever she wanted? Summer breathed a quick prayer of forgiveness for her attitude. She would do what she had to do.

TWO

Christian Titus leafed through the thick ream of papers he kept in his satchel. Today would be his last day on the road, and by this afternoon, he would reach his destination. The papers felt weighty in his hand. He glanced through the key aspects of the case even though he didn't need another review; he knew every word by heart. If he could sum up the whole stack in one word, it would be this: deception. And that was the one thing he could not abide. Just the thought of the word made his blood boil. His past had been ruled by it. Now his one goal was to annihilate any lie that stood in the way of truth.

Putting the papers back in his bag, Christian packed up his camp and made ready to head for the coastal Virginian town of Waterford Cove. By this time tomorrow, his next mission would begin. But much to his consternation, he knew he would be forced to use what he despised in order to bring about justice. A temporary disguise cloaking the essence of who he was. But he would do what had to be done. And in the end, an entire town would be the better for it. Christian settled his hat on his head to shield the morning's light and steered Sadie onto the roadway. His short-lived duplicity was a small price to pay.

The salty air came off the ocean as Christian Titus made his way into an area near Waterford Cove's docks. Tonight, he would take a room at a boarding house and get a good night's sleep. The last job had taken longer than expected, and he hadn't been able to regroup at his own home before heading to his next assignment. Hopefully the inn's beds were comfortable, for he needed to be fresh in the morning. A sharp mind and a ready tongue would serve him well as he applied for employment at the home of the notable George Wilson, former governor and current candidate for senator.

Men who'd had too much to drink that muggy August evening littered the boardwalks as Christian found a livery to keep Sadie for the night. Riders on horses vied with buggies in an attempt to make the road their own. Women who plied themselves for trade made their services available to any sailor or businessman who would look their way. It appeared the boarding house that the Agency was paying for wasn't in the seemliest part of town. Ah, well. In the morning he could put this behind him and tomorrow night be warm and snug in one of George Wilson's bunkhouses.

"Anyone here?" he called. The livery held many horses yet appeared to be unattended.

When no one answered, Christian tied Sadie to a hitching post inside the open-aired building, then watered and fed her. It always amazed him how people treated their animals like they didn't have needs. Christian took pride in tending what was in his care. His horse had come to him abused and underfed. It had been his honor to bring her back to health and life. The mistreatment of animals angered him almost as much as deceit did. Almost. Unfortunately, Mr. George Wilson encompassed both of these unfortunate attributes. The man owned numerous racehorses and made a fat profit using horseflesh for his own personal gain. Many would not consider racing horses to be cruel, but Christian had a different opinion.

"You looking for a place to stay too, mister?" came the question in the half dark of the livery. A boy, not much older than fourteen, appeared in suspenders and dirty brown pants.

Christian sized up the young man. "You the keeper?"

"Sure am, mister. That is, when Pa's away at the races." The boy's eyes lit with excitement. "Wish I was old enough to go along. I could take a day's pay and turn it into a week's! Then I wouldn't have to hang around a place like this." He kicked at the hay littering the walkway.

Christian wished he could set the youngster straight on the effects of throwing good money away on such an activity, but he didn't feel he would be within his rights. "I think I've already got a place, but if you could keep my horse for the night, I'd be much obliged. I've already watered and fed her, but her brush is in the saddlebag if you wouldn't mind giving her a good once over."

Christian tossed the boy a coin and gave his horse a final pat. As he walked toward the boardinghouse, Christian thought of himself at that age. Oh, the places life could take a man in just a few short years.

He had been on his own since he was fourteen, trying to make it alone in the world. His father had been the king of lies, swindling his way into and out of one shady transaction after another. Christian's poor mother had put up with it all, doing her best to keep food in her son's stomach. But all his father's fiddling with the family's finances had cheated Christian and his mother out of a decent life.

Christian had decided to take matters into his own hands just as soon as he could. He left home, determined to make his life count for something and use integrity as his badge of honor along the way.

He had done pretty well, too, until she came along. Tabitha. Every time thoughts of her came to mind, they taunted him with their cruelty. Christian had been so blinded by puppy love that he had up and married her before he knew who she really was. And now he was going back to the city where their tragic story had begun.

He had been totally blindsided when Tabitha had left without warning. Some days he felt as though he was still recovering. That had been ten years ago and Christian prided himself on not being dumb enough to fall for that kind of woman again. Yet sadness still tore at him when he thought of the letter he had received from one of her friends several months after she left. Tabitha and the baby he hadn't even known about had both perished in an especially difficult labor only a short train ride away from his home.

The circumstance had burned him, leaving him with an insatiable desire to uncover the lies that ripped people apart. To discover the truth about a situation; a situation that from the outside seemed perfect, yet inside held a deeper secret. His experience with Tabitha had fueled a fire already kindled, one started by his father. Life had not been fair, but his job gave him the opportunity to right some of the wrongs in the world, and most of the time, that was enough.

And so, tomorrow morning, he would begin a new assignment. A quest to expose the lies this city seemed to hold. He couldn't wait to get started.

Elizabeth came down the stairs of her two-story brick Victorian home to find Summer seated in the parlor. Muted pastel tones graced the room, the feminine decor a result of never having a man in the home.

A mirror in the hallway gave Elizabeth the opportunity to check her hair before greeting Summer. She gazed back at her reflection in silent contemplation. Fair skin with a splash of freckles, light blonde hair piled high on her head, and a figure that reflected her willpower to not eat too many tea cakes. But at thirty-eight, Elizabeth had resolved her life was useless. Unmarried, lonely, and guilty of unacceptable sin, she knew it didn't matter what her outward appearance looked like. No one would ever want her as a wife. She had no other choice but to live out the rest of her days knowing what was done, was done. Regret wasn't strong enough to turn back the clock.

Summer seemed preoccupied as she gazed out onto Lumière Square. Eight homes made up the unique block, and Elizabeth enjoyed the common garden that graced the center of the square. But although the neighborhood was held in prestige in Virginian society, Elizabeth knew it came at a high price. Too high a price.

Pasting a smile on her face, Elizabeth greeted the younger woman.

"What thoughts take you away, my dear?" Elizabeth hoped she could lend an ear to Summer. How she longed to reach out to her and connect in some way. They had shared many an afternoon tea and had gone out and about together on occasion. But Elizabeth ached for a friendship to form between them. She told herself to just give it time.

Summer turned toward her, and Elizabeth caught her breath as she realized once again how much Summer's presence here affected her.

"Aunt Elizabeth. I didn't hear you come in." Summer settled her skirts around her and reached for a cup of tea. "Are you in need of respite? I could have Laura bring another cup."

Elizabeth wavd her hand in an air of dismissal, declining the offer. "Actually, I was coming to ask you if you wouldn't mind taking me to the orphanage this evening."

At the surprised look on Summer's face, Elizabeth laughed softly. "I know, I haven't been too keen on wanting to accompany you in the past, but as they say, wonders never cease. I just thought it would be nice to see the work you have been doing down there. It will help me get to know you better if I understand your interests."

"I was planning on heading over there after dinner." Summer smiled, a smile so like her own. "I would be happy to show you. Remember, though, it's just the temporary location until the King's Castle is finished. And its current location isn't in a very nice part of town."

Elizabeth sincerely hoped Summer didn't think her too snobbish to go into the factory district. True, Elizabeth had never been to that particular area, but this situation called for an exception. It was important she take every opportunity to connect with Summer. In fact, it was more than important. As the days passed on, Elizabeth felt it was imperative.

The carriage rolled along past shoddy homes tucked between factories with billowing smokestacks, and Summer turned to her aunt to gauge her reaction to their surroundings. Elizabeth seemed to be taking in the scene of children in rags and women doing the wash in the waning evening light. Even in the twilight, it was easy to see the squalor in which these people lived.

It was for the parentless children who lived in such desolate conditions that Summer volunteered her time and energy. The orphanage ministry had sprung from her aunt's church, and Summer had gotten involved from the first time she had heard of the need. It had been her pleasure to help Garrett Cole and Justine Davidson get the project off the ground. Summer thought again of her relief that Garrett was indeed not available for courtship. Summer had worked side-by-side with Garrett and Justine and felt they were perfect for one another. She was glad things worked out the way they did. She considered them both good friends and was happy to help their endeavors to champion the orphans of Waterford Cove.

"Oh, I wish Uncle Dustin could see this," Summer said. "He would be so impressed by all the inventions being produced in mass quantities down here. Isn't it exciting?"

"Yes. Dusty." Elizabeth's face took on a far-away look as she answered Summer's question. "I wonder what he is up to now."

Summer raised an eyebrow at the familiar use of her uncle's name but was even more surprised to see Elizabeth's face flush a bright red.

Elizabeth ducked her head and fiddled with a button on the leather upholstered seat. "Dustin and I used to be close, but we grew apart a long time ago."

This was news to Summer. "When was the last time you saw him?"

Elizabeth put a hand to her throat. "Goodness. I was unable to attend your parents' wedding, so it must have been about six months before that."

Summer's brow furrowed as she considered these new revelations. Why had her aunt not been able to attend the wedding of her own sister? *How odd.* Summer's mother had shared little about her sister's life and for the first time, Summer wondered if there were secrets to be discovered. Could this newly revealed detail about Dustin and Aunt Elizabeth be her next undercover quest?

Before she could formulate a question to voice her thoughts, Matthew stopped the carriage and helped the ladies disembark, abruptly putting an end to the conversation. So much for prying into the past.

Summer and Elizabeth stood gazing up at the factory that was serving as a temporary orphanage until Garrett and Justine completed construction on the King's Castle. It was hard to believe before this orphanage was organized the homeless children of Waterford Cove had nowhere to go. Now with donations from the church, numerous contributors from around the city, and Garrett and Justine's selfless caretaking, it looked as if the children would be very well provided for.

"It still amazes me that the previous owner of this place, Eric Waverly, employed children and paid them atrocious wages, not even enough to buy the food they needed to survive. They had to go scrounging for food, many times resorting to thievery." Summer shook her head. "Unbelievable."

"But look at it now," Elizabeth commented as they opened the door.

Beds with fresh sheets lined the walls on three sides, while a temporary kitchen and dining hall occupied the other. In the middle of the vast room, comfortable davenports and settees that had been donated made up a makeshift parlor. Wooden toys and handmade dolls were being loved on and played with by the clean and well-fed children who occupied the floor.

"You've done good work, Summer." Elizabeth took Summer's hand in hers and gave it a squeeze. "I'm so proud of you."

Summer smiled in return. It did her heart a world of good to know she had played a part in making the orphanage a reality, but she felt warmed to her toes on hearing her aunt's words of affirmation.

The old factory offices had been turned into the nursery area, and Summer led Elizabeth in that direction. The babies were by far her favorite to visit, and she was anxious to see how the little ones were thriving and growing.

A young girl named Amber whom Summer had gotten to know in recent weeks was helping the babies' caretaker. Elizabeth hung back by the doorway and watched as Summer said hello to her new little friend and then swung a little one up into her arms. He had black curls that near to covered his ears and dark brown eyes framed by thick lashes. "Isn't he sweet?" she asked her aunt.

Elizabeth's face had gone from the red it was in the carriage to a ghostly white. Maybe she wasn't feeling good. Summer would make her visit quick even though she felt she could stay all night.

When she set the baby back on the soft carpet, Amber handed her a small bundle. "She's just come to us yesterday. Got dropped off at the doorway without so much as a note." The girl looked from Summer to the baby and back again. "Come here, Lucy!" she said to another little helper. "They look like twins, don't they?"

A cry that belongs especially to newborns filled the room as Summer tried to make the little one comfortable. Within moments, the wee babe had quieted and Summer got a good look at her face. Sure enough, soft blue eyes that might be green one day stared back at her while wisps of blonde hair graced the top of her head. Summer was just about to ask her aunt's opinion on the matter, but looked up to find she was gone.

Handing the baby back to the caretaker, Summer went in search of Elizabeth. She found her standing outside, taking huge, heaving breaths.

Summer placed a hand on Elizabeth's shoulder and could feel the woman shaking. "Aunt Elizabeth, what is it? Are you ill?"

Elizabeth turned red-rimmed eyes toward Summer. "No, no, I am fine." Summer could see she was trying to pull herself together. "Just needed a bit of fresh air is all. What do you say we head back home, hmm?"

By the time the carriage was rolling along, Elizabeth seemed her old self again. Summer couldn't imagine what had caused such a reaction. It appeared to have something to do with that new baby, but Summer couldn't fathom what. Boldly, yet gently, Summer asked, "Would you like to talk about it?"

Elizabeth grasped Summer's hand for the second time that night, catching her by surprise. "I can't, Summer. But know this. I am so glad you have come to visit and my true wish is to know you better. Please consider this an open invitation to come to me about anything, anytime."

Summer was completely taken aback by her aunt's forthrightness. At the same time, it was extremely refreshing. She had been raised to keep her feelings to herself, and the society that surrounded her did the same. But there was something about her aunt that invited an openness, called out for a bond. And Summer would be happy to oblige. But not yet. If Elizabeth wasn't ready to talk about what had upset her in the orphanage, Summer's secret could wait too.

Suddenly the day's events came rushing back to her mind. The secrecy, the heart-thumping adventure, witnessing a murder, overhearing incriminating information. Summer wished she could share it all with her aunt, wished she didn't have to carry her burden alone. Instead, she pushed the images and feelings inside, knowing she needed more time to process everything that had happened.

The sharing would have to be put off, at least until tomorrow.

THREE

The wind picked up outside her guest room window as Summer turned over for the countless time in the down bedding. The breeze brought in a much-needed respite from the heavy summer air. Oh, how Summer longed for the cool days of autumn. Fall had always been Summer's favorite season. But after tomorrow's confession, she wouldn't be in Virginia long enough to get a taste of it in this new place. No, by the time the leaves turned, she'd be back within view of the North Carolina woods.

Flipping over yet again didn't provide the comfort she sought and instead only served to wrap her nightgown more tightly around her. Summer resolved to lay flat on her back for however long it took to fall asleep. Adjusting her nightgown and pillows, she settled in and tried to calm her mind. But it mocked her as it raced with thoughts of the morrow when she would go to the authorities with the information she alone held.

What would the police ask her? What if she couldn't answer their questions? Summer started to roll to her side but caught herself. She had to get some sleep if she was going to be sharp in the morning. Closing her eyes, she tried to imagine herself at the police station. She would approach the desk and ask to speak to the officer in charge. He would want to know, of course, what a woman of her standing had been doing at a horse race. Heat would fill her face as she would try to explain her reasoning. He would then proceed to ask her what she saw and heard and question her as to why she had waited until the following day to share her knowledge.

Since arriving at her aunt's home after the race, Summer had done a stellar job of not thinking about the horrid incident. Every time it had come to her mind—the shouting, the greed, the anger, the blood—Summer had busied herself with another task. Going to the orphanage had proven to be a smart diversion. The situation had only crossed her mind momentarily during the conversation in the carriage. But once they had arrived back home, Summer had excused herself to her room, even refusing to let Laura help her undress and get ready for bed.

She knew, though, that in the morning, the police would require every last detail of what she saw. She began to roll over yet again, but a verse came to her mind. The general gist was about a lazy man rolling over on his bed. Well, Summer wasn't lazy, that she knew. But another verse quickly made its way into her thoughts, one that made her squirm with its pointed truth.

"Be careful for nothing; but in every thing by prayer and supplication with thanksgiving let your requests be made known unto God."

Ah, yes. One of the first verses she had committed to memory as a child. She would sit on a tall stool in Uncle Dustin's workshop, her long legs dangling while he taught her the ways of Christ. Summer had been more than willing to soak up his knowledge and love for the Lord. Then, what had once been childhood stories from a beloved relative soon turned into a faith of her own.

Be careful for nothing. She knew it meant she should not be anxious. That indicated a lack of trusting God. Hmm. It seemed that wasn't going very well.

Suddenly, she had a thought. Maybe if she wrote down everything she knew of the altercation, it would serve to clarify things for her and she could finally fall asleep. Summer got out of bed, went to a small writing desk in her guest room and lit a lamp. As she formulated her thoughts, an idea occurred to her. If she wrote everything down in detailed manner, tomorrow she could simply hand the paper to the officer and be on her way. That was a fool-proof way to avoid the inevitable censure and awkward confrontation she would have with her parents when they came to fetch her and bring her home. All embarrassment would be avoided, and Aunt Elizabeth would remember Summer as a blossoming young woman who could take care of herself, not an immature girl who needed to be watched by her parents.

Oh, who was she fooling? Just because she wrote down what she saw wouldn't make her any less liable to testify in a court of law. The truth would come out, her parents would still know what happened and Summer's future would be put on the chopping block. But she could still write down what she remembered to keep the details straight.

Closing her eyes, she tried to conjure up images of the horrible afternoon. The race had been a blur with her nerves taking center stage. Then that man in front of her indicated he had won and mentioned something about George Wilson. Wasn't that the former governor of Virginia? Well, there was something. The next thing she remembered was the man who had been in front of her fighting with another man who claimed the money was his. And before anyone could break it up, the blonde man had reached into his coat pocket and a shot had gone off. Wait. If her memory served her correctly, his hand had still been reaching inside his coat when the shot rang through the air. That didn't make sense.

Her mind was spinning just as it had when she'd opened her eyes on the bench at the track. She had heard two men deep in discussion as she had stood there listening. She never had the chance to see the one man's face, but would describe him as being lean with closely cut brown hair. And when he'd turned just slightly, she had seen the edge of a pair of wire rim glasses and a thick, brown mustache. The bald, heavier man was named Frederick, and Summer was sure she could pick him out of a crowd. He had seemed anxious, and Summer racked her mind to think of the exact wording of their conversation. Snippets came to her in bits and pieces.

No one will ever know it was not his gun that killed Nigel Fairbanks. The thin man was referring to Landon Moore, her lady's maid's brother. That proved it was a set up. But why frame someone for murder? He had also said something about this Frederick fellow taking the dead man's job. Would someone really murder another just for the sake of employment? Both men had been well-dressed, so maybe this whole ordeal involved money. Perhaps a great deal of it.

There was one other portion of information she felt she was missing. Summer sent up a prayer of supplication, asking for her Father's wisdom and help. Her eyes flew open as she again remembered the name George Wilson. This Nigel Fairbanks who had been murdered uttered the name George Wilson just moments before he was shot. Then the two conspirators had mentioned George Wilson's name shortly after the man was dead. Surely this was not a coincidence. Summer thanked the Lord for bringing this to her memory. She picked up the quill, dipped it into ink and began to write.

But as the first few paragraphs on the page began to take shape, so did an idea in Summer's mind. An idea so preposterous, it could be called absurd. A plan so absurd, it could be called impossible. A plan so impossible, it could only be made viable by God Himself. Yet even with the odds stacked against her, something in Summer's heart came alive as she stopped writing and tore the paper into a hundred tiny bits. Tomorrow suddenly looked brighter, her future viewed in a whole new light. Yes, if this plan worked, tomorrow would be a new day, not a day of going back to a self-made prison, but a day of looking straight into the storm, face to the wind. A day of sweet freedom.

The sun was just making its early morning ascent as Christian peeked out through the rented room's window that overlooked a small park. He could see the dew lingering on the green grass that dared to show its face through the fallen leaves of last night's wind. Christian let the curtain drop. Usually, dawn was a welcome sight. But not today. Between the storm and the excitement of a new job, Christian had been awake more of the night than he cared to admit.

He quickly made ready for the day, packed his travel bag, and returned his room key. Looking Sadie over at the stables, Christian could see the young livery boy had done a good job brushing his horse down last night. Sadie's glossy red-brown coat gleamed in the morning's rays. However, the boarding house had lived up to Christian's expectations. Hot, loud, and uncomfortable. But that was behind him now. It was time to get to work.

Christian took pride in having honed his undercover skills in the years since he had joined the Pinkertons. His knew his brown hair, brown eyes, and medium build blended into the scenery the same as his demeanor did. Sure, he was generally a driven fellow with little time for the niceties of society. But he could make conversation with anyone, be it a governor or common scullery maid and had made an art of being able to fade into the background of any scenario.

The Pinkerton National Detective Agency was extremely choosy with whom they trusted for their detective work. Many who joined the agency worked as personal security guards for high-profile citizens or government officials. Others acted as strikebreakers in the event of a labor unrest.

Christian sat a little straighter in his saddle when he remembered the day he was chosen to investigate an assumed assassination plot against then President Arthur. Since that assignment almost eight years ago, he had been trusted with prestigious undercover detective work and was considered one of the best in the agency. As a result, he had received assignments all over the country and even as far as Europe.

Murder plots, kidnappings, and extortion schemes made up much of what Christian did in his duties. But this particular job excited him like no other. If the truth could be brought to light, a corrupt political voice would be silenced. George Wilson had much influence in his arena and should the supposed accusations be true, the former governor's voice would no longer be heard in Washington. Many people would be the better for it, for no one needed a cheat for a leader.

But Christian would have to be crafty to catch this particular cat at play. And if the counterfeit money operation headed by George Wilson had been going on as long as rumor indicated, this cat was sure to be an expert at covering his tracks.

Christian adjusted his work coat collar, then tightened his grip on Sadie's reins, anything to distract himself from itching his newly grown facial hair. A goatee, some called it. But being required to put on a disguise for his role as an undercover agent for the Pinkertons, Christian needed to put aside his own feelings on the matter. Truth was what he sought. It was the driving force behind his desire to do his job. But masquerading as someone else always left a bad taste in his mouth. It brought to mind his past, Tabitha, and the unborn baby she had taken with her.

Tabitha had worn a mask of sorts. A bright smile to cover up her dark heart. An attractive body to camouflage a calloused soul.

So be it then if he had to feign different personalities and images to do his job. They were merely means to an end.

"Just a little farther, Sadie." George Wilson's estate was located about a fifteen-minute ride out of town. Christian caught sight of a long country lane flanked by massive oaks on either side. *How fitting.* A grand entrance for a grand thief.

Summer knew she had an ally in Uncle Dustin. When she needed someone to listen to her, Uncle Dustin had always been there to offer the wisest advice. He also did not hold to the many traditions of the family. Her father's younger brother, Dustin tended to go against the family's long-held way of life. When they shunned him for speaking his mind, he would just smile graciously and continue in his train of thought. If they frowned on his wonderful sense of humor, he would simply do something silly to try yet again to make them laugh. His love for science and experimenting with gadgets served him well in his manufacturing business, and Summer admired him for not wearing a stuffy suit and sitting behind a desk all day like her father did.

No, Dustin did not fit the standard mold of North Carolina high society. But that was one of Summer's favorite things about the man. He took the life he had been handed at birth, and rather than kowtow to what was expected, he became his own person, all the while not caring a whit what others thought. After spending as many hours in his shop as her mother would allow, Summer held a deep respect for the godly man she knew as Uncle.

Uncle Dustin had also taught her that people were people. One did not rank above another in God's eyes, so why should social class and status matter here on Earth? He often quoted Scripture where Jesus ate with tax collectors and talked with prostitutes and lepers. Summer felt she had learned this particular life lesson from her uncle and it had great reward. She felt she could talk to anyone, no matter their background or the size of their bank account. Even at her home in North Carolina, where social class was strictly observed, Summer had befriended many of the staff. Her parents never approved of such associations. *It is not permitted to socialize with those who are beneath you,* she had heard on more than one occasion. So, even though Summer had a way with others, she was still in disbelief that when she'd laid out her plan this morning that Laura had agreed to it.

Her lady's maid was surprised to hear the account of what went down at the horse race but her anger at her brother's dishonesty prevented her from being overly alarmed. When Laura heard Summer's plan to try and ferret out more information before going to the police, she was hesitant at first but promised to give it a fair chance and told Summer she'd be visiting Landon that afternoon to hear his side of the story.

Summer's heart beat fast in anticipation of the day ahead. She tried not to second guess her ruse, instead choosing to focus on her disguise.

"I wish you luck, Miss Summer," Laura offered as Summer made her way out of the room. The maid wiped her eyes but smiled bravely and waved her hanky in a farewell gesture.

Summer's stomach fluttered in a most unsettling manner as she crept ever so softly down the stairs of Aunt Elizabeth's home. *Lord, I pray I am right in that I am sensing You're leading me to do this.* Summer had never prided herself of knowing the Lord's will, but last night as she had composed her thoughts, something almost supernatural took hold of her, giving fresh hope for the future. Maybe the circumstance she was placing herself into this morning was a result of her own willful nature, but she hoped it wasn't. She sincerely wanted to do the right thing. For Laura, for Landon, and for herself.

She hadn't told her aunt where she was going and could only pray Elizabeth would not ask too many questions when Summer came home later that day. Summer had decided that if anyone asked her what the truth was, she would not lie to them. But was omission of the truth the same as being dishonest?

The foyer clock read seven fifteen, and Summer hadn't seen her aunt up and about yet this morning. Laura knew Summer's whereabouts and since Cook was at market purchasing her goods for the day, Summer knew she was free to escape the house without being noticed. The driver, Matthew, wouldn't be around at this hour, of that she was sure.

Her favorite horse, a beautiful black mare, nickered as she entered the stable behind the house. "Good morning to you too, Miss Bess," Summer greeted as she tied on her baggage. If only she knew exactly where George Wilson's house was located. Ah, well, she could always stop and inquire. She knew the general direction of the estate and figured she would happen upon another rider on the road.

"Awfully early in the morning to be heading out, isn't it, Miss Edwards?"

Summer's heart jumped into her throat, beating twice its normal speed. "Matthew," she gasped. "I didn't expect to see you this early in the day." She tried to take a calming breath and hoped her face didn't show anything amiss.

He held up two buckets of feed and shrugged his big shoulders. "Sorry I startled you, Miss. You can always find me here tending the horses, seeing to the day's work." He grinned, revealing a gap in his smile. "Someone's gotta get up early 'round here."

Nodding politely seemed to be the best option for not responding to his inquiry. "Mind if I take Miss Bess out for a while?" Summer finished tying her bag to the horse and quickly mounted.

The big man shook his head. "Don't mind a bit. Where you off to so early?" Matthew persisted.

Her palms were sweating as she grabbed the reins. "Just to see to some business."

Matthew tipped his hat and Summer sighed inaudibly. *That was close.* He had asked where she was going and Summer resisted to answer. Guilt tugged at her heart. This wasn't going as well as she had planned. She had thought that if asked, she would tell the truth at all costs. But she hadn't even made it off of the property before she was tested. And clearly, she had not passed.

The morning sun was rising as she made her way north and west out of town. Just as she had hoped, a young man on the road gave her precise directions to the former governor George Wilson's estate. What she needed now was a nice little spot in the trees, tucked away from peering eyes, in which to change her dress. She doubted George Wilson's butler would hire a fancy dressed socialite for a housekeeper. A smile crept over her face at the thought of putting on a different persona today. She and Laura were about the same size, and Laura had wanted to help by loaning her a simple dress. It was, after all, her brother's incarceration on the line.

The trees had thinned out and Summer was giving up hope of finding a place to change. George Wilson's long, tree-lined driveway came into view. But a small copse of dense trees jutted out behind a rock near the entrance to the drive. Perfect. Summer led the horse behind the rock and dismounted. If she got the job, she would have to come here daily and change. She couldn't be seen leaving her aunt's house in maids' garb.

The thrill that overtook her heart as she put the finishing touches on her attire tickled her all the way down to her toes. How exciting it was to be someone else, to become a different person. No expectations hanging over her head to act just so. No pressure to say things just the right way. If all went well, she would only be asked to dust and scrub and run to and fro to please the master of the house.

Miss Bess nickered as her shiny black body took its rider down the drive toward the imposing mansion at the end of the lane. Summer could already see that Mr. Wilson's estate encompassed a massive home, numerous barns, small dwellings, and land as far as the eye could see.

Today she would be Summer Edwards, common maid and undercover mole. A new status for a new identity. A new identity to nail down a killer with a hidden agenda.

FOUR

Christian watched as a young woman with light blonde hair came out from behind a large rock near the entrance to George Wilson's estate. Her back was to him so he backed his horse down the lane a bit to stay out of sight. The woman carefully folded a light blue piece of fabric, probably a dress, and tucked it carefully away in her satchel.

How odd. The dress she was wearing was nice enough, but seemed more the kind a maid would wear. Maybe she had stolen the beautiful fabric and intended to sell the piece. It would bring a high dollar down on the wharf.

She mounted her horse, and Christian was surprised to see her heading in the direction of the large mansion. Suddenly it dawned on him. She was a prostitute by night and a maid by day. He had yet to see her face, but she was probably a beauty who used her charms to make an extra buck or two. But who was he to make such rash decisions about a person? He blamed it on his deductive mind, always working overtime, always trying to figure things out.

He let her have a good lead ahead of him, making sure she didn't see him. If he was going to be working here, he would need to keep an eye on all the comings and goings of the place. Keeping close tabs on the employees, guests, and residents of the home would be his top priority. For it was when one of them stumbled and made a mistake that the secrets of the home would be revealed. And Christian had a hunch the mysteries held within these walls would bring down the whole house.

"Miss Anton. Good Saturday morning to you. Here is your tea." Laura Moore came into the parlor bearing a silver tea tray that had come straight from London.

Elizabeth knew her entire home could be considered a museum of carefully chosen items from around the world. A hutch, handcrafted from the finest mahogany wood from Columbia, graced the far side of the parlor. The chandelier, which hung suspended in the foyer like a thousand tiny diamonds, was made from premium crystals mined in Madagascar. Floors from Italy, bedding shipped directly from Sweden, cutlery and dishes that normally served kings and queens. And pictures, pictures, everywhere of places and cities and foreign lands. Yes, this was what Elizabeth had traded for a life without her daughter. Tears pricked her eyes as she thought of the choices she had made.

"Miss?" Laura had set down the tray but had yet to leave the room.

It dawned on Elizabeth the young woman might have something to say. She looked pale standing there in her threadbare wool skirt and white maid's shirt. Perhaps the girl needed a raise. Or a favor. Elizabeth realized at that moment how truly alone she was. She had isolated herself from being known and knowing anyone else in return. Why, she didn't even know her staff well enough that they would feel comfortable coming to her for a need.

Hoping to put the girl at ease, Elizabeth motioned toward a nearby overstuffed chair. Laura looked positively mortified that she would be invited to sit with the mistress of the house. "Do have a seat, Laura. Is there something on your mind that you wish to speak of?"

The girl perched on the edge of the chair, looking ready to bolt at any moment. Then a soft sob came from her frail form, catching Elizabeth completely by surprise. Elizabeth reached into her reticule to find a clean handkerchief. She held it out to Laura who took it tentatively.

"It's just that, that—" Laura let out a wail.

Elizabeth's heart was moved by the girl's obvious distress. Was it something about her work environment that caused her to sob? Elizabeth felt she had always paid her employees fairly. She only remained aloof for the strict purpose of never wanting to give the wrong impression that her safely walled-off heart was penetrable. She had made a royal mess out of the relationships God had blessed her with early on in life and couldn't stand the thought of failing again.

"It's just that my brother, Landon, has been framed for murder and now he's in… in…jail!" Laura continued to talk, but Elizabeth couldn't understand one word of what followed.

"Now, there, there. Try saying that again, dear. You say your brother is in jail? For murder?"

"Yes, Miss Anton. But he didn't do it. I know it. Summer, I mean, Miss Edwards saw the whole thing and thinks she knows who did. At first, I was so mad he lied to me about the bank account I told myself he could rot in jail for all I cared. But they framed my poor Landon, and now Miss Edwards is off to find the murderer! What am I to do?"

More crying ensued, giving Elizabeth a few moments to process this information before asking any more questions.

How in the world had Summer been witness to a murder? And how did she know Landon Moore wasn't guilty? Where had this taken place and why had Summer not said anything to her about it? When the two of them had left the orphanage last night, Elizabeth had felt reassured that the communication between them would improve. She had offered a listening ear whenever Summer needed it. That was a huge olive branch for her to extend.

Obviously, Summer didn't trust her enough to come to her with what was happening. The realization cut Elizabeth to the core. When Summer asked to come stay with her, oh, how Elizabeth had hoped the two of them would become close. Opening her heart to this new relationship was Elizabeth's first brave step into a great unknown expanse, and it scared her to the core. But truly, how could she blame Summer? Elizabeth hadn't been open with her either. It appeared they had a long way to go.

Opening the small secretary desk that sat under a window in the parlor, Elizabeth withdrew monogrammed stationery and dipped her quill into the inkwell. "Laura, if you want me to help you, you need to tell me everything you know. Now, let's start at the beginning." And Elizabeth began to write.

"But certainly, you have some position here for me?" Summer took a deep breath and tried not to panic. It didn't work. She could feel the blood drain from her face and her breathing remained rapid. She needed to be hired today if she were to find out the truth about the man who had been shot and what had gone so terribly wrong in his life that someone would want him dead. She needed this for Laura Moore and her incarcerated brother. She needed this for herself.

The head butler who sat across the desk from her shook his graying head.

"I assure you, Mr. Moss, I bring many competencies to the table."

"I am certain you do, young lady."

A booming voice drew her attention to the doorway and Summer was stricken mute as she stared at the man standing there. His eyes were a pale green, contrasting nicely with his silver hair and strong broad shoulders. But it wasn't his appearance that made Summer stare. No, it was something else altogether. Summer felt at once she knew this man. Knew him well. But that couldn't be. She had never seen him before in her life.

"Do forgive my rudeness, miss." He strode into the room and went to stand next to Mr. Moss's chair. "I assume you are here seeking employment?" The imposing man peered at her with his green eyes.

Summer somehow managed to nod. Who was this man?

"Mr. Moss, do we have a position here for this young woman?"

"No, sir, we do not. I spoke with the head housekeeper yesterday and she assured me—there are no openings at this time. Not for a woman, at least."

"Looking for more stable hands, I assume?"

At Mr. Moss's nod, the man continued. He spoke with such authority, Summer wondered if this was the famous George Wilson. She swung her foot anxiously as she waited to see how this would play out.

He rubbed his strong hands together and paced the room. "You know, Mr. Moss may not have room for you in the household staff, but depending on what skills you possess, young lady, I may be able to use you as an assistant secretary in my offices located in the other wing of the home." He raised a silver eyebrow in her direction.

Remember why you're here, she told herself as she gathered her composure. This could be the opportunity she was hoping for. Even better, in fact. She would be inside an office, close to paperwork, close to those of high position on Mr. Wilson's staff. And if this man was in fact George Wilson, she could get close to him as well and find out why someone would need to pull the wool over his eyes, as the man at the racetrack had so imperiously stated.

"Sir, I assure you of my abilities in the office as well as the home. I was raised with a good education, especially excelling in numbers and ledgers. You will not be disappointed; of this I am certain." Summer forced herself to meet his eyes as he seemed to ponder her answer. When he nodded his approval, Summer let out the breath she had been holding.

"Mr. Moss, see to it she gets a full tour of the home so as to familiarize herself with the layout. Miss, you will report each weekday, beginning Monday morning, at eight o'clock. Sharp." He turned to go but stopped at the door and looked back. "Oh, by the way, I'm George Wilson."

"It was very nice to make your acquaintance, Mr. Wilson. I am Miss Summer Edwards."

Mr. Wilson looked at her with a peculiar expression on his face. Then his confident air once again controlled his features. "Glad to have you onboard. There is much to be done—a campaign for Senate to run, you know." He ran his gaze down the length of her skirt. "Miss Edwards, if you can manage it, wear something a little nicer tomorrow."

❦

Must be quite a looker, Christian thought as he stood outside the door to the head butler's office that was tucked away to the side of the foyer. A servant had met him at the front door and directed him to wait until Mr. Moss was available. Christian inclined his ear to the interesting conversation inside the room with no intention of interrupting. Sometimes a man could learn a lot just by being quiet. And in this case, staying out of sight.

He hadn't seen, or heard, rather, a man fall all over himself like that for a long time. Imagine, to give a common maid the position of assistant secretary to the former governor of Virginia without so much as a business reference. Beauty could be a strong pull for a man, and clearly this was no exception.

Christian backed up against the wall as Mr. Wilson made his way out of the room. The older man nodded to him, and Christian tipped his hat. He held his place in the foyer as Mr. Moss made small talk with Miss Edwards about her pay and new position.

A chair scraped against the wood floor and Christian knew his turn was next. But before he could go in and inquire of a position at George Wilson's home, the young woman stepped out and for a moment, the world seemed to stand perfectly still. This was the girl he had seen next to the rock. Now her hat was in her hand, leaving her golden hair exposed to the incoming daylight from the windows. It fairly gleamed as it accentuated her exquisite green eyes and fine Norwegian features. Her common brown dress and serviceable shoes couldn't hide her smooth fair skin and dainty, unsoiled hands.

This woman was no maid. She was a true beauty. Something inside Christian was drawn inexplicably to her. Her silky hair begged to be let down. What he wouldn't give to run his fingers through the length of it.

Gradually it dawned on him he was staring at this most magnificent of creatures. He cleared his throat and removed his hat. "How do you do?" he greeted her, feeling a sense of victory at getting out the smallest of phrases.

She smiled and curtsied, and Christian felt his heart fall to his stomach. He waited in anticipation of what she would say. His mind wandered to what she would wear tomorrow and if he would have the privilege of seeing her again. This Summer Edwards. This enchanting lady in maid's clothing.

Summer had always considered the home she was raised in to be very well appointed. She paused for a moment just outside the doorway of Mr. Moss's office to take in the home's sheer size and craftsmanship. Looking up, brilliant chandeliers sent their sparkles every which way across the venetian plaster on the ceiling. On the floor, the hardwood gleamed clear and smooth, catching the image of its surroundings. But as her eyes took in the huge mirrors reflecting arrangements of hydrangeas, they locked in on a man standing to her side.

Suddenly, all rational thought left Summer's head and she could not force her eyes away from his warm brown ones. He was looking at her with the most tender expression she had ever received. She took a step closer to him and realized his eyes held the most remarkable hint of gold, like a priceless, rare treasure found at sea. He removed his hat to reveal wavy brown hair that looked like it had been combed by the wind. His facial hair had a hint of red and covered only his upper lip and chin. A most becoming asset.

When Summer had stepped out of the house this morning, she felt like she was breaking down long-standing borders of expectation and fear. She had found her way to the former governor's home, dressed the part of a maid, and had managed to acquire a position in the politician's office. But none of these new experiences were more earth-shaking than her almost physical response to the man standing before her.

"How do you do?" he had said in a voice that was deep and rumbling. What was the appropriate answer to such a question? She could answer graciously in a number of ways but none seemed fitting to the feelings tumbling around inside her chest. It was probably just nervousness she was feeling in response to all that had taken place this morning. Yes, she was certain that's what it was.

She curtsied while trying to think of something to say. "Very well, thank you."

He held out his hand to her and she was powerless to do anything but give him her own. He kissed it gently and spoke in that amazing voice again. "Christian Titus, at your service, Miss?"

"Edwards. Summer Edwards."

He let go of her hand. "I'm new to town and looking for work. Do you happen to know if Mr. Wilson is hiring?"

Feeling useful and grateful she knew the answer, Summer said, "Mr. Moss, the head butler, just mentioned they are looking for a stable hand." She blushed as he continued to look at her with those amazing eyes. "I wish you all the best in your search for employment, Mr. Titus. I myself was just hired. Perhaps we will speak again."

They bade each other farewell and Summer made her way to the other wing of the home to find her tour guide. As she walked down the wide hall, she looked back over her shoulder. Christian Titus was watching her, too. Summer smiled in return and sent up a prayer that they would indeed see each other soon.

Dear Ruth,

I pray this letter finds you and Marvin doing well. Late summer has been beautiful here in Waterford Cove. I hope you have not worried too much over Summer being here with me. I know you and Marvin were not in complete approval about her coming here, but I assure you she has found out nothing concerning the past.

Truly, she keeps incredibly busy and has yet to ask uncomfortable questions. It is an honor to have her as a guest in my home. She has proven to be quite the accomplished young lady—volunteering her time at one charitable cause or the other. Her quest to attend church never wavers, nor does her time spent in the parlor reading her Bible. I am most proud of the young woman she has become.

I write to you today, however, with a concern. It has been made known to me that Summer might be privy to a very sensitive situation. The information she possesses may put her at risk. I assure you she happened upon this information unknowingly and that it does not concern her relationship to me in any regard.

What I ask of you today is for a favor. Three favors, in fact. First, that you allow Summer to stay on with me for a bit longer. She does not know I have this information concerning her, and it would break her confidence if she knew I was writing to you about this matter. Next, I ask that you trust her. She is bright, if not a little headstrong. But I believe she seeks the will of our heavenly Father on every matter. And finally, if this letter gives you pause about her current situation, rather than come to collect her, send someone to check on her instead. Perhaps another family member or close friend. I believe that would be honoring to everyone in this circumstance. I pray you will agree.

With much love, your sister,
Elizabeth

As Elizabeth set her seal upon the stationary, she felt only a small twinge of guilt in her stomach. Summer may be a capable young lady, but for all Elizabeth knew, Summer also might be in over her head. If what Laura Moore related to her earlier today were true, Summer's life could be in danger.

Elizabeth had contemplated going straight to the police, but within moments decided against it. Laura was right. If they went to the police now, the real truth as to why this Nigel Fairbanks had been murdered may not ever be discovered. Reason deemed that the police could handle it. It was their job to investigate murders and the like. But Elizabeth rationalized that by Summer going undercover, her daughter was taking after her in her love for adventure. Even if the closest to adventure Elizabeth ever came was a jaunt on a rented sailboat, it gave Elizabeth a feeling of connection to Summer.

Elizabeth also felt that by sending a letter to Ruth, she was absolving herself from all culpability. She had revealed the right amount of information to Ruth and Marvin and now they could respond suitably.

They could come and whisk Summer away, take her home to North Carolina, choosing not to trust their grown daughter. Or, as Elizabeth ardently hoped, they would see Summer for who she had become. A bright young woman with a good head on her shoulders.

Oh, how she prayed they would.

FIVE

Summer's heart kept up its unsteady off-rhythm beat for the rest of the morning. She felt wholly off kilter after meeting Christian Titus. Throughout her tour of the gorgeous home, Summer had forced her mind to focus on the details she was being shown. George Wilson wasn't joking when he'd requested Summer have the entire tour. She had been shown everything from the glass atrium in the rear of the home to the private bedroom chambers of the former governor himself.

Her personal tour guide was a young maid who ran errands and messages around the house for George Wilson. Natalie Paul appeared to be an intelligent girl, not more than twenty years of age.

"If you will follow me, we will take the exit next to the kitchen that leads to the rear grounds behind the home."

Summer nearly tripped over Miss Paul as she led the way out doors.

But it wasn't Summer's lack of attention to the tour that caused her feet to stumble. It was the amazing sight of watching Christian Titus's strong arms and broad shoulders load hay into the back of a wagon.

Summer had been undercover for an entire work week now, fulfilling her role as one of many assistant secretaries. A week doing whatever assignments the matronly Mrs. Harris, lead secretary, handed out for the day.

Summer sat at her small desk in George Wilson's wood-paneled first-floor office and stared out the windows. Six whole days without seeing Christian Titus. Well, that wasn't exactly true. The long windows that flanked two walls of the room afforded Summer an excellent view of the expansive green area on the southern side of the home. Frequently, men would walk by, going about their work in the garden or stables. Often a bit of reddish-brown facial hair and well-built shoulders would catch her eye. Christian never looked her way when he passed, but to Summer, it was a delight merely to catch a glimpse of the man. Though they had only spoken the one time in the grand foyer of the mansion, the tender look he had bestowed upon her that day had stayed with her.

Six. Whole. Days. It felt like an eternity. Not only was she empty handed when Laura greeted her at the door of Aunt Elizabeth's home each afternoon, she had not one chance to speak to Mr. Titus. Six days of dreaming of who he was and she still didn't know one detail about him. She took great pains to come to work a little early each day in hopes of seeing him when she brought her horse to the stable area. Each time she arrived, a young man with a head of curly, dark hair would greet her with a smile, take Miss Bess to her stall and leave without a word. Summer felt more than awkward standing there in the muck, trying not to look conspicuous, all the while seeing if she could spot Mr. Titus. Oh, to hear the rumble of his voice in her ears. Just the thought of him made her stomach flutter. It was a welcome feeling.

But she must be sensible. She had work to do. Focusing on the task at hand was the order of the day, not daydreaming about a handsome stable hand she had only met once.

Paperwork, deadlines, errands, and a murder to solve. That was the agenda. Summer shook her head at this new world she now called her life.

Oh, she wasn't foolish enough to think it would go on like this forever. But one key detail couldn't be ignored—Frederick Ellis had Nigel Fairbanks killed to get his job as accountant to George Wilson. Senior accountant to the possible future senator of Virginia was a prominent position, to be sure. But was it worth killing over? Summer doubted it. There had to be some other reason the murder had taken place.

On her first day there, Summer had recognized Frederick Ellis right off. Office rumor had it George Wilson was lost without his long-time friend and accountant, Nigel Fairbanks. Frederick Ellis seemed to be an adequate replacement, if not a planned one. She didn't quite have him pegged, but figured him to be a pushover. He asked how high when told to jump. But Summer knew he would have to have at least a little bit of gumption to be at the center of a murder plot.

A thin man walked into the room just then, heading straight for Mr. Ellis's desk. He flipped out gray coattails and made a grand motion of sitting down. "Frederick, good to see you. How goes the new job?"

She watched the interchange between the two men at Ellis's mahogany desk through lowered lids. Summer gasped softly. Why, this was the other man from the track! His build plus wire-rim glasses and brown mustache gave him away at once.

Her ears strained to hear their exchange. Perhaps something in the men's conversation would give Summer a lead as to how to proceed in this situation. Maybe even some good news to bring home to Laura later on today.

"The new job?" Frederick pulled at his shirt collar as if it were choking him. "Uh, yes, Andrew, it's going just fine." Mr. Ellis cleared his throat and took a handkerchief from his pocket with which to wipe his brow. "What brings you up this way today?" He glanced toward Summer, the only other person in the room.

Andrew turned his head and nodded politely. Summer quickly shifted her eyes back to her work, hoping they didn't think she was listening.

"Just stopping by to say hello." Out of the corner of her eye, Summer saw this Andrew person glance her way again, then pass a white, square piece of paper across the desk to Mr. Ellis. He tapped his finger on the paper twice, then turned and left the room.

Summer kept up the appearance of preparing a form letter to potential campaign investors but glanced now and again at the perspiring

Mr. Ellis. She took a deep breath and prayed for patience and wisdom. Whatever was on that slip of paper could be the key to unlocking the secret these two men held and the key to unlock the prison cell in which Landon Moore sat daily.

A large grandfather clock against the far wall revealed the time. Quarter past four. No wonder Mr. Ellis's co-conspirator had come to pay him a visit. Andrew had not anticipated anyone else still being there for the day.

What if the men had recognized her as someone they had seen at the track? Panic seized her momentarily as she considered the implications of such a discovery. She knew they would not think twice about snuffing out her very life. *Thank you, Lord, for keeping me safe,* Summer breathed. *And for causing me to forget the time.*

That paper could hold an answer to the growing list of questions Summer kept filed in her mind. She needed to get close to Mr. Ellis's desk before he put it out of sight.

"I didn't realize what time it had gotten to be." Summer stood and straightened her dark pink linen dress. She was ever so grateful she didn't have to hide behind that rock to change every day when she reported to the mansion. Now she could leave Aunt Elizabeth's house without drawing too much undue attention.

Draping her shawl across her arm, Summer walked across the room. *Lord, help me.* "Excuse me, Mr. Ellis?"

"Yes?" The heavy man looked up from the note he was holding. The very note Summer needed to lay her eyes on. From where she stood, Summer could see the ink had bled through the thin paper. The numbers "0" and "0" appeared next to each other. Next to the zeros, a mark or two of sorts. Then a backwards "5." Then a strange looking symbol. All other characters were hidden by his beefy hand.

"I wondered where you might be from, sir? I used to live in North Carolina and your accent sounds familiar to me." Summer hoped she wasn't revealing too much information about her own background by asking.

"Why, I hail from a small town, just north of the North Carolina border." His brown eyes sparkled for just a moment, making Summer wonder about this man. Had he once led a normal life that had some-how spiraled into his current circumstance? "No one has asked me that in a long, long time. Good memories of that place, I tell you." He smiled then, the first time Summer had seen such an expression from him since taking this position. "You just made my night, little lady."

At that, the man stood and proceeded to stuff the note in his pocket. Summer watched as he donned his hat and headed for the door. But she was not dissuaded or discouraged. On the contrary. This was her first real chance to unlock a piece of the mystery.

It was obvious what the two zeros and backwards five meant. Es-pecially since they had a marking in between them. It was a time. Five o'clock. Summer quickly put on her shawl. The days were getting short-er, the sunlight already beginning to dip a bit toward the west. But as Summer stood covertly looking out the office windows, she was thank-ful there were hours of daylight left to find out what Mr. Ellis was up to. His first stop would parallel her own. The stables.

It had been Christian's experience that the stable area was a perfect location from which to observe the comings and goings of a house-hold. It was from this one location that no one could come or go with-out first passing through, for every horse was required to find its tem-porary home there no matter their owner's errand to the Wilson estate.

He surmised working in the stables would have two additional ben-efits as well. He could take good care of the horses owned by Mr. Wil-son, both the race horses and the ones for daily use. Plus, each day, he would have two opportunities in which to engage Miss Summer Edwards in conversation. If truth be told, he was besotted with the girl. She never looked out the window as she sat at her small desk, but even so, he took every opportunity to pass her way.

Unfortunately, the foreman had assigned Christian to run errands in town during the early morning hours. By the time he arrived back at the estate, he had already been at work for more than four hours, and

Summer sat much occupied at her desk. And since he began work before the sun barely tipped the horizon, he was dismissed to the bunkhouse before she left for the day.

Pure cowardice. That's what it was, plain and simple. Each day for the past week, he could have waited for her to exit the mansion. Each day, he could have come back from the bunkhouse and talked to her. He chuckled to himself as he lay in his bunk. All it would take was a little courage. And the reward would be worth all the stomach butterflies in the world. Just to gaze upon her serene face, carved by an angel. Just to see those green eyes flicker in interest in his direction.

Tabitha had been gone a long time. He needed to move on. But how would it feel to be burned again by a woman? Turning on his bunk, Christian didn't think he wanted to know. No, he was *certain* he didn't want to know, which was exactly why he had avoided the female population for almost a decade.

Then a little wisp of a woman had laid her enchanting eyes on him in a grand foyer in Virginia. He slammed his fist down on the lumpy mattress. Dash it all! Why did he ever have to lay eyes on that girl? He was doing fine. Just fine, indeed. He needed to get her off his mind. Maybe he should get out of there for a while. Clear his head. Snoop around some more like he had done on occasion in the past few days.

He grabbed his coat and hollered to anyone who cared to listen, "Be back before long." A couple of grunts were his only responses.

Christian stepped out into the late afternoon air and breathed in the scents of late August. A few dry leaves crunched under his feet as he made his way to the stables. George Wilson employed an entire team of gardeners and wouldn't tolerate leaves anywhere on his grassy yard. Christian shook his head and smiled. He felt sorry for the young men who worked tirelessly to keep the area free of debris. And that included the thousands of leaves that would begin to fall from the towering maples and aspens and oaks in a few weeks' time. One more reason to be glad he had been hired on as a stable hand.

As he neared the biggest barn in the group of outbuildings, Christian slowed his steps. He spotted golden hair shining in the sunlight.

Hadn't he just made up his mind to steer clear of women?

And yet, there she was, practically running across the lawn from the house to the stable. It seemed unusual to see a young lady moving so fast her stockings showed beneath the ruffles of her skirt. What could be so important to get her in such an all-fired hurry? Well, he wasn't one of the head detectives at the Pinkerton National Detective Agency because he was good at standing around.

After she tore out on her black mare, he quickly mounted Sadie. Something told him he should find out where she was going and what was so urgent. She may be in trouble or would find herself in need of help. Maybe it was a hunch. Or maybe, he just wanted to be near that sweet little gal again.

"You have got to be kidding me." Summer watched as the thinner man called Andrew paced back and forth, back and forth. Crunch. Crunch. Crunch. "Are you saying I came all the way out here and you're empty handed?" His voice rose in anger, a chilling sound to the bones.

"Sir, please take into account the situation. It's not like I can produce it out of thin air," said Mr. Ellis.

Andrew stopped pacing and faced Mr. Wilson's new accountant. An evil laugh echoed against the hardwoods that surrounded them. "Sure you can! And that's exactly what you will do. Now when will I see my money?" He bore a bony finger into Ellis's chest.

The heavy man held up his hands. "You'll get it, I promise!" His voice was shrill and panicked. "We—we had a deal, remember? I—I'm good for it, you know I am!"

"I don't know nothin' except if I don't have the cash in hand by this time next week, you'll regret it." He laughed again, venom dripping from his lips. "But you won't see the end of my gun until I have brought you to utter humiliation first." He paused. "And you should know, I look forward to the opportunity."

Summer squeezed her eyes shut and wished she could make herself invisible in the dense forest. Her pink dress would shine like the sun if the afternoon light caught her in its grip. She must stay in the shadows until it was safe to leave.

The breeze had taken away some of their words, like feathers floating on the wings of the air. Shadows dappled their features as sunlight made its way through the thick foliage, but not enough to disguise their identities. Summer had yet to learn the last name of Andrew, but she knew he was the same brown-haired, thin man from the track and Frederick Ellis the other. The two men had not revealed much new information but they had revealed their meeting place and the fact that they weren't on cordial terms. Summer also knew Frederick was holding out the payment he owed Andrew. Payment made for killing Nigel Fairbanks.

Summer thought she could hold her breath no longer when she heard one horse being mounted and prodded into a gallop heading west. Then another, a short time later, this time headed north. She dared not breathe, dared not move. A few moments went by, and she took only silent, shallow breaths. Another minute, then two. Listening. No more rustling of forest carpet could be heard. All was quiet. She could breathe easy now. She was alone. Maybe that wasn't such a comforting thought after all. If she got to Aunt Elizabeth's home at this very moment, she didn't think it would be soon enough.

Christian watched as Summer picked her way back to her black horse tied to a tree a good hundred yards away from where the men had argued. Whatever her purpose for following the men, she knew enough not to give away her presence. Although, a different choice of attire may have served her better. But if Christian had the chance, he wouldn't tell her so. The pink linen she wore today had made her look like a soft rose petal.

When he had made the choice to follow Summer, he never would have expected this. It felt odd spying on someone who was very obviously spying too. The question was, why would she trail these men out into the deserted woodland? The Pinkerton National Detective Agency was the only operation on this case as far as he knew. That meant she had some involvement with these two men. Could it be that such a beautiful angel could be an adversary in disguise?

He thought of his observations the first day they had met. The way she carried her person, along with her flawless skin and impeccable speech, all gave clear evidence she was not a maid by trade. No, Christian now felt sure she was something else altogether. And he would take pleasure in finding out just who exactly she was.

Christian mounted his own horse, lost in thought. By the time he had settled in on the saddle, Summer was gone. She was going to distract him from his work at this rate. A small smile was hard to resist, though. An attractive distraction at that.

He'd had to keep his distance to not be seen by the men or Summer so he didn't catch all of their conversation. But he had clearly seen the face of one of the men arguing. An accountant that had been hired about the same time Christian had arrived in town. At least now he knew where to look next. And it was no further than a stone's throw from where Christian went to work every day—George Wilson's office.

SIX

Sometimes, Elizabeth didn't think she could sit one more day in this tidy museum of a home. Simply sitting and waiting. Waiting for what? For another bank note to be mailed to her address on this exclusive Virginia square? What good had any of that money ever done her all these years? It offered nothing but confinement. Each dollar sent was like a brick in the walls of a giant fortress of hurt and secrets, barricading her in until she couldn't see out anymore. Maybe if she had been brave enough to jump out when the walls were low, her life would look differently. But now they were so high, no light could make its way inside.

Elizabeth ran her hand over the Holy Bible sitting on the carved marble table next to her, its embossed letters raised against her fingertips. Once in a while, a small beam of light from this beloved book would pierce the dark of her heart where the fortress was kept. A tiny beacon of hope would lift Elizabeth's eyes from her mistakes and regrets.

All too quickly, though, the illumination of God's grace and mercy toward a woman such as she would be snuffed out by lies that were easier to believe. *You made your bed, and now you get to lie in it.* Or *You think you deserve better than this?* That one never left her in peace for long. *Just look at the mess you've made of everything.*

Enough! Elizabeth swiped at her eyes and hastily grabbed her shawl, handbag and the newest camera she had acquired, a "Folding" Rochester. If she didn't get out of there, and now, she was going to go mad.

She flung the front door open and stepped forcefully forward at the precise moment a man lifted his hand to knock on the door. Their opposing forces threw them into each other awkwardly, toppling them both to the porch floor.

Elizabeth found herself tangled up with the poor man. But try as she might, she could not find a way to become upright once again without her skirt becoming more awry than it already was. She had never been more mortified in her life. As she made to apologize to the unfortunate fellow, strong hands lifted her gently up and seated her on her bottom.

"Oh, sir, I do apologize." She couldn't bear to look the man in the eyes. "Please find it in your heart—"

Those same strong hands that had set her down now cradled her flaming face in their cool embrace, slowly lifting her chin so her eyes finally had no choice but to land on his.

"Lizzy."

As if a miracle had taken place, strong rays of pure hope shone through the shadows with just one simple spoken word.

For as long as she lived, Elizabeth knew she would never forget the moment when Dustin Edwards stepped back into her life.

"Some refreshments for your guest, Miss Anton." Laura dipped a curtsy at the handsome gentleman sitting on a green brocade settee across from her mistress.

The man tipped his head in greeting at the girl, but Elizabeth knew his attention was wholly focused on her.

Elizabeth squirmed in her rose-patterned chair, not knowing where to let her eyes land. Dustin Edwards could not be sitting in her parlor, stirring sugar into his tea like this was an everyday occurrence. This simply could not be happening.

She dared a look in his direction. Just as she suspected, his bright blue eyes were fixed on her and they made the silver in his black hair shine like the moonlight. Elizabeth looked away quickly, finding great interest in a loose thread on the arm of the chair. Over the last twenty years, Elizabeth had daydreamed many times about seeing Dustin again. But never in all that time had she pictured the two of them falling down on top of one another in a most embarrassing event.

Nothing was right about him being there, seeing her like this. Nothing, that is, except for that fabulous smile currently spread across his face. Dustin had always had the ability to melt her heart when he gave her that look. The one that said she was special, that no one else in the world existed but her.

"It's good to see you, Lizzy."

"You…you, too, Dustin." Elizabeth's nerves were jangling like the bells on a market door. "What brings you here? I have to say it was more than a surprise seeing you after all these years." Elizabeth had to resist the urge to repeat a childhood habit of crossing her fingers as she waited for his answer. *Please let it be that he came just because he wanted to see me.* She fiddled with her teacup, thinking about the timing of the letter. It wasn't possible he could have received it and then made the trip to Virginia. He must have already been on his way when she'd mailed the letter. Maybe Ruth and Marvin had sent him here to collect Summer. *But please let it be that he came to see me.*

He gazed at her from across the room, those blue eyes settling on her own green ones. What would it have been like to have spent all these lonely years with this dear man? Elizabeth was sure it would have been pure heaven. But choices had been made, whims followed, consequences paid.

What felt like a lifetime ago, Elizabeth Anton and her sister Ruth had lived in North Carolina with their parents. Close in age and sisterhood, the young ladies were thrilled when their parents invited the Edwards family—including two handsome young sons—for dinner one evening. It didn't take the young people in attendance long to realize the reason for the invitation. The four parents had in mind to unite their two families in name and business. Dowries would be paid in the form of shareholdings in the Anton's profitable timber business and both couples were assured wedded bliss. For what could be better than adjoining these two bloodlines who shared the same social and religious values?

Ruth had taken to the older brother, Marvin Edwards, immediately. Shortly after dinner that evening, the two had settled in on a game of cards. Not too many calendar pages were turned before a proposal was made and all the arrangements for a wedding were set.

Elizabeth had been thrilled that Dustin Edwards was left for her. The instant she laid eyes on him, she knew he was the one. Not only was he by far the most handsome man she had ever met, he had an innate ability to make others feel comfortable. His integrity was extraordinary and he believed in the same God as she. If that wasn't enough, Elizabeth admired him for his resistance to go with what others told him to do. He claimed God was his only guide, and his actions showed he was no hypocrite.

Dustin soon became Dusty to her as they spent more time together. He would come to call and they would take strolls in the garden and talk for hours. How Elizabeth's heart would thrill at the sound of his voice, the feel of her hand in his. She was head-over-heels in love and waited daily for his proposal. But it never came. Weeks turned into months, and Elizabeth began to lose hope that something would ever come of their relationship.

Then one night, it happened. Dustin was set to pick her up for a charity ball at a quarter to eight. When he didn't come by nine o'clock, Elizabeth decided to go alone. She had her driver drop her off at the palatial home where the ball was to be held and told him to pick her up at midnight. A golden gown of the finest silk caught many an eye as she entered the ballroom, unaccompanied.

The crowd seemed to part as a tall, well-built gentleman came to her side. He stood a shoulder above all the others in the room, and Elizabeth couldn't help but think Dustin was actually quite short. This man's eyes were green like her own, while Dustin's were blue. Then the stranger asked for a dance and took her arm. She remembered feeling his strong hands on her waist as they swung round and round the dance floor. She blushed when he whispered things in her ear she had never heard from a man's lips. Even so, she had encouraged his flattery to continue.

Elizabeth's heart sank as she remembered what happened next. Dustin never came that night. To this day, she didn't know where he had been. But she knew what she had done. When the driver came to collect her at midnight, no girl in a golden gown could be found. The next morning at the breakfast table with her parents, Elizabeth knew she was no longer their innocent daughter. What had happened in the night changed everything. Nothing would ever be the same.

"Lizzy?" Dustin got up and came to kneel in front of her chair. He took her hand in his, and she felt both the sudden urge to flee the room and to reach out to touch his beloved face. Oh, the betrayal she had held out to him on a platter! If only she hadn't let her desires get ahead of her heart. She had traded one night of unfulfilling lust for a lifetime of unfulfilled passion with the man who knelt in front of her.

The shame and harsh reality of it all was too much to bear. Seeing Dustin gaze at her with forgiveness and adoration in his eyes was all wrong. Elizabeth knew she didn't deserve it and she certainly wouldn't accept it.

"I can't Dustin, I'm sorry," was all she said before she jumped up from her chair and ran outside through the kitchen. The slam of the door as it closed behind her echoed the door shutting in her heart, snuffing out long-held dreams that had tried to pierce the darkness.

Summer had taken the weekend to mull over the interchange she had witnessed in the woods, inform Laura of what she knew, and spend time in God's house on the Lord's day.

It was a new week now and something different needed to happen. Maybe she should get out of the office for a while. Being trapped inside all day was not Summer's idea of fun, although her heart still thrilled at this new adventure. Maybe a change of scenery would propel her forward in her hunt for answers to the questions churning in her mind.

This morning, as usual, she had brought her lunch with her to work. She leaned over the side of the saddle to peer into the bag. Perfect. Cook had packed a meat and cheese sandwich, accompanied by some fruit and a few apple fritters. It would make a splendid picnic lunch. Normally, she ate at her desk in hopes of overhearing a conversation or having the office to herself for a few minutes so she could snoop in the other desks. But not today. Certainly, there had to be a place close by where she could enjoy God's creation and have some time to pray and think.

Summer's horse approached the barn where Miss Bess spent the better portion of the day. She could see the hands working to groom the horses, load hay, and muck out stalls. Orders were given by the foreman, a middle-aged man with a mustache. Men scurried to and fro to meet his demands.

Summer looked around for the young man who normally took her horse. But instead of him, someone else altogether came up and took the reins. Christian Titus. Summer's heart nearly stopped at the sight of him in the morning sun. She was so taken aback that she put her hand to her chest.

He grinned up at her, one side of his mouth higher than the other. "Good morning, ma'am." Tipping his hat, he led Miss Bess into her stall. Normally Summer dismounted quickly when she arrived. She had never been into the stall before.

Christian tied the horse's reins to a ring in the stall wall and held out his hand to help her down. Summer merely looked at his hand, speechless.

"All right, have it your way, beautiful." And with that, Christian took her by the waist and she had no choice but to allow him to assist her down.

Summer's feet hit the dirt floor and she could do nothing to make them move. Her focus was completely on the man before her. The foreman's calls, the scent in the late summer air, even her undercover job awaiting her inside the big house, all of it faded away. It seemed they stood there like that, with his hands still at her waist, for endless moments.

Finally, Christian's neck began to turn red and he cleared his throat.

Taking a step backward, he smoothed down his facial hair. "Thanks for the tip on the job, Miss Edwards. I hope you are enjoying your new position as well?"

Summer straightened her skirt in an effort to buy time to calm her racing heart. "Yes, thank you for inquiring, Mr. Titus. I understand it is unusual for a woman to work in an office setting such as George Wilson's, but my time there has brought many new opportunities."

They began to walk out of the stall and Summer noticed Christian seemed oblivious to the activity going on around them. Didn't he have a job he needed to do?

"Titus! Quit socializin' and get on over here!" Christian and Summer turned to see the foreman marching toward them.

Christian stopped and bowed before her. "I consider it a great privilege to have had the opportunity to speak with you today, Miss Edwards." He gave her a grin that could have charmed the stripes off a skunk. "I count the minutes until we meet again." And with that, he tipped his hat and jogged away to answer to his supervisor.

For a heartbeat, Summer simply stood there. The hustle of a busy Monday morning continued around her as she willed her feet to move. She lifted up her skirt and hurried inside, all the while feeling giddy at this turn of events. Christian had never met her at the stables before today. Perhaps this meant she would have the chance to speak with him more often. She hoped with all of her heart it was true.

It had taken three hands of poker, his gold watch, and an entire weekend of convincing, but Christian had done it. Young Benjamin, with his dark curly hair, had finally agreed to take on Christian's early morning errands so Christian could be at the stables every day when Summer arrived. The foreman had grunted in reply when Christian mentioned the switch last night, and the man hadn't blinked an eye when it was Christian who did today's early morning mucking. Christian felt like he had come in by the skin of his teeth on that one, and was grateful no one had objected. He needed to keep an eye on Miss Summer Edwards. There was something more going on than met the eye when it came to the beautiful maid-turned-secretary.

The memory of seeing her hidden behind a tree in a dense forest listening to two men fight about money sent red flags flying for Christian. He needed to find out why she had been eavesdropping on Friday. It was entirely possible that she was somehow connected to the counterfeit ring that was rumored to be centered at George Wilson's home. Possible, but not probable. Christian just couldn't correlate the two. Summer was such a soft, sweet, beautiful young lady; she couldn't truly be wrapped up in something this sinister. Then again, sometimes money drove people to do things they never thought they would or could. Christian had seen his fair share of that in his time as an agent and from years of watching his father chase down one money-making scheme after another.

Memories of Tabitha came rushing at him as he thought of how a woman could fool a man so easily. Tabitha had been beautiful and endearing too, but in the end, she had proven to be a devil in disguise. Christian forked hay into the next awaiting stall with renewed vigor. His heart burned with anger toward the one lady he had ever allowed near his heart. Women. They just weren't worth it. Back then, Tabitha and God had been his whole life.

God. Ha! He forked another load of hay and threw it for all he was worth. Christian would admit to anyone who asked that he had turned his back on God. He wasn't ashamed to say it. God had turned His back on him, so he had just returned the favor.

Since he'd started looking out for himself, though, he could say with pride that most things had turned out pretty well. He had worked his way up in the agency, and now he found himself as the top pick for high-profile jobs like this one. Yes, he was the best, and Christian knew he had no one to thank but his own hard work and determination.

The stalls were mucked out and new hay had been laid for the day. Christian stood back and looked at his work with satisfaction. It may not be a glamorous job at times, but he didn't mind the hard work. Especially when he got the chance to be near the horses. They always had a way of soothing him, calming his soul.

Sweat dripped from his brow, and Christian wiped it with his chambray shirt sleeve. He went to the front of the barn to fetch his drink. As he downed the last of the canteen, he surveyed George Wilson's property. Clipped, manicured lawns gave way to at least a hundred acres of both treed and pastured land. Numerous stables, barns, and outbuildings showed the utmost in care. A creek cut through the south side of the property, offering the livestock and home a much-needed fresh supply of water.

Maybe someday, Christian would settle down, buy a place of his own. The instant he had the thought, he squelched it. Home meant family, and that was something Christian knew he would never have. Right now, it was just him and his job. He nodded decisively. *And that's the way it's going to stay.*

SEVEN

The wind was fresh as it rolled off the ocean, calming Elizabeth's spirits as she strolled along the shoreline.

Sometimes, when she needed to clear her mind, she would take her favorite horse and gallop down to the sea. Of course, the sand usually teamed with activity, but she found that if she came early in the morning, before the sun even rose, there was no one around. There, she could be alone with her thoughts. That process, however, usually compounded the problem. Each time, once she began sorting through her heartaches, she wondered why she had believed coming to the shore to think would be any different than staying at home where she would inevitably do the very same thing.

Then, as the sun would rise above the horizon and skim the sand and the water with its warmth, Elizabeth would be reminded of how great and powerful God really was, how big and wonderful He had made the world, and things would slowly fall into perspective. A bit of Scripture would be brought to her remembrance by the Holy Spirit as the treasured words of her Bible washed over her heart. Her toes would feel the soft squish of the sand, and she would picture her Lord carrying her along, leaving only one set of footprints behind.

On a typical day in her life in Virginia, Elizabeth would spend the better part of it berating herself for the choices she had made in life. It was a miserable existence, always looking back, never ahead. Gazing at the photographs that hung on the walls but never having the courage to answer the beckoning call to explore their reality. But then there would come a day like today, when she would venture beyond the security of her beautiful home. A moment would come when she would feel a small release from her past and for that brief span of time, her mistakes would fade into the background and she would dare to dream of a different life.

Today, she would take up one of her favorite activities as the sun climbed higher in the morning sky. She waved a hand to the man whom she always hired to take her out on his sailboat. She was a glorious vessel, made for pleasure, and cost a small fortune to rent. But Elizabeth didn't mind. She would happily pay the hefty price if it meant a few moments of peace with the wind and salt water spraying her in the face as the captain took her far from shore. A light breakfast would be served and she could sit in the sun and soak up a much-needed respite.

She went to the old captain, who had the boat docked. He was shining the already glossy wood of the deck and had a huge smile for her this morning.

"Hope you don't mind some company today."

A voice from behind caused Elizabeth to swing around. At that precise moment, a breeze off the ocean caught her hat and took it on a lilting ride. It landed with a soft *whoosh* at the feet of the man who had once captured her heart.

It had been two whole days since Dusty had shown up at her door. Two torturous nights wondering why he had come and where he had gone after her hasty departure. Yet, there he stood, bringing all her years of remembering to a sharp point.

The feelings he had dredged up in her during their brief moments together had rocked her to her core. Elizabeth tried to push aside those feelings. She did not deserve to even be in the same state with the man, let alone have him treat her with tenderness in her own parlor.

And now, here he was again.

Elizabeth bent to retrieve the wayward hat, only to find Dustin's hand had gotten there first. Her fingers brushed his and their eyes locked. Both stood up straight, Dustin's hand clutching the hat, Elizabeth's hand clutching his. Try as she might, she couldn't let go. His blue eyes searched hers as if looking for an answer. An answer she was not prepared to give.

A call from the captain broke the moment. "What say there, Miss Anton? Do we have two guests for the morning's journey?"

Elizabeth tore her eyes away from Dustin's with much effort and waved again to Mr. Monroe. "Be with you in a moment, sir."

Elizabeth looked down at her bare toes in the sand and blushed at how inappropriate this must seem to a wealthy man from North Carolina. "I—I was just—well, going to—you know." Oh, that went really well.

"Do you come out here often, Miss Anton?" Dustin teased with a glint in his eyes. Instead of waiting for her to answer the elderly captain, he linked arms with her and walked toward the lovely boat. "I wouldn't blame you a bit if you did, pretty lady. Who wouldn't enjoy a quiet morning such as this?" They stepped up the short plank and he helped her onto the ship's deck. Turning to her with a wink he said, "Sure am glad your maid likes to share the details of her mistress's day."

Elizabeth stared in shock as the man she had loved for more than twenty years made himself perfectly at home in her carefully protected little world.

"This is what I want to know: what's she doing here?" The whispers behind Summer's back could not be ignored today. Rumor had it that the entire house was abuzz as to why a common house maid would get a position in the famous George Wilson's campaign office without so much as a reference.

Every day since coming to the estate, Summer had begun to feel more and more unwelcome in her new environment. She would arrive home in the afternoons completely deflated. Whenever Aunt Elizabeth asked where she had been all day, Summer would just avoid answering all together. If she'd had more success in uncovering the truth, maybe she could have mustered up the courage to tell her aunt about what was happening. As it was, it was getting harder and harder to come to work each day on the far-fetched hope that she would learn something new about why Nigel Fairbanks had been murdered and Landon Moore framed.

Summer glanced up from her work to look at the two maids currently talking about her. They pretended to be dusting the many bookshelves in the wood-lined room, but Summer could feel them looking at her as they spoke behind their hands.

Enough was enough. A glance at the grandfather clock announced lunchtime was upon her. Summer got up from her desk and hurried from the room, tears burning her eyes. She hadn't asked for this. All she wanted was to have a little adventure, to break away from the norm, to help a friend. But the only thing she was accomplishing was being deceitful to her aunt and undermining her parents' wishes for her life.

She came out of the house with her lunch bag in hand and started stomping in the general direction of the creek. Summer swiped tears out of her eyes and kept marching, following the flow of the water as it wound a path away from the house and road.

It seemed the faster she walked, the faster the tumult of emotion that had been bottled up inside came rushing out. Tears of anguish at being forced to live up to everyone's expectations her entire life came pouring down her face. Her lack of success at trying to help Laura and her brother tormented her with each passing step.

It dawned on her after she had walked for a while that her distress had turned into a prayer for help. Her parents had never encouraged praying aloud, unless it was to impress a visiting vicar, but Summer had always felt closer to her heavenly Father when she did.

"Father God, I need your help! Can't you see I am in way over my head here? How in the world did I end up in this mess?" Summer stopped and covered her face in her hands and sobbed softly. She could feel her hair upon her shoulders, but didn't care that her pins had fallen in her haste to get away. It wasn't her hair that needed repair now, it was her heart. Her life.

The house now well out of sight, she dropped to her knees and faced the murmuring creek. Head still in her hands, Summer asked God for guidance and wisdom. As she lifted her burdens to the Lord, she felt a peace come over her, a peace she hadn't felt in a long while. Not since that fateful day at the racetrack.

As the tears subsided, Summer prayed, "What should I do now? Do you even want me here? Or should I just go home and live in the box my parents have created for me?"

Clear as could be, a voice whispered in her heart, *Tell Aunt Elizabeth.*

That's what she should do? How strange. Summer had thought the Lord would have told her where to look for her next clue or possibly to even go home to North Carolina. What did Aunt Elizabeth have to do with any of this?

The words echoed in her heart once more, and Summer nodded her head in answer as she got up and began to look for a place to eat her lunch. "Yes, God. I will."

"Your new employee certainly left in a huff."

Christian watched covertly through a door that was open just a crack as Harriet Wilson regarded her husband with suspicious eyes.

"This wouldn't happen to be a lover's quarrel would it, dear?" Her cold gray eyes matched her silver hair.

George Wilson's frame seemed to take up the small room in which they spoke, but Mrs. Wilson didn't appear intimidated in the least. Instead, she held her ground and pinned him in place with a simple look.

The powerful politician slammed his hand down on an end table. "Dash it all, woman! Why do you go around making trouble where there isn't any?"

Harriet Wilson circled her husband, ending up eye to eye with him again. She ran a hand down his lapel and smiled demurely. "So, you aren't having an affair with her? I must say, she is the most beautiful young lady I have seen in quite some time."

"No, I am not having an affair with her. How could you even ask such a question? Wait, don't answer that. Although, it has been years since I have wandered from home."

"Maybe she's part of your scheme, then? A lovely distraction perhaps for your highest bidders? I dare say some of your cronies would have a heyday with her and maybe even fatten your coffers more than you thought."

"My scheme? The highest bidders? Harriet, what are you talking about? If this is about my gambling, I assure you, I have that under control as well. You know once I became a team owner, it was easy to give that up." Mr. Wilson began to pace the room, dominating the space three strides at a time. "Just because I like to go to the track and watch my horses compete every now and then doesn't mean I have a problem."

"Check your accounting books, dearest. I hear rumors they are fatter than ever." Harriet made her way to the door, causing Christian to walk down the hall and miss her final comment.

As Mrs. Wilson walked in the opposite direction, Christian let himself out the nearest door and took a moment to examine what he had just heard. He leaned up against the side of the home, breathing freely once again.

Could it be true? Was George Wilson completely oblivious to the counterfeit ring being housed somewhere on his own property? He had sounded incredulous when his wife inquired about his *scheme*, as if he had no idea what she was talking about. It was more probable that Mr. Wilson just didn't want his wife to know about his underhanded business dealings. Then again, it sounded as if she already knew. But why try to throw her off his scent if she was previously aware?

Christian began heading to his next chore, lost in speculation, when he saw the lovely Summer rushing headlong toward the south side of the property. It looked like she was going out alone and by the looks of her posture, she was quite upset. There were plenty of ranch hands who had commented on her attractiveness, making lewd jokes at her expense. Christian felt compelled to follow her, just to make sure she was safe. It had nothing to do with how her tiny waist had felt in his hands this morning as he'd helped her from her horse or how her hair would look if she let it down from her tight chignon. It certainly didn't have to do with the reality that he couldn't get her off his mind, night or day, no matter how hard he tried. Nope, that wasn't it at all.

It had been Christian's experience that if a sudden change took place after a horrific event, something other than tragedy was at play. Frederick Ellis was a fine example of just that. The man's recent employment as George Wilson's chief accountant was highly suspect. That simple change of staff in George Wilson's office could be a giant clue that he had been overlooking. Christian didn't know why he hadn't seen it from the beginning. But after witnessing the odd exchange between Mr. Ellis and the stranger in the forest, Christian knew a deeper investigation of the man was in order. And the sooner the better. He would send a letter by messenger this very day to the head office so they could do a thorough background check on the man.

It had also been his experience that if someone broke away from their regular routine, like Summer was doing now, it usually proved useful to follow that person and find out what they were up to.

Summer seemed to be following the course of the river, whether she meant to or not. From the looks of her heaving shoulders, she didn't care where she was going. She simply stumbled along, nearly missing a fall at times.

Christian kept his distance at first, though as he closed in just a bit, he doubted she could hear his footsteps over her weeping. She slowed her steps and began to speak out loud. Christian felt his mouth drop open as he realized what she was doing. Praying? She was praying? Go figure.

When Christian had followed her into the forest, he had assumed she was part of the whole counterfeit ring. Why else would a lady risk life and limb to spy on a couple of men in the middle of nowhere?

But seeing her now kneeling in prayer, straight blonde hair hanging around her shoulders as the sun lit it aglow, he wondered how she could have anything to do with evil. She was simply a girl, praying to a God she obviously believed in, obviously trusted.

"Miss?" Christian could take it no more. Although she had stood again, he knew she was a woman in need. How could he ignore that? He lightly touched her on the shoulder and she jumped about a foot in surprise.

"Oh!" Summer quickly swiped at her eyes, but Christian would be a fool if he chose to look past the torment he saw there. "I didn't realize anyone else was out here." She dipped her head formally. "Please accept my deepest apologies, sir."

Bowing slightly, Christian tried to find his voice. The combination of those green eyes and gorgeous blonde hair down to her waist were enough to leave any man speechless. Her tears had caused her eyes to take on the look of light green emeralds shimmering in the sun, and her cheeks had blossomed rosy spots on each side. Her lips trembled slightly and Christian had to hold himself back from taking the two steps that separated them and kissing those lips until Summer Edwards could no longer remember why she had been crying in the first place.

But instead of giving into impulse, he did his best to formulate a reply. "No harm done." He gestured toward a smooth, flat rock perfectly positioned along the bank of the river. "Would you care to eat your lunch over there, Miss Edwards?"

She looked, nodded, then settled in and smoothed her skirts around her ankles.

Christian took a place beside her and began to throw small pebbles into the river that played a lovely melody as it wove along the ground. He stole a glimpse of Summer's sweet face and realized she looked a little more relaxed as she seemed to take in the natural beauty surrounding them. It wasn't a mountainous area, but time and the river had forged a small natural valley bordered by numerous trees. If Christian didn't know it, he would have thought they were far from civilization, not a mere half-mile from the main house.

"If you were looking for the perfect picnic spot, I think we may have found it."

She smiled slightly and placed a bag onto her lap. "I have plenty to share, if you would like. I always bring my lunch to work with me, but usually eat at my desk."

"I know." Summer's eyes flew to his. "I mean, I figured you did, since you're probably so busy in the office." Fool. He should just keep his mouth shut. But in this case, changing the subject would have to do. "Forgive me for asking, Miss Edwards, but when I first saw you the day we both arrived to seek employment, you didn't strike me as a common scullery maid." She frowned. "That was supposed to be a compliment, but I fear I may have fudged it a bit."

"No, no. No offense taken. You're right; I have never been a maid." Summer hesitated. "I came that day looking for work and was blessed to end up in Mr. Wilson's office instead." She held out half a sandwich to him. "I think Cook may have put some apple fritters in here, too."

EIGHT

G reat. How many servants or working-class girls had cooks in their employ? How in the world was Summer going to talk her way out of this one? She remembered with utter clarity the promise she had made to God about not telling anyone a lie about why she was working for the former governor. Now here she was sitting next to a man she would very much like to get to know and the moment of truth was before her. Christian had said she didn't look like a common maid when she first arrived. It wasn't a question exactly, so Summer figured she could avoid answering—for now. But she had a feeling getting to know anyone around there meant the truth would eventually come out.

Summer took a bite of the thick slices of ham on the stone ground bread and closed her eyes. The combination of the good food and the music of the creek were doing wonders to calm her heart.

It's so peaceful here. She felt she could spend all day sunning in this very spot and not spend one moment on the worries that plagued her. All thoughts of murders and jail, clues and conversations flew out of her head as the sound of the water brought the serenity she sought.

She thought about her prayer on her walk out to this spot. Two things stuck in her mind the most—how much more peaceful she felt now and how she needed to talk with Aunt Elizabeth about all of this as soon as possible.

Summer's mind had wandered from the broad-shouldered man sitting beside her until he cleared his throat. "It's good to see a woman's cares melt away. I hope it is okay to say that I saw you praying earlier." Christian gave her a slow wink that sent her heart skittering. "What is going on in that pretty little head of yours?"

Summer felt her face fill with heat. She finished her sandwich and started in on the fritter, buying time to calm her nerves. This man had such an effect on her. His brown eyes held a depth that Summer wanted to discover. But, oh, what was she thinking? She was no common girl, but the daughter of one of the most prominent businessmen in North Carolina. Her father would have her hide if she got tangled up with some livery boy. Marvin Edwards hadn't spent dollar upon dollar raising his only child to choose such a man. No, instead he had his eyes open for just the right man to come along, someone who would be a good addition to the family, someone who brought with him prestige and power and wealth.

But as Summer watched Christian, thoughts of her father seemed very far away. Christian didn't look away when he caught her gaze, but instead seemed content to be just where he was. And so was she.

Elizabeth leaned back on the deck of the *Morning Princess*, letting the summer sun soak into her skin.

She looked at Dustin from beneath lowered lashes and smiled to herself. Dustin Edwards was every bit the gentleman he had been when they were close so many years before. From his perch near the bow of the sailboat he caught her looking and smiled that charming, multi-layered smile that could light up the entire cove.

He beckoned her with his finger, making her heart slam against her chest. All morning, Dustin had been trying to pry her open little by little with his tender ways. She could feel her heart slowly cracking under the pressure of his care for her. But what would happen if she handed him a sledgehammer to knock a peephole in her carefully protected fortress? Oh, she was just being silly. What would a man of Dustin Edwards' caliber want with used garbage like her?

Dustin had told her, as they ate their light breakfast on board, that he had come in response to the letter Elizabeth had sent to Ruth. Elizabeth smiled ruefully at the speediness of the postal service. But never in a million years had Elizabeth suspected her sister to send her brother-in-law, Dustin. Didn't Ruth know what a loop this would send Elizabeth for when her first love showed up on her doorstep? Obviously not, otherwise she would have sent a servant, or even herself. And what would Summer think when she found out her uncle had come to see if she was behaving? Summer and Elizabeth's budding relationship would wilt before it ever had a chance to grow.

Giving in to Dustin's summons, Elizabeth crossed the deck to where he sat. She could taste the salt on her lips as she took in the sight of the water that surrounded them. This view, this feeling of freedom was why she came out there. Because when she did, everything else faded. But today, Dustin's presence unsettled her more than any past recollection could.

"How've you been, Lizzy?" He smiled, encouraging her to respond.

"Um, I've been good. Time passes, little by little."

"What keeps you busy these days?"

If she was honest with him, he may leave before she had the chance to connect with him. But then again, Dustin always had the uncanny ability to read right into her soul, whether she wanted him to or not.

"Well, as you can probably imagine, having Summer here keeps me occupied. She is a delight to have around." Did he know? Had her secret been revealed to him at some point over the years? Did he know why she had to leave North Carolina?

Dustin laughed, a jolly sound that threaded its way deep inside Elizabeth. "I'm sure she keeps you hopping. She is certainly wonderful to have around. I can attest to that." He paused and reached out to catch her hand up in his own. "Oh, Lizzy, you should have seen her at her debutante ball when she was fifteen. She was so full of life, so beautiful."

His eyes suddenly misted, and Elizabeth pulled her hand back and turned her face away. He knew. How horrible! And how wonderful. Oh, to be released from the burden of this life-swallowing secret! To be able to share it with someone else. Or perhaps to be embarrassed beyond belief in front of this man she had spent almost half of her life loving from afar.

"Elizabeth. Look at me."

She slowly turned his way and blinked back the tears that threatened.

"Ruth and Marvin sent me here to check up on Summer." Dustin took her hand once again. "I accepted their request without hesitation." With his other hand he stroked down her cheek. "But I knew Summer could hold her own. What I'm trying to say is that I wanted to see you. Lizzy, I came here for you."

Boy, was he in trouble. Christian rolled over for the hundredth time on his lumpy cot in the bunkhouse, trying to get to sleep. But as tight as he closed his eyes, the image of Summer crying out to God wouldn't go away. He pictured again her genuine tears as she brought her requests before a Lord she obviously believed in. He shifted again, remembering the days when he himself would turn to the God his mother had taught him about. Even back then, in his childlike faith, he wondered what kind of God would give a boy an abusive, lying father. His faith had grown, though, as he left home and had the chance to become a man without his father's deception to taint his view of life.

But then, like a flame suddenly snuffed out by a torrential downpour, his faith had been extinguished by the pain of Tabitha's betrayal. The final embers had faded when the news of their baby's death reached him. Christian had walked away from his Lord and never looked back. Until today.

That confounded woman! First, she had the gall to look like an angel, then she had the nerve to possess a sweet disposition. Now she was making him remember the days when he felt close enough to call on God and have communion with Him.

He rolled over in bed again and was rewarded with a thump from the bunk below. Christian kicked off the twisted covers, jumped down and got dressed in the dark. Just because sleep was as far away as the nearest desert didn't mean everyone else in the bunkhouse had to pay for it.

Pulling on his boots, he stepped out into the night and leaned against the bunkhouse. He didn't want his heart to be seen for the black hole it was, so the darkness was a welcome sight. But before he could squelch it, a Scripture he didn't even know he remembered came bubbling up to the surface, its words piercing his heart. "If I say, Surely the darkness shall cover me; even the night shall be light about me. Yea, the darkness hideth not from thee; but the night shineth as the day: the darkness and the light are both alike to thee."

Christian slammed his fist into the bunkhouse wall and pushed off, trying to outrun the words from the psalm that now banged around inside his head. "O lord, thou hast searched me, and known me. ... Whither shall I flee from thy presence? ...Search me, O God, and know my heart: try me, and know my thoughts."

Christian started to run, his feet carrying him wherever they pleased. His eyes felt blinded as he tried to escape the truth of the words that were haunting him. How terrible that God could see his thoughts and know his heart! He wanted to hide, but the Bible said that was impossible. God was everywhere, had seen everything he had done. Knew his prideful heart and the places his feet had carried him all these years. Oh, the shame he felt at trying to be independent from the Lord. He was a fool to think God had turned His back on him. It was Christian who had done the turning. He could see that now.

A movement in the near pitch black of the night caught his attention. Christian was near the atrium at the rear of the Wilson's home and watched as a shadowed figure stooped to slip through a small door only two and a half or three feet in height, probably used for shoveling out old mulch and plant clippings. All of the tumultuous feelings he had been experiencing were suddenly gone as his eyes scanned the interior of the atrium through the glass enclosure. There was no one in sight. But Christian was smart enough to know when he had been put in the right place at the right time. He ducked through the small door frame, then hid behind a nearby fruiting tree, trying to spot any sign of movement.

There! The man was going into the home by means of the heavy double doors that opened onto a hallway. Christian quickly removed his shoes so he could silently follow the prowler. Since coming to work for Wilson, Christian had yet to find any clues that led to the whereabouts of the counterfeit ring or any evidence that would hold up in a court of law. None of his covert questioning of employees had generated helpful information. The report he had requested from headquarters on Frederick Ellis had yet to come back. Christian felt empty handed. George Wilson was obviously a master at disguising his devious ways but Christian knew witnessing this clandestine breech of the Wilsons' privacy could be his first big break in this case.

Christian remained out of sight as he followed the man through the house and was not the least bit surprised when the fellow slunk down the hallway that led to George Wilson's offices. Of course, this had to do with money. Didn't it always? If this were an average burglar, he would have perused the parlors of the home, pocketing crystal or possibly raiding the safes for jewelry. But only trouble could be found in the offices of a crooked politician and his counterfeiting ring.

He watched from the shadows as the man went to a desk bearing a nameplate that read *Frederick Ellis* and lit a small candle. Since the home was built a few miles out of the city, it did not have the modern convenience of electric lights. But it was more than risky to light a candle; anyone from the outside could see light from the windows of the first-floor office and anyone from the household would be able to see light spilling into the hallway.

Despite this misstep, the man obviously knew what he was looking for. For who could harbor the secrets of Mr. Wilson more than his own accountant? *Blackguard,* thought Christian. Then for the first time in his detective career, he felt a pang of something uncomfortable in his chest. He could almost picture God looking at him, knowing his movements and thoughts. Did He approve of what Christian was doing? Was it wrong to break and enter into a home when you were trying to gain information that could potentially help many people? He dismissed the disturbing thoughts and continued to watch from his hiding place.

The intruder slowed his movements and sat down almost reverently in Mr. Ellis's chair. The fellow had a hat on, so Christian couldn't see his face, but he could see him reach into his pocket and produce a key. He tried the key in each of the drawers, but it didn't seem to match any of them. The burglar got up and walked all around the desk, looking, Christian supposed, for a hidden compartment. Not finding one, the man ducked under the desk and in less than ten seconds, Christian first heard a gasp and then the satisfying click of a lock being turned. The man quickly emerged with a large portfolio-type book in his hands. Setting it on the desktop, he ran his hands down the length of the first page. If only Christian could get closer to see what was written there. He had a hunch it had everything to do with the production of fake money.

As Christian crouched in the shadows, he pondered his next move. Should he confront the burglar and risk the possibility of a shoot-out? Obviously, this man knew what he was looking for and had confiscated the key for this very purpose. Should Christian wait until the man was gone, then pick the lock to find the valuable information he may need to break this case wide open? Or should he follow the man to find where he was taking his stolen information? Yes, he decided. The latter was the best of the three options.

The intruder produced a small notebook and appeared to be copying whatever was on the page.

It was only a matter of minutes before the book was replaced and the key the fellow had used was put in what was likely its normal hiding place. There appeared to be a secret compartment just under the center drawer for such a purpose. This bit of information would be highly beneficial for Christian, for he would certainly return and investigate that portfolio on his own.

Christian followed the man outside and watched him ride away on a horse that had been tied to a tree. Christian quicky mounted his own steed and set off down the road, keeping a safe distance so as to not be discovered. It had taken years of tracking criminals to hone this particular skill. Now he was a master at it.

After a good fifteen minutes, they finally entered what appeared to be an extremely well-to-do neighborhood. Christian would not confront the individual tonight, but now that he knew where this low-life thief took his information, Christian could learn who resided in this most beautiful of homes and find the next link in the chain of criminals who were corrupting this city.

As horse and rider drew near the house, Christian expected the intruder to hitch his horse and deliver whatever message he had written down. Or perhaps go around to the back and slip a note under the door or call on the master of the house away from neighbors' prying eyes. Instead, the thief put his horse in the stable and slipped through the darkness to the back door of the home. Christian quickly dismounted and let Sadie stand. Just in the nick of time, Christian saw the man turn a key, thereby letting himself inside. Christian's heartbeat picked up a bit as he watched from the shadows. Why, this was no common thief but rather what appeared to be a rich man poking his nose around George Wilson's office in hopes of getting richer.

That new accountant had better watch his back. Christian couldn't help but wonder if Frederick Ellis would be the next person to lose his life.

NINE

Summer didn't think her heart had ever pounded so hard. She could hear nothing but the blood pulsating in her ears. She leaned heavily against the servants' entrance door, taking deep calming breaths. It didn't work.

Her hands shook noticeably as she patted the inside pocket of the masculine coat she wore. The matches and candle were contained there, along with her scribbled notes from the ledger. Her nerves tingled at the thought of the revealing evidence she'd just garnered.

Earlier that afternoon, she stayed late in the office with the excuse of finishing an assignment. Her patience had paid off when she had made pretense of leaving for the day only to come back less than a minute later. Mr. Ellis was the only person left in the room and Summer had come back just in time to see him pull open a small drawer and withdraw a long skeleton key. He pocketed it immediately when he saw her enter, and she had watched sweat break out on his forehead. She had ducked her head demurely and mumbled something about forgetting her umbrella. It had been a worthwhile ruse.

Going back to the Wilson mansion after midnight was risky, but she knew her find of the little door leading into the atrium would be the perfect entry point. Each step in her action plan had led to this small victory. It was abundantly clear why the accountant kept this particular ledger locked away. Undoubtedly, George Wilson was into something illegal. Summer was sure of it. Even if he had under-the-table campaign supporters, all their contributions would never amass to that much money. Now it was a question of where the money was coming from and who was involved.

She looked down at her getup and couldn't suppress a chuckle. Boy, did she look a sight! It calmed her beating heart a bit to remember Laura helping her don some of her brother's clothes, including pants four sizes too large and an oversized hat to hide her blonde locks. Laura had taken several dozen pins and tucked under the hat every last one of Summer's strands so no one would recognize her mistress. Summer wondered if Laura would be able to wait until the morning before getting a full account of what had transpired. Summer wanted to lend her friend some confidence that her brother would someday be released from jail. That is, unless Landon Moore had somehow gotten himself entangled with George Wilson. Summer doubted it.

A white envelope on the kitchen work table caught her eye. Her name was scrawled on the front. *Miss Summer.* Only the household staff called her that, and she had a feeling it was neither Cook nor Matthew who had left her the missive. She tore it open to reveal Laura's handwriting.

Inside was a brief but apologetic paragraph from her friend. Laura had received permission from Elizabeth to stay with a grandmother until the situation with Landon was resolved. Laura promised to pray for Summer and to visit Landon on her way out of town. She left the address of her grandmother's home, about an hour's travel by train from Waterford Cove. Laura apologized for not having the nerve to withstand the circumstances and hoped her time with her grandmother would be an encouragement to the entire Moore family.

Truly, Summer tried to understand but suddenly felt very much alone in her quest. She reached down to untie her black boots and gasped suddenly. All thoughts of self-pity flew out of her head, for right next to where she was standing lay a pair of very large dark brown loafers of the highest quality. *What in the world?* The only man who ever set foot in this house was Matthew, and that was only to take his meals between outdoor chores.

Her boots in one hand and Laura's letter in the other, Summer quickly climbed the back staircase in the darkness and felt her way along the hallway wall to her bedroom door. Her question about whom the loafers belonged to would have to wait. The first order of business was to shed her disguise and get into her nightgown. Her hand shook slightly as she turned the knob in the darkness.

Summer had not anticipated Laura leaving town. She had been looking forward to sharing what information she had gleaned tonight. It would have bolstered the girl's anticipation of a good outcome for her brother.

Rolling her borrowed clothes into a bundle, she remembered her earlier conversation with God and how she'd felt Him direct her to tell her aunt everything. She would not ignore God's leading on this. Summer was sure He had led her to ferret out the truth; now, she would continue to obey Him.

As she changed into her nightgown and stashed the bundle under the bed, she wondered about the men's shoes she'd seen downstairs. Was it possible her aunt was keeping company? Summer never would have suspected that from Elizabeth. Summer instantly berated herself for thinking such a thing. Why, Elizabeth was a Christian and would never succumb to such temptation. Her aunt most likely had a visiting relative or was offering hospitality to someone from the church. Yes, that must be it. Needing time to mull over what she had found in the ledger before turning in for the night, Summer made her way back to the kitchen.

She didn't want to risk turning on an overhead light for fear of waking her aunt, so she made her tea by candlelight then sat down at the kitchen work table. As she sipped the hot drink, she kept glancing at the shoes by the back door.

Suddenly a light flipped on and two female screams resounded in the kitchen.

Summer stood up on impulse from the start she'd just received and bumped her thighs against the table. "Oof!" She sat back down with a thud as the amber tea crested over the rim of her mug. "Aunt Elizabeth!"

Elizabeth looked equally as startled, her face turning white enough to match her nightgown. "Why, Summer, it's past midnight! What are you doing in here?"

Summer was suddenly grateful she had changed out of men's clothing before making herself something to drink. If Elizabeth had seen her earlier, she would have had to tell her aunt she'd just broken into someone's home. That would clearly mean being sent back to North Carolina before she figured this whole thing out. And she wasn't ready to do that yet.

"I, um, was just thinking of having a nice hot drink to make me sleepy." Summer cleared her throat and got up to fetch a rag. "What are you doing here?" Summer decided to try to take the attention off of herself so no more questions would be asked.

She got her reward when Elizabeth's face went from stark white to blazing red. "I, um, was just thinking the same thing."

Summer cast her eyes at the shoes sitting beside the back door. "Whose are those? I don't recall Matthew having such expensive taste."

Elizabeth waved a hand in the air. "Oh, no, no. Those aren't Matthews." She turned her back and busied herself at the counter preparing hot chocolate for herself in a stoneware mug. A few moments of silence followed, and Summer waited to see what her aunt would say.

"No, they aren't Matthew's at all." Elizabeth turned around and appeared to be trying to compose herself. "Summer, your Uncle Dustin is here." She went on in a rush, "Now before you get all—"

"Uncle Dustin! I can't wait to see him. When did he get here? Why is he—?" Reality slammed into Summer like a wall of waves crashing over her. "Oh. Mother and Father sent him, didn't they? To collect me and bring me home." It was more of a statement than a question. Tears pricked her eyes and she leaned her forehead on her hand. What had she been thinking? Her parents weren't going to let her go so easily. She had only been fooling herself to think their arm of control wouldn't reach to Virginia. Her shoulders felt tense at the realization that it was all over. She was about to be hustled back to North Carolina where for the rest of her life she would be required to be the perfect wife and daughter. Hot rage burned inside her chest at the confinement her parents were about to put her in.

"There, there, dear. Don't get yourself all worked up. I know what you're thinking, and your uncle is just here to see how you are doing. Once he sees you're getting along just fine, he's sure to head home and deliver the good news." Elizabeth sat down across the table from Summer and looked her in the eye. "I know you've enjoyed the freedom you've found here away from your parents. Rest assured and simply take advantage of the time you do have here in Waterford Cove, hmm?"

Summer looked at her beloved aunt and wished her own mother was so comforting. Oh, yes, her mother had parented her, but not in a sweet, tender way. When she spoke, she used more of an authoritative tone, always leaving Summer feeling like she was never good enough. She sighed and thanked her aunt. They sat that way for a while, and even though Summer didn't choose that moment to confide in Elizabeth, she felt now as she had each time in her aunt's presence—there was something special about this lady.

Elizabeth put her hand to her head as she made her way up the staircase to her room. What a predicament she had gotten herself into. Now Summer knew Dustin was here, and Elizabeth was positive Dustin knew she was Summer's mother. The walls of secrecy and protection that had taken two decades to build were slowly but surely crumbling down around her.

A hand on her shoulder as she turned the knob of her bedroom door made her gasp and whirl around. "Dustin!" she whispered loudly. "You scared me half to death! What are you doing up at this time of night?"

Even in the darkened hall, Elizabeth imagined she could see the clear blue of his eyes boring into her own green ones. Instinctively, she put a hand to her hair, knowing it was pure foolishness to worry about her appearance in the darkness. *My goodness, this man has an effect on me.*

"I was up doing some praying and heard you coming down the hall. Or at least I hoped it was you." There was a smile in his voice and he laid his free hand on her other shoulder.

Now she was trapped for sure. But what a wonderful trap to be in. Normally, her natural impulse would be to run and hide, but the butterflies doing a dance in her stomach wouldn't let her get out of this so easily.

She started talking to distract herself from wondering what Dustin's lips would feel like on hers. Not that she didn't know, but right here, right now, would they feel different than they had all those years ago?

"Elizabeth." Dustin's voice came out low and husky. "I want you to know I was praying for you. You are such a special lady, but I know you've hid yourself from real life for fear of being hurt again."

Elizabeth turned her face away and tried to shrug out from underneath his hands. Before she could get one step away, there was Dustin, turning her face to his. Never had he used force with her, but always a gentleness that reminded her of her Savior. She imagined this is how Jesus would look at her—an absence of condemnation, an assurance of grace and love.

"I know God placed me here at this time, in this place. And I will do all I can to encourage you to face your demons and let God and others love you." And with that, he caressed the side of her cheek then turned to walk to his room at the other end of the hall.

Summer stayed in the kitchen listening to the sounds outside the window. The crickets repeated their chirping song while the wind tickled its way through the late summer leaves. They were the sounds of change, sounds that ushered in a new season. Summer got up from the table, blew out the candle, turned off the light, and thought of her own season of change. She'd had twenty years in the summer of life's sun. Would the beauty of autumn fade too quickly into winter the deeper she went into this venture?

When Summer had stowed herself away in her room, she took a good, long look at her reflection in the mirror. She still looked like the same girl who had left North Carolina, but she felt entirely different inside. Some of the changes were good; some not so good. She certainly felt more alive than ever before, but there was also a sense of trepidation, a feeling of tenuousness that threaded through her middle, emotions that had never been there before. *Honesty is the best policy*, Uncle Dustin used to tell her. Maybe that was the reason she felt she was on shaky ground.

Taking her hastily scribbled notes from the ledger to bed with her, she sat up against the oak headboard. She remembered seeing deposits and withdrawals when she had first looked at the ledger, in addition to seeing a pattern of large sums of money being recorded on the first and the fifteenth of the month. But it was the amounts in the columns of the ledger that she had recorded for her own notes, amounts that were just as astonishing as she studied them a second time.

What in the world could George Wilson be doing to earn such a sum? Summer knew the world of politics was affluent, but never in her life had she even imagined such numbers. She was fairly certain even her father's healthy business didn't turn such profits.

Suddenly, Summer's mouth felt dry as a realization struck her. This was dirty money. No one could come by such sums naturally. Of course. The murder! With clarity she saw it now. Ellis was in his seat of power, in the perfect position to extend some of these monies to the man who had gotten him the job. The same man who Summer saw talking with Ellis in the woods that one evening. Andrew.

She thought back to the conversation she overheard in the woods; Andrew making threats at poor sweating Mr. Ellis. Had the man gotten his payoff yet? He certainly had been angry, threats spewing from his mouth. Summer shuddered. How she would hate to run into him face to face.

Putting her notes on the bedside table, Summer got out from under her covers and knelt by the bed. She spent some time in prayer until her heartbeat returned to its normal pace. As she prayed, she remembered what God had spoken to her. Clear as a bell, she had heard she needed to tell Aunt Elizabeth what was going on. And yet tonight, she had been deceitful, changing her clothes quickly so no one would know what she'd been doing. She had hidden her actions and been duplicitous.

Well, that's going to change, she decided as she turned out the light and crawled under the soft downy covers. *Lord, give me the strength and courage to tell Elizabeth by the end of the week.* Summer resolved she would put on her bravest face and talk with her aunt, even if it meant she had to pack her bags and leave on the fastest train bound for Charlotte.

TEN

Christian turned and faced the bunk window and watched as daylight turned the morning a pale gray. In his mind's eye, he kept seeing the events of the previous week unfold. The intruder slipping inside the Wilson mansion. Covertly observing the man taking information from what appeared to be a secret ledger. Following the intruder to a fashionable neighborhood where the man let himself in by a back door he was obviously familiar with. And then the best parts, picnicking with Summer every day by the river.

He never thought it would happen. But the fact of the matter was, he was growing quite attached to the young lady. She was private about certain areas of her life, but Christian let it slide. He hadn't exactly been forthright with her about everything. How could he? Various aspects had to be avoided but when they talked, Christian decided to divulge as much as he could.

In half an hour's time, the property would be teeming with activity, everyone ready to tackle the day. Christian smiled to himself as he quickly pulled on his clothes, donned a hat with a large front brim, and put his lock pick in his coat pocket. How he loved the chase, the unique opportunity to catch a snake like George Wilson and pull the rug out from under him.

The atrium stood sentinel against the brick of the house and Christian questioned using this entrance with the light just beginning to break. Maybe a different door that was surrounded by shrubbery or trees would provide a better cover. He decided to risk it, hoping the dawn would provide just enough darkness for him to make his way to the little glass door that would give him entrance.

Movement from the corner of his eye caught his attention and Christian froze, still as a statue up against the wall of the atrium. He should have gone with his first instincts, knowing the glass was practically worthless in disguising his presence there. Hopefully whoever or whatever was in the half-dark with him, had no knowledge of his presence.

A voice, thin and demeaning, cut through him like a dull saw blade. He felt his face grow hard and his body rigid as Shaw, a fellow Pinkerton, sauntered around the corner like he owned the place. "Christian Titus. I should have known they'd put the likes of you on this case. No wonder old George is able to continue his politician ruse." The smaller man laughed as he stopped a foot from Christian. "Good thing I'm here now. A real man on the job is what they need. And now they've got it."

"Shaw," Christian breathed through clenched teeth. "Who sent you? I was doing just fine on my own." For reasons unknown to him, Christian felt the need to defend himself to this lowlife excuse for an agent. "In fact, I was just about to locate some very important documents, but now I'll have to wait. It's too light but it wouldn't have been if you hadn't delayed me."

Christian started walking away, not able to stand the sight of the man. He and Shaw had been on a case together a few years back, and Christian had always felt in his gut that the man was a cheat and a liar. He'd never had any proof, but just the same, he'd avoided the man at all costs. Now it appeared they were assigned to the same location. Christian was so mad he wanted to spit.

He got about ten paces away and whirled around. Shaw just stood there, leaning up against the atrium, cleaning his glasses. "Titus, you can just pack your bags and go on home. Tell the bosses at the main office I don't need you. I'll have this thing closed up in less than a week."

Shaw's needling, whiny voice followed Christian as he stalked over to the stables. A good ride was what he needed. Swinging up onto his bareback horse, Christian rode like the wind toward town, all the while hearing Shaw's voice saying he wasn't good enough, just like his father had always told him. Just like his father.

"I'd like to talk to you, Miss Edwards." George Wilson stood like a giant next to Summer's desk. His booming voice rang around the room, bouncing off the wood paneling and every ear in the place. "Have lunch with me today in the atrium. Say around noon?"

Before Summer could barely nod her head, the broad-shouldered man walked away and was starting a conversation with Frederick Ellis. What was it about this man that drew her so? Without question, he was handsome and powerful in his field of influence, but something resided just under the surface whenever Summer spoke with him.

Up until now, all of their conversations had been business related. File this, run an errand for that. Now she had a lunch invitation from the man? She earnestly hoped he didn't have anything up his sleeve. He was twice her age and a married man! Her cheeks burned with the thought. She felt as if every eye in the room was trained upon her and after she dared a look, it appeared her suspicions were not unfounded.

Already she was subject to much gossip. Now this. Her reputation would go down the drain. What would possess a prominent politician to ask a humble—at least in his eyes—employee to have lunch with him? In the atrium, no less?

Summer looked at the clock and realized she would find out soon enough. It was nearing ten o'clock even now. She had come in early the morning after her little caper. That was days ago now and her heart still pounded at the possibility of being caught. If anyone knew she was privy to confidential information about all that money, she would become a target. Summer took a deep breath and tried to focus on the paperwork she had been assigned to that morning. The letters and numbers crossed in front of her eyes, and she couldn't seem to get a breath as she thought of losing her life. Was all of this worth it?

She stood up and felt a bit woozy, but made her way to the head secretary's desk just the same. She had to get out of there. With disgruntled permission to take a break, Summer ran down the stairs and nearly flew outside. Christian Titus stood not twenty feet from her, and she drank in the sight of him like fresh water.

He was making his way toward her, and Summer tried to school her face into something that resembled a ladylike expression. Years of training and practice in her mother's drawing room had taught her never to show her true emotions.

"Miss Edwards," Christian tipped his hat and smiled at her. "Looks like you were headed somewhere," he asked with a question in his voice. "It's a little early for lunch."

Summer laughed lightly. "Oh, you know me, always looking for a reason to get out of the office." She smoothed down her dress distractedly.

"Actually, I'm really just beginning to know you," Christian replied as he gave her a slight wink. "But I can't wait to find out more."

"I meant—"

Christian laughed, a jolly sound that made Summer feel at ease. "I know what you meant. Have no worries." His smile disappeared and he looked soberly at her. "But the hours we've been able to spend together have meant more to me than you'll ever know." He kicked at a tuft of grass then looked back up at her. "How about we meet right here at noon?"

Summer knew her cheeks were even more flushed now than they had been when everyone had been staring at her after George Wilson's lunch invitation. "Well, I—" She hesitated, not knowing if it was wise to tell him that she was having lunch with someone else. But how could she not? He would wonder and just ask questions.

Christian looked embarrassed at her hesitation. He started to back away as he said, "Forget I said anything."

Summer reached out and touched him on the arm. The warmth from his body radiated through her hand all the way up to her shoulder. It was unlike anything she had ever felt before. "No, wait," she said breathlessly. Why was it so hard to get oxygen right now? She attempted to fill her lungs then tried again. "I can't have lunch with you. Something else came up." Summer saw Christian's brow furrow. She went on quickly, "But I would love to see you after work."

Hope, pure and bright, filled Christian's face. "You would? I mean, great. I mean, may I pick you up tonight for dinner? With a chaperone, of course."

"Actually, come to think of it, I have plans this evening." As Christian's face fell, Summer had an idea. "What if you came along with us? My aunt and uncle and I are going to help at the orphanage over on Mangrove Street. Maybe we could all get dinner after. If you'd like?"

Christian looked thoughtful for a moment, as though his mind was far away. Then he gave a decisive nod and asked when and where they should meet. A minute later, she felt a thousand pounds lighter as she watched Christian walk away with a skip in his step.

Forget the gossiping servants and staff. And who needed the worries of controlling parents? So what if she was having lunch with a future senator in less than two hours? None of that mattered. In her mind's eye, all she could see was a pair of amber brown eyes looking back at her.

Christian's heart felt like it might have grown wings the way it was flapping around in his chest as he went about his morning chores. The hay felt lighter as he forked it in the stalls. The foreman's gruff commands rolled off his back. Not even thoughts of his run-in with Shaw earlier that morning could dampen his mood. Summer Edwards floated like a dream through his mind, and he counted the minutes until he would see her tonight.

But his heart fell when around lunchtime he walked past the rear of the home. Summer's shiny blonde hair caught his eye. She sat at a table in the atrium with none other than George Wilson. She smiled demurely at something he said and daintily ate what was on her plate. Christian knew he couldn't just stand there outside the glass wall of the atrium without drawing someone's attention. Either Summer or Mr. Wilson were bound to see him unless he hightailed it out of there.

Begrudgingly, he moved his feet, and soon Summer and the politician were out of sight. But they certainly were not out of mind. At first, he seethed inside, wanting to demand Summer not be near that crook. Then reason won out as he realized Summer probably had no idea who she was working for. She was just a beautiful girl who had gotten a good job in an office. Christian should not be surprised she had captured George Wilson's attention. She was a stunning beauty who had an intrigue about her that made a man want to be near her. No wonder the prominent politician had his eye on her. She was pure gold. It was probably why he had hired her in the first place.

Christian only hoped Summer would be sensible enough to see what the man was ultimately after. He also surprisingly found himself praying she would keep her morals and remember Mr. Wilson was a married man. Maybe Christian would ask her about the strange lunch when he saw her tonight. And maybe, just maybe, he would find that he could trust Summer Edwards.

Elizabeth was good at keeping busy. It was what had allowed her to remain halfway sane all these years, cooped up in her stately mansion on Lumière Square. Pretending was her other strong suit. Looking at the pictures that graced every wall in her home, she could get lost in their beauty and find herself in a daydream of faraway places. In her heart, she was a true pioneer. It would be unwise for a single woman to travel alone, she knew. So, she acquired as many photographs of the wild world as she could and added her own photographs of the sea whenever inspiration struck. These distractions allowed her to go through an entire week and never once let herself think of the past, Summer, or the love she lost the night she threw caution to the wind.

Thoughts of her mistakes were waking up as quickly as the morning, and she knew she'd better get busy before they had time to trap her again. She hadn't seen Dustin yet this morning, and with Laura gone visiting family, Elizabeth decided today was as good a day as any to give the upstairs rooms a good airing out before winter began to set in. Oh, how she hated when things smelled musty. Deciding to start with Summer's room, she bustled in the door and started stripping the bed.

Elizabeth folded the coverlet neatly but as she turned to remove the sheets, something inside her snapped. She grabbed the cotton sheets as though they were an offensive remnant of something best left in the trash bin. When they had felt the wrath of her hands, she turned to find something else to unleash upon. Her heart felt angry, and she knew she was being irrational, taking out her pent-up emotions on inanimate objects.

The rug was next. She took a broom from the hall closet and began to beat the rug until dust flew in every direction. She didn't even care that she was making a bigger mess with all the dirt flying through the air. No, it didn't matter. Nothing did. Nothing ever had. Not since she had sinned against God and ruined her future.

Taking one final blow to the rug, she felt a hand on her shoulder. *I should have known*, she thought, as the fire left her and she slowly set down the broom. Dustin had heard her. How could he have not? Maybe all during her tantrum she had known he would hear. She was trying to push him away. Maybe if he saw her at her worst, the inevitable would come. No one could care enough to stay and love her. Elizabeth knew she couldn't take the rejection of him leaving. The answer was simple. She would push him away. What man in his right mind would want a woman who wasn't in her own right mind?

Her heart both sank with despair and leapt with elation as she turned her face to look at his. It made her want to scream the way he looked at her. What right did he have to possess such compassion on such a despicable piece of the human species? And yet, he stood next to her, looking at her as if he was there to stay.

Elizabeth wasn't capable of having him in her presence any longer. The week had been torture, sitting with him for hours on end without really talking about anything of significance. Having dinner every night with Summer and Dustin and not being able to push from her mind the scenario of what it would have been like to have married Dustin and to have shared Summer as their daughter.

She needed to take action. She would have one final conversation with him, one hideous revealing of the truth and that would be that. No longer would she have to endure his loving gazes, his sweet caress of her cheek, only to know he would discard her the moment he knew the facts. Yes, it was clear now what she must do to protect her heart from further entrapment of this wonderful man. As it was, it would take the rest of her life to get over seeing him this one last time.

But before she could lay it all on the line, Dustin spoke first. "Why don't you meet me downstairs in about ten minutes, Lizzy? There are some things that need to be said." And with that, he walked away.

ELEVEN

Elizabeth forced her feet to carry her to her bedroom. She needed to collect her thoughts and freshen up a bit. Her emotions made it feel as though her body had been the recipient of a boxing glove. A hot bath sounded nice. And a good book, one she could lose herself in and not have to think about the wreckage of her life.

But one look in the mirror reminded her that there was a man downstairs, a wonderful, considerate man, who was waiting for her. When she thought of it, she had been mentally preparing for this conversation for twenty years. As she redid the pins in her hair, Elizabeth went through the conversation she had rehearsed so many times.

At first, after she found out she was expecting a child, she wondered what it would be like to talk with Dustin after she came back from her hiatus. She would picture herself at church or the market, running into Dustin. He, of course, would have moved on and his beautiful new wife would be hanging on his arm and smiling her charming smile.

But Elizabeth never came home. Instead, she had taken a deal, one that welded her prison bars together with money and beautiful material possessions. From there, the rehearsal of the conversation had changed. She imagined their reunion wouldn't be until she was old and gray. Finally, the years of pain and captivity would have faded and she would judge that enough time had passed and she could finally go home. A train would pull into the station in Charlotte, North Carolina. Elizabeth would use her cane to step foot onto her native soil once again. Dustin would be the first person she saw. He, of course, would be surrounded by his numerous grandchildren, while she stood there, like lamb before the slaughter. No, Dustin would never verbally throw her mistakes in her face, but seeing him with his loving family would be retaliation enough.

A quick look in the mirror told her no one would want to spend even a minute in her presence. She might as well get this over with. She wasn't the woman in either of those scenarios, but she could hold her ground while she took the final blows she deserved.

Dustin stood as she entered the parlor that was filled with morning light. His bright blue eyes stood out against his black suit coat, beckoning her with their warmth. For a moment, Elizabeth let her heart absorb him, taking in every detail of this man. Even though she knew she was setting herself up for a lifetime of dreams never fulfilled, she breathed him in one last time.

"Come sit by me." He gestured to the velvet davenport as he made himself comfortable again.

Elizabeth waved her hand in dismissal. "No, no. I couldn't." She took a chair by the fireplace where there was the least amount of light streaming in from the large picture window overlooking the square. That way if she blushed at her revelations to the man she loved, at least she would find some semblance of comfort in the shadows.

"Lizzy, I—"

"No, Dustin. Let me start. There is so much to be said that if I don't jump right in, I may never get it all out."

A look of patience combined with expectation settled on his face, and he sat forward with his elbows on his knees.

Elizabeth took a deep breath and began. "What I am about to tell you will probably make it so you never want to be near me again. Let me say in advance that I won't blame you for walking out and never looking back."

"Lizzy, I would never—" Dustin started to stand up.

"Just sit down and listen." Elizabeth said firmly. She cleared her throat. "I don't know where you were the night of the ball." Dustin started to answer, but Elizabeth held up her hand. "And I don't want to know. It doesn't matter now, because everything changed that night. I was feeling rejected and abandoned as I waited for you to come and escort me to the dance." She looked at her lap and shook her head. "But you never did. I went alone. And I was never the same after that night. Mind you, it wasn't because of you." She needed him to understand this one thing even if she muddled up everything else. "You are not to blame in any way. What I did that night was of my own choosing. I won't give you all the details, but I—" Elizabeth faltered for the first time.

"Go on," Dustin said encouragingly. "I'd like to hear them."

Oh, why did the man have to be so confounded loving all the time? If he wanted the whole story, then so be it. She would deliver the sucker punch and he would be gone. Good. She couldn't wait.

Her voice shaking, she stared at the carpet and plunged ahead. "I slept with a man that night, a man I didn't even know. He was tall and dashing and an up-and-coming politician. I was miffed my sister had an engagement ring on her finger and you hadn't so much as hinted at marriage. Your brother and Ruth were planning their future while I waited on you. So, to get even with you, I went home with this fellow." Here it came. "And if you didn't already know, as a result of that night, Summer is my daughter." There. It was said, and now he could leave.

But instead of looking shocked, Dustin smiled. He actually smiled. Was he daft? He must need one final kick to get him out the door. Fine. She could deliver that, too. "When I found out Summer was on the way, I moved here to Waterford Cove. The man who is Summer's father lives here. That way I could keep the embarrassment out of the family name and Summer could know her father." Elizabeth turned her face toward the window. "But he didn't want to know her. He wanted the whole thing kept quiet. He was so determined he made me an offer." She gestured around the room. "One I obviously didn't refuse. He bought my silence. And buys it still. We haven't spoken in almost twenty years but his bank account and mine have an excellent relationship."

Elizabeth laughed, a hollow mirthless laugh that spoke volumes of her cynicism. "So, you see? I made a trade. And for what? A lifetime of loneliness without you or my daughter." Elizabeth got up and crossed the room to where he sat. She pointed at the door. "Now that you know the truth, you can leave. I'll telegram my sister and let her know you are headed home and that all is well with Summer."

He pulled her down to him in an awkward embrace. A hug good-bye? Yes, she supposed that was appropriate. But then a chuckle rose from deep within his belly and made her shoulders shake as he clumsily held her to him.

"This is comical to you then, is it?" Elizabeth straightened.

Dustin put a hand to his chest and took a deep breath to calm his laughter. "Oh, Lizzy. Come here."

"I most certainly will not." She stood up tall. "You are well informed of the truth and there is nothing left to be said but goodbye."

"But I already knew all that. Did you think by admitting everything I would take my leave and never look back?" At her hesitant nod, he continued. "Nothing could be further from the truth. You see," he said, looking at her with those eyes of his, "I've known the truth for quite some time. For years now, I've made myself stay away because I thought it would bring you more pain. That was in the beginning. Then I told myself that you had moved on and that coming here would be the worst thing for you. But I never stopped loving you."

"You loved me?" Elizabeth asked with a mixture of skepticism and hurt. "Then why didn't you ask me to marry you like your brother did with Ruth? I waited and waited, every day we were together, hoping you would propose."

Dustin succeeded this time in pulling her down to sit next to him. "Oh, how I wanted to, my sweet Lizzy. But I was just a boy and didn't have the maturity to see two days into the future. You see, I needed to grow up. Your leaving helped me to do just that. Pain can do that to a man."

She had always known she had been a source of hurt to him, but to hear it from his own lips was almost more than she could take.

108

"It wasn't until recently that I learned you were taking money in exchange for your silence. Every day since, I have prayed for you. Prayed you would be released from the past that holds you captive." He looked down shyly, then back up at her. "Then I prayed God would restore you to me." He paused and held his breath for a moment. "I have never stopped loving you. All those years watching Summer grow up, I knew deep in my heart I would always belong to you. The question is, will you let your heart belong to me?"

The velvet on the davenport was the recipient of the swirls Elizabeth's fingers were making in the fibers. "How could you want that, after knowing what you know? I am the lowest of the—"

Dustin held a calloused finger to her lips. It felt like the rough sand touching the smoothness of the water. "I am going to say something, and I hope you hear me. If you don't, I will continue to tell you the truth for the rest of your life, no matter how long it takes you to understand: we are all sinners and have fallen short of the glory of God. You are no worse than anyone else. We are all the same."

"But you don't understand! Every day I look around me and my sin screams in my face. I can't get away from it, Dustin. I can't!" She felt the familiar panic rise up in her throat.

"That's just it. You can't get away from it. Not on your own. But there is One who can overcome your darkness with His marvelous light."

"But I've tried! I pray and pray and never seem able to break free."

"How could you, though? You are still entwined in the lies that bound you in the first place. Does Summer know you are her mother? No. Do you still accept money from this man who is her father? Yes." Dustin grasped her hand with intense fervor. "Elizabeth, you can escape. The truth must come out in order for you to be free, the way Christ wants you to be free. And I am determined to help you. I know you well enough to know you thought I would run the minute I heard the truth. Am I right?"

Elizabeth looked down. "Yes," she said quietly.

But she looked up when she heard the tone in his voice. "Well, have I got good news for you. I'm not going anywhere. Like I said, I will hand you the truth on a platter for the rest of your life if that's what it takes for you to get your freedom." He placed a quick kiss on her cheek and looked triumphant as he stated boldly, "Elizabeth Anton of Charlotte, North Carolina, and Waterford Cove, Virginia, I love you."

TWELVE

And this is Justine Davidson. She and her fiancé, Garrett, turned this place into a safe home for orphaned children earlier this year." Summer watched as Christian took Justine's hand like a perfect gentleman. For a hired hand who worked in the stables, he sure had a way with people. Almost a professional-like quality to his demeanor. If Summer didn't know better, she would think he was a businessman of some sort. But what did she know?

"The pleasure is all mine." Christian had arrived separately from her and her aunt and uncle. Summer watched as he looked around the massive building with appreciation written in his expression. "I can see this used to be a factory of sorts."

Justine spoke up. "Mr. Titus, if only you could have seen this place before. The poorest of working conditions, I'm sad to say. And if you can believe it, mere children made up the vast majority of the laborers." She smiled at Garrett. "But God had a different plan in mind for those little lives." She squeezed her fiancé's arm affectionately. "And for ours. Who would have thought the Lord would bless us so much."

They chatted a bit more and casually watched the children play. The center of the factory-turned-orphanage was like a large living area, full of couches and toys and chairs in which to read books. Elizabeth and Dustin were already engrossed in reading to a group of toddlers on the large area rug. Summer couldn't wait to introduce them to Christian. She wondered what they would think of him.

She had so enjoyed the ride over to the orphanage with Elizabeth and her uncle. It had helped take her mind off of her luncheon with Mr. Wilson. What a strange conversation. He had inquired about her past, her parents and how she had come to be in Waterford Cove. Then he had invited her to be his special guest at a ball to take place the following evening.

Repressing the unsettling feelings, Summer turned to a more pleasant matter. She secretly hoped Uncle Dustin would stay on for a time in Waterford Cove. His presence always gave her a large measure of comfort. He was like a second father to her. And during this tumultuous time, she could use his godly wisdom.

A boy about ten years of age rushed past, then skidded to a halt. He looked at the group of adults and asked if anyone would be willing to supervise a game of ball outside. Summer knew Justine and Garrett had strict rules about the youngsters going out-of-doors on their own. This was a pretty rough neighborhood and they should not be unsupervised. So whenever an extra adult came to volunteer or visit, they were bound to get dragged into a game or two.

Summer was taken aback when Christian immediately volunteered. His eyes took on a playful light, and Summer wished she could follow the group now forming at the door just so she could see Christian in action. She had never pictured him as the fatherly type, but watching his natural interaction with the boys gave her something new to think upon.

The next two hours flew by as Summer played with the children and chatted with Justine and Garrett about the latest happenings around the orphanage. They reminded her the King's Castle was having a grand fundraising event Saturday evening, just two days away. The way construction was progressing, it looked as though the children would be settled before the holidays. The Cole family owned a large parcel of land, and Garrett's parents had been more than willing to allow him and Justine to build the massive new home at the rear of the property, just near the creek. It had been a long time since Summer had been out to see it. In the course of conversation, Garrett and Justine encouraged her to bring a guest to the fundraiser. Summer's mind immediately pictured her and Christian dancing at the event, he donning a black tuxedo and she in a stunning green silk dress, her blonde hair braided and arranged in loops on her head.

She didn't know if that was possible, but despite who her escort was to be, she planned on giving all the pay she had earned to Garrett and Justine. That was worth all the papercuts she would ever have to endure.

Summer didn't have much time to dwell on the daydream as their time at the orphanage drew to a close. It wasn't until she and Christian made their way to the carriages that Summer had the opportunity to introduce him to Elizabeth and Dustin.

"This is Christian Titus. We met recently. Mr. Titus, this is my aunt, Ms. Elizabeth Anton, and her brother-in-law, my uncle, Dustin Edwards. Elizabeth is my mother's sister and Dustin is my father's brother. He is visiting from my hometown in North Carolina."

Christian gave a slight bow, his cheeks still rosy from his skirmish with the boys. "Pleased to make your acquaintance. I hear the four of us will be dining out together this evening. Did the three of you have any place in particular in mind?"

Again, Summer was struck with Christian's impeccable manners. Come to think of it, all the times they had spoken, he had been the perfect gentleman with none of the stable lingo slurring his vocabulary. Summer studied this man she was coming to know in a new light. Who was he really? Sometimes, she felt as though she knew him intimately. Then he would do something unexpected and she would be reminded once again that they had only just met.

"Why don't we meet at Rue De Flores on Madison. I hear they have the most exquisite French cuisine," Dustin replied. With a wink he added, "Christian, why don't you drive Summer in your carriage and Lizzy and I will follow you there?"

Summer felt her face turning what was sure to be a most unbecoming shade of pink at her uncle's suggestion. It would be her first time in a carriage with a gentleman unaccompanied by a chaperone. What would they say to each other? Would she be nervous? If her dry mouth and sweating hands were any indication, it appeared that was a foregone conclusion.

Summer and Christian agreed to meet them at the restaurant, and Summer shyly took Christian's hand as he helped her to the carriage. It wasn't nearly as ornate as Aunt Elizabeth's and no driver directed the horses, but just the same, sitting next to Christian in the open air as the horses began their trot down the lane, Summer thought she just might be in heaven.

Christian's heart seemed to skip every other beat as Summer sat close to him on the seat. His hands were very much occupied with the reins of the horses, but if they were free, he would be tempted to hold her hand. He glanced at Summer and caught her looking at him, too. His heart tripped over itself, and he had to force his eyes back to the road. If he wasn't mistaken, Summer Edwards was just as interested in him as he was in her.

As their arms rubbed up against each other with the horses' jostling, Christian couldn't help but think of Tabitha. Wasn't this the way he used to feel about her? Like a schoolboy in love. Would Summer rip his heart out like Tabitha had? One could never tell, for appearances could be deceiving. A guise of truth could conceal the most deceitful of hearts. Was it worth the risk to take another chance? All these years he had convinced himself that the stakes were too high. But one look in her green eyes and Christian wanted to forget everything else on earth. Including his doubts.

"One thing I haven't learned about you is what brought you to Waterford Cove. Or have you always lived here?"

A trickier question she could not have asked. Best to answer the last part of her question and ignore the first. "I haven't always lived here. Actually, I am from around our nation's capital."

"Did you come here looking for work?"

Not exactly, thought Christian. "Yes, in a manner of speaking." Her arm brushed up against his again, sending shivers up his spine. "What about you? Are you originally from here? I guess not, since you mentioned your uncle is visiting from your hometown in North Carolina."

She looked nervous for a moment before she answered. "You are right. I am from North Carolina. But I have been in Waterford Cove for a little while now. I came here to stay with my aunt. She has lived here for many years. When I first arrived, I mostly helped out with the orphanage. But now, as you know, I spend the majority of my time in Mr. Wilson's office."

At the mention of the politician, Christian felt a surge of jealousy. Should he mention he saw Summer and Mr. Wilson dining today in the atrium? It was now or never, and it would eat him alive if he didn't know why they had met for lunch.

"I couldn't help but notice you had lunch with Mr. Wilson today." At her surprised look, he rushed on. "I'm sorry, I didn't mean to embarrass you. I took the pathway behind the house to do a chore when I saw you. It was just the two of you, wasn't it?" He held his breath, hoping he was wrong.

Summer looked away and took a few moments to answer. "Yes, it was just us. He asked me this morning to join him for lunch, though I am still at a disadvantage as to know why. Don't get me wrong, he is a nice man, but I don't understand what a man like him would want with a girl like me."

Christian huffed out loud. He couldn't help it. Couldn't she see what he was after? Was she that naïve? Summer had always made the impression on him that she had a good head on her shoulders. Maybe she was simply innocent when it came to men. She had seemed shy to ride with him alone. Perhaps that was a good sign of her virtue. He liked that in a woman. It meant she wasn't after a hidden agenda.

"Be careful around him, Summer. You are a very beautiful young lady. Anyone can see that. Just remember he is a married man. I would caution you to never be alone with him."

At first, Summer seemed to take offense at what he said, then her eyes softened and she put her small, delicate hand on his arm. "Thank you, Christian. You are becoming a good friend."

Christian wondered if he should take this opportunity to let her know he wanted to be more than friends. No, not yet. They were pulling up near the restaurant now. If or when he told her how he was beginning to feel about her, the timing had to be right. For how could he tell her his feelings without telling her his true purpose for being in Waterford Cove? No, now was definitely not the right time.

Dinner was a grand affair, with candlelight, wonderful food and brilliant conversation. Christian did not go into great detail about his past or present jobs, but even if he had, Summer would not have been embarrassed. So what if he worked in a stable? He loved horses, that was plain to see, and wasn't that what most people wanted out of life? Doing what they loved? She knew Uncle Dustin would understand, for he himself had bucked tradition and followed after his heart in his career.

Both Elizabeth and Dustin had warmed immediately to Christian and so the conversation flowed naturally. Summer was content to listen most of the time, just getting to know this dashing young man who had become part of her daily thoughts. Her mind kept drifting back to the events of the evening, from Christian's eagerness to help with the older boys at the orphanage, to his shoulder touching hers for the duration of the ride to the restaurant, to the fact that he had called her beautiful.

She sighed a happy sigh. It wasn't that no one had ever commented on her appearance before, but for some reason, Christian's opinion of her mattered. She wanted him to notice her, and it appeared he had. But more than that, she wanted him to know her. Know what she liked and disliked, know what God meant to her, and know how her heart hammered in her chest whenever he was near.

One thought saddened her as they made their way to the carriages again after dinner. How could Christian ever truly know her if she was living a disguise? Would she ever be able to reveal who she was and her purpose at the Wilson home? Or was she destined to keep her secret and give up this man she was coming to treasure? These questions and more would have to remain just that—questions.

"It was lovely meeting you, Mr. Titus. I hope you will grace my home with your company for dinner sometime very soon. How about Sunday after church?" Elizabeth looked expectantly at Christian, and Summer's heart was all too happy to hear she would get to see him again so soon.

"I'd be delighted, Miss Anton. I'll plan on seeing you all then."

"Say, Christian, would you be willing to take my niece home this evening? I need to make a stop on the way back to Elizabeth's place. That wouldn't be too much of an inconvenience for you, would it?"

Summer cast her uncle a sidelong glance as they left the restaurant. It was almost as if her uncle was trying to give her and Christian time alone together. The rascal. She would have to give him what for later. And a great big thank you.

"Not at all. It would be my pleasure. I'm sure Miss Summer here will show me the way."

"You two might as well make a stop in the park first. It's such a beautiful night," said Elizabeth. "Good night then, Mr. Titus."

"Good night." For the second time that evening, Christian helped Summer up into the carriage and settled next to her. As her aunt and uncle rode away, Christian reached over and laid his big, calloused hand in hers. "Summer, it has been an honor to escort you this evening, and I count the minutes until we shall see each other again on Sunday."

"It sounds as if we shall have a few more minutes together tonight before we bid each other ado." She couldn't help a small giggle that rose up in her throat.

"What are you laughing at?" Christian asked, but by the look in his eyes, it appeared as if he already knew.

"My aunt and uncle. If I didn't know better, I would think they were trying to give us some time alone." Summer sighed as the carriage began to roll. "They certainly are different from my parents."

"How so?" Christian inquired as he skillfully maneuvered the coach down the lane.

Should she open up more to this man? If she started to, where would she stop? Summer refused to lie, especially to Christian. But how did she share part of her past without sharing all of it? The answer was simple. She would tell the truth. But her heart caught in her chest as she planned what she would say. It would not be the whole truth. She would skirt that issue like a lady in full hoops at a ball. She would only reveal what she thought pertinent to the questions he asked. And if he happened to ask more than she was willing to share, she would either not answer or tell the truth. She would not lie.

"You see, my parents can be very controlling. They have had a plan for my life for as far back as I can remember. I was never out of their sight for more than a moment, unless I was in my room, of course. I am an only child, and I fear they may have pinned all of their hopes and dreams on me." Summer laughed self-consciously. "It can be quite stifling."

"Is that what brought you to Waterford Cove?"

This she must share. "Yes. My Aunt Elizabeth and I have never been close, until last year when we began to write letters to one another. I found her to be a good friend, and when I mentioned my desire to be out on my own, she invited me to stay with her. I accepted, even though my parents disapproved." She looked down at her hands twisting in her lap. "And I hope I never have to go back."

"You sound ashamed of that fact. Well, I don't blame you. What grown, lovely lady would want to live under such restrictive circumstances? You made the right decision, going against their will. I would have done the same."

"Oh, but Christ would not have. And He is my ultimate example. Why, if I followed His way in all this, I would be headed home on the morning train."

"You sound very close to God," Christian commented with a faraway look in his eyes. "If you are such a devout follower, why don't you obey Him?"

A good question, one Summer had asked herself many times. But she always came up with the same answer. "I also feel as though God has given me a purpose here in Waterford Cove. A purpose I cannot leave until I see through to the end."

"Would you care to explain? That sounds intriguing," Christian stated as he pulled the carriage into a park.

He helped her down, tied the horses, and put her arm through his as they began to stroll the path. Gas lights lit the way but not so brightly that one could not see the stars twinkling overhead. They were dazzling in their brilliance. Summer didn't want to answer his question. She looked up at Christian as they walked and wanted nothing more than to make this moment last forever.

THIRTEEN

What could be so important that Summer would abandon what she thought was right? Its magnitude must outweigh her initial thoughts on the matter. Again, Christian remembered the way he used to think of everything in light of his relationship with God.

Recently, Christian had felt a softening of his heart in spiritual matters. When he finally acknowledged that it was he who had run from the Lord, not God that had forsaken him, the rough edges of his blackened soul began to be sloughed away. He could feel the Holy Spirit working in him, and although Christian was still hesitant to open his heart up completely, he knew that was what he wanted to do. What he needed to do.

He had even taken an afternoon devoted just to prayer. He had ridden Sadie out on the Wilson's grounds, finding the solace he was looking for as he followed a path that led to an old log cabin. His horse had seemed skittish as they neared the dilapidated building, so Christian had turned and ridden the other direction. But it was during those moments of solitude that he had sought the Lord concerning some of his most pressing issues, mainly his lingering feelings of hurt about Tabitha.

"If it's all the same to you, I'd rather not say what is keeping me here longer than I anticipated. It's kind of a private matter." Summer squeezed his arm with her hand and Christian decided he didn't care why she was there, just that she was with him now.

He wasn't sure what made her hesitant, but he felt free to share how he had recently come back to the Lord. It turned out to be the best part of the night so far. Summer didn't judge him, as he feared she might. Instead, she opened up about her own spiritual hiccups, sharing verses that had helped her trust in their Savior grow.

He felt lighter than he had in years, walking next to this woman who had made him examine his heart once again, this woman who shared his faith. She was so lovely, with her hair piled up high, revealing her long, slender neck. The dress she wore this evening didn't look like the garments she usually wore to work. It had intricate roses sewn along the bodice and the soft yellow brought out the color in her cheeks.

The couple strolled through the park until a man on stilts came through to extinguish the lamps. They talked and laughed and Christian held Summer's small hand in his, their fingers intertwining in the starlight.

"Looks like I'd better get you home," Christian said reluctantly. He stopped on the path and held her gaze.

"Yes," she replied, a bit breathlessly.

"Summer," Christian said, the word lingering in between them.

Her face shone up at his even though the only lights now were the ones God had provided overhead. Christian put his hands on her arms and brushed her soft skin with his thumbs. "Summer," he said again, this time it came out more like a caress.

Her mouth felt like pure heaven as their lips met in a modest kiss. But it was enough for Christian to know he would never be the same. He knew now that Summer Edwards had changed his life forever.

"Turn right at the next block," Summer said as she stole a glance up at Mr. Christian Titus. What a man he was. Full of surprises. She found herself thinking of what it would be like to have him in her life forever. She sobered at the thought of introducing Christian to her pretentious parents, but she comforted her heart with the feelings of love she was beginning to feel for this man. Not once had any of the suitors who had

ROOTS REVEALED

come to her North Carolina doormat made her feel like she felt when Christian was near. The only thing better would be feeling this way for the rest of her life.

"Then take another right onto Lumière Square." Summer pointed to her aunt's home, the most beautiful one on the unique block. "That one right there, with all the scroll work."

The horses were brought up short at the small front gate. Summer didn't want to go in, but knew she had probably overdone the bit of freedom she had been given this evening. There was a soft glow in the parlor window, and Summer secretly hoped her aunt would be awake. She wanted to share some of her thoughts with her.

Summer turned from the house to bid Christian farewell. She noticed his normally tanned skin had turned a pasty white and he was breathing heavily, small beads of sweat breaking out on his forehead.

"Goodness!" she exclaimed. "Christian, you look like you've seen a ghost." She tried to look him in the eye, but his were fastened on the home. She took his shoulders and tried again to get him to look at her. He just kept staring at the house.

"Christian." No response. "Christian!" Summer said a bit more forcefully. "Let's get you inside and call the doctor. I fear for your health." Perhaps he had some sort of medical condition. Summer had never witnessed anything so odd in her life.

Before she could try and drag him from the carriage, she heard Aunt Elizabeth calling out. "I thought I heard you two coming back." When she came closer, she too noticed Christian's peculiar behavior. "My goodness, whatever is the matter?"

At that, Christian's eyes snapped straight to Summer's, and the way he looked at her made her want to crawl under the nearest rock. Hatred and rage resided there, such as she had never seen. His face quickly turned from stark white to blazing red.

"Christian, would you care to come in for a cup of tea? I'm sure Aunt Elizabeth knows of a good doctor that would come to call on you." She reached for his hand but he jerked away. "Do come in. We are worried about you."

123

"Sure, you're worried," Christian said sarcastically. The next sentence came out in a growl. "Get out of my carriage."

Summer scrambled down and stood next to her aunt, gaping up at him. The kind, romantic Christian seemed to have bizarrely turned into this seething man, whose anger obviously boiled just under the surface. Clearly his ire was toward her, but what could she have done in the short distance it had taken them to get from the park to home?

As soon as her feet hit the ground, Christian flicked the reins harshly, and the horses jumped to do their master's bidding. He flew around the square and down the road before Summer could think of what to do next.

"Summer, are you all right?" Elizabeth put her arm around her niece as they began walking up the path to the home.

Summer thought of their kiss in the park, snuggling up next to Christian and feeling as though her heart would burst with love. And now, in one confusing moment, what she had held briefly in her hand, had been suddenly taken away.

The soft light of the lamp in the parlor and the smell of sugared tea beckoned as Elizabeth gently led Summer to the settee. The elder woman took Summer's hands in her own, looked into her eyes and said, "Tell me everything."

Christian's heart beat fast and furious like the poor horses' hooves as he veered and swerved through the city streets. He wanted to take the nearest rock and smash it on his head. How could he be so stupid? "Christian, I love being with you," his heart mocked the words Summer had said to him only minutes before he knew her underhanded dealings.

He urged the horses faster as they entered the country road that led to the Wilson estate. He would get even with Summer for ripping his heart out if it was the last thing he did. But his heart proved a traitor as he remembered a verse from a borrowed Bible he had read just the other night. Something about God being the only one to seek vengeance on a person. He slowed the horses to a walk as everything came crashing onto him at once.

Between realizing he had been bamboozled once again by a beautiful woman and knowing he was a sinner who had also received undeserved forgiveness from his heavenly Father, Christian didn't know what to do. The horses lost interest in pulling the conveyance and began eating mouthfuls of grass at the side of the road. Christian barely took notice as he sat in silence and tried to pray. The stars that had glittered hopefully overhead only a short time ago now mocked him with their brilliance.

As he sat silent under the heavens that were made by the same hands that formed him, Christian realized no matter how he felt, God was still God. He was in control. Not only that, He cared. Christian saw that now. He had blinded himself to God's love for so many years. The blatant rebellion in his heart had earned him nothing he treasured. So, Christian resigned to commit himself to letting God be the Lord over every area of his life, including his budding relationship with Summer. He needed God, knew he couldn't live without him. And if he needed a Savior, he would do well to remember that Summer was just that—a sinner in need of saving. At the core, they were no different.

The horses began a slow plod as Christian urged them forward once more. The Wilson estate loomed not far in the distance as Christian debated what to do next. He must push his feelings of hurt and anger aside and focus on his assignment—the reason he came to the Wilson house in the first place.

First, there was the matter of the counterfeit money. Christian had yet to learn much information regarding who was behind the entire scheme, if indeed there was one. If he could only learn of the location of the printing press, if it existed, that would be a win.

He also felt in his gut that the new accountant, Frederick Ellis, had something to do with the counterfeit ring. Christian had tried to garner information about the man during his stay in the bunkhouse, but he hadn't learned anything that pointed to Ellis being a key player.

Then again, there was that conversation Christian had observed in the woods between Mr. Ellis and the other man, whose face was never seen. If only he could get his hands on that ledger in the locked drawer in Mr. Ellis's desk. He was sure it held a vital piece to this puzzle.

And how was Summer involved in all of this? Christian had overheard Harriet Wilson accusing her husband of having a dalliance with Summer. Could it be true? Christian had witnessed them having lunch together. And Christian suspected it was Summer who had copied from the ledger in George Wilson's darkened office. Maybe the lunch was to pass along what she had learned. Perhaps she was a spy for Mr. Wilson, and in the process, had become his mistress.

Christian berated himself as he parked the borrowed buggy and unhitched the horses. He was certain the answer to all of the questions floating around in his mind was right in front of him. One didn't hone years of skills in this business without having a little intuition on a situation. But right now, he felt very naïve to the answer. And it was all his fault. If he hadn't allowed himself to be distracted by a charming girl, he wouldn't be in this predicament. Perhaps that was why Shaw had shown up. Christian really hadn't reported much to the home office. In turn, it appeared they had sent another agent to do his work for him. Since their run-in behind the atrium at dawn this morning, Christian had yet to see the man. Christian sincerely hoped Shaw wouldn't get a job at the estate and end up bunking with him. He shuddered at the thought.

Well, no matter. he had business to attend to and he wasn't just going to hand this case over to another Pinkerton, no matter what the home office decreed. It was nearing ten o'clock in the evening, and he knew not many would be awake in the house. Now would be as good a time as any to snoop around Frederick Ellis's desk, see if he could locate the key that opened the locked drawer, and possibly find some sort of evidence that the ring existed.

Going around back to the entrance Summer had used to slip into the home, Christian let himself inside. He stole through the atrium after removing his shoes by the door and began to make his way to the business wing of the home.

A door stood open just down the hall from where he was, allowing light to spill onto the polished wood floors. Voices, whispered and harsh, came from the room. Foregoing his original plan to find the ledger, Christian crept closer to the door and hid himself in the shadows, trying to make out what was being said.

"Harriet, I promise, nothing is going on between Miss Edwards and me." The sound of a kiss on a cheek. "You know you're the only one for me."

The sound of a slap startled Christian. Harriet laughed harshly. "I cannot tolerate being lied to. I can see with my own eyes the way you look at that girl. Don't lie to me, George. You're so in love with her, you can barely see straight. And don't deny it. I heard about your little tête à tête in the atrium." Her voice seethed with rage. "I'm sure you're looking for a way to dump old Harriet so you can have your fun with Summer." The last word was said in a sneer.

"Harriet, be reasonable. I told you before and I'll tell you again—I have not had an affair since that one time many years ago. Please forgive me that transgression and allow me to get close to you again. I swear, you are the only one for me."

Silence ensued, and Christian wished he could see what was taking place. Mr. Wilson sounded sincere in his request to be close to his wife. If he was, then what interest did he have in Summer? Perhaps only a business relationship that profited him in his counterfeit ring? Something inside Christian wanted so badly to believe that. If Summer was only guilty of helping out in an illegal scheme, it would appease Christian's heart just a bit. If she wasn't a mistress of a wealthy politician, he could forgive her just a little easier.

"Then tell me this," came the whispered question. "Why have I seen you two together? What is your interest in Miss Edwards?" Harriet's voice was much softer now, and Christian leaned as close as he could to hear George's response.

"Harriet, you wouldn't believe me if I told you."

"Try me."

George cleared his throat. "All right, then. Follow me."

127

The couple came out of the room, so Christian quickly made himself invisible by tucking his frame behind a tall, potted plant. Then to his dismay, George and Harriet Wilson began heading to the southern wing of the home, where Mr. Wilson conducted his business affairs. It appeared Christian would have to find another time to search out the hidden ledger.

FOURTEEN

The sun was skimming the horizon and bursting with pulsing beams of light when Summer awoke the next morning. She stretched and threw back the beautiful down coverlet. She felt new this morning, the weight completely gone from her shoulders.

When Christian had thundered away the night before and Elizabeth had led her inside to the cozy parlor, Summer knew the time had come. At first, she sat before Elizabeth, ashamed to confess all she had been trying to cover. But Elizabeth had been kind and understanding, telling Summer she already knew some of what was taking place and how she had covered Summer with her prayers since the day Laura had told her what was happening.

Summer had hugged Elizabeth and her fondness for her aunt only grew. Summer then confessed everything—the conversation she had observed in the woods, the ledger she had copied from, the feeling she had that Frederick Ellis was somehow behind the trouble that was happening. And finally, how she had really met Christian. She even confessed to her aunt that she felt she was falling in love with him.

"I don't understand, Elizabeth," she had said. "It's like my heart finally found its home with him." She had laughed self-consciously. "I probably sound like a love-sick fool."

Elizabeth had looked around the room and even peered out the doorway before responding. "Actually, I know exactly what you mean. I've been going through some of the same emotions myself lately." Her cheeks had turned a charming shade of pink at the disclosure of her feelings.

Summer's heart picked up a couple beats as she put two and two together. "You don't mean…" She had let the sentence hang in the air and pointed to the library where Uncle Dustin was reading the paper.

Summer finished scrubbing her face and then began brushing her hair as she remembered the remainder of their conversation.

Elizabeth's face had turned a darker shade of red, and she slowly nodded her head. Summer had gasped and then giggled like a school girl. Elizabeth joined her but modestly refused to divulge any more information. Summer was itching to know what was going on between the two of them. Maybe cornering Uncle Dustin later would get her the answers she longed to hear.

She smiled at her reflection in the mirror as she admired her white day dress with blue satin ribbing. She felt it made her look like the sunshine, with bits of blue sky peeking through puffy summer clouds. A perfect outfit for a day when she felt so sunny and bright. Now that she wasn't hiding any secrets from her aunt, she felt more light and free than she had in a long time.

Summer knew the time had come to write to Laura and tell her that she could no longer go on with her ruse at the Wilson home. Secrecy had its price, a price that was too high to pay. She had promised Elizabeth last night that today would be her last day of working for George Wilson. She would spend her final hours there giving her best to find out why Laura's brother had a murder conviction on him when he hadn't pulled a trigger. What lay before her would not be easy, but Summer knew it must be this way.

The realization gave her a lighthearted feeling as she stepped into the kitchen. She sobered though as Cook handed her a letter. It was from Laura. She forgot about breakfast and raced up the servant's staircase, shutting the door to her room behind her. She didn't know what the letter had to say but wanted to be alone when she read it.

The news was not good. Landon's trial had been set for two weeks from Monday. In her letter, Laura lamented that Summer had made no progress but also pleaded with her not to go to the police. She trusted Summer's original instinct to not involve them and instead urged Summer to try everything she knew to clear Landon's name.

Two weeks wasn't much time to find proof, but Laura's despair lit a fire under Summer. She *would* do it. She would do everything in her power to see the innocent brought to freedom and the guilty brought to justice. There was only the issue of Aunt Elizabeth now. Summer had made a promise to her. Well, no more secrets, at least between the two of them. She would ask her aunt's permission to continue in her position at the Wilson home until the two weeks were up. If she had not discovered why someone would frame Landon for murder by then, then she would wash her hands of the whole thing.

Summer responded to Laura's letter with a quick missive reassuring Laura that God was on their side and that His desire was to see justice prevail. She signed the smooth paper with a flourish then ran it out to Matthew to take to the post. Summer rushed back inside and found Elizabeth and Uncle Dustin sitting in the dining room having breakfast.

"Why, don't you look like a fresh buttercup this morning," Uncle Dustin drawled. "Wherever are you off to in such a hurry?"

"Aunt Elizabeth and I had a talk last evening after Mr. Titus brought me home." She looked at her aunt, trying to determine if she had told Uncle Dustin what she had said.

"Don't worry, Summer. I told Dustin everything this morning. He is privy to all of your secrets."

Uncle Dustin put a hand affectionately on Elizabeth's hand, and Summer wished she had more time right now to find out what was going on between the two of them. "Are you off to your last day at work?" he inquired.

"Aunt Elizabeth, Uncle Dustin," Summer addressed them with hope in her voice, "I am praying you understand that there needs to be a change in plans." She swallowed. Despite what their response might be, she must be honest with them from here on out. Even if that honesty bought her a one-way ticket back to North Carolina. She had to swallow again before continuing.

"You see, Laura informed me this morning by letter that Landon's trial is set to take place in two weeks. With no one trying to clear his name, he is sure to be sentenced to a life in prison, if not worse." She reached both of her hands out to grasp one of each of theirs, and for a moment, they were an unbroken circle of family, a family Summer was more grateful for now than ever. "May I have your permission to stay on working for George Wilson? At least until Landon's trial?"

She held her breath, but need not have worried. Her uncle squeezed her hand and looked at Elizabeth. At the slight nod of her head, he gave Summer their blessing, with firm instructions that if Summer got over her head and felt like her life was in danger, she was to go to them or the police immediately.

"Oh, I will, I will. Thank you both for trusting me. It feels so good that the two of you know all that is happening." She looked fondly at both of them. "I love you both so much. I hope you know that."

With quick hugs all around, Summer grabbed a muffin from the kitchen and headed for the stables. She had work to do in the office, a murder to investigate, and a ball to attend tonight as Mr. Wilson's guest. This was going to be a very interesting day.

Christian huffed in frustration as he went through his morning stable chores. Last night after overhearing the conversation between George and Harriet Wilson, he was more confused than ever. How was Summer involved in all of this? If only he could prove her innocence. It was possible, wasn't it, that it hadn't been her that evening sneaking into the mansion and getting information from Mr. Ellis's desk? Yes, but not likely. He had never seen the face of the prowler but the hat could have obscured her hair and the person's build was just about right for Summer. But why would she dress in men's clothing to do such a thing? There were too many questions and zero answers.

Speak of the woman and here she came. All white and blue this morning, a vision with her long golden hair flowing out behind her in all of its glory. Despite his suspicions of the girl, he stopped in his tracks as she came near on Miss Bess.

"Good day, Miss Edwards. You look most enchanting this morning."

"Enchanting, you say? That word seems more suited to a ball or gala dinner. Which, by the way, I will be attending this evening. But why should you be speaking to me at all? Last night, you seemed in quite a hurry to get away." She dismounted with his help, and he couldn't help but stare at her flawless skin and mesmerizing green eyes. She was stunning. And he couldn't have her. She was sullied by the things of this world, and he had determined to follow after God wholeheartedly. He simply could not accomplish that with such a woman at his side.

Trying to remain nonchalant, he kept his back to her and led her horse to a clean stall. A high-society ball might be the perfect place to gather information on this case. "If you look this good now, I can't imagine what you might look like tonight." He turned to face her now, his look sober. "Summer, please forgive my behavior last night." He truly did want her forgiveness; he just couldn't tell her why he had been so angry. That would blow his cover. So, for now, he needed to appear relaxed.

Summer smoothed her skirts and looked around, everywhere but his eyes. "Of course, not a problem," she said coolly. "Now, if you'll excuse me, I have a job to attend to."

He caught her arm, and she turned a hurt expression toward him. She had feelings for him. He could see them clearly on her face. And he had seared them last night with his behavior. Whatever she had done illegally, she was still a person with a heart, a heart he was going to have to hurt. He would have to tell her he could not continue this relationship. To not tell her would be wrong.

"Summer, I wonder if you might consider another picnic with me today?" When she hesitated, he rushed on. "There's a whole estate to explore here. I am sure we can find a spot we've never been to before."

She lifted her lunch pail in response as she began to walk away. "All right," she called over her shoulder. "Meet me at noon in the stables."

As he watched her graceful gait eat up the distance to the office, Christian tried to convince himself he simply wanted time with her to break off the relationship and find out additional information he could use to help this case. He hated to admit that deep inside he wanted to jump up and kick his heels together. This afternoon, he would have Summer all to himself.

FIFTEEN

Summer swung her foot back and forth, back and forth, as she languished at her desk. All this sitting and waiting and watching and wondering was enough to drive her crazy. But she must be patient. There had to be a way to find out more about who was responsible for putting an innocent man in prison and why all those excessively large figures were recorded in that hidden ledger. But what could she do? Sitting here wasn't getting her anywhere.

A thought crossed her mind as she filled out repetitive forms for the head secretary. She tried to remember the route she had taken the afternoon she had followed Mr. Ellis and the other man into the woods. Could she find it again? Was that location a key to some of the mysteries she needed answers to? Maybe tomorrow on her day off she would take Miss Bess and do some exploring. It couldn't hurt. And it was certainly better than waiting for something to happen.

Her mind drifted to what she would wear to the ball. It was to be held at the home of the Mayor of Waterford Cove. Thank goodness she knew how to behave at such an event. Her upbringing hadn't been a complete waste. She would wear her best gown, put on her most charming smile and keep her ears and eyes open to information about anything that would help her cause.

She glanced around the room, and for once, no one seemed to be looking at her with disdain. Word must not have gotten out yet that she was going as a guest of Mr. Wilson's. If it had, the rumors would be flying wild.

Lunchtime finally came around, and the butterflies in Summer's stomach began to take flight. What would Christian say to her on their picnic? Would he be charming like he was in the park last night when they had shared a sweet kiss? Or would he be angry with rage, coming from an unknown origin? Summer truly did not fear him, but she was curious as to what in the world would make him act that way when he dropped her off. She would ask him. She had a right to know after all they had shared.

Christian was leaning against the stable wall when she came outside. She put her head down to study the grass as she walked toward him. There was something very disconcerting about his gaze, and she didn't want to meet his eyes. They were full of curiosity and had the hint of a question in them.

"Shall we? I have Miss Bess and Sadie all saddled and ready to go."

"We're taking the horses?"

"Sure, why not? It will allow us to explore a little."

"You're sure Mr. Wilson won't mind?" she questioned.

Christian helped her up on Miss Bess's back and straddled his own horse. "Naw. No one will mind." He nudged Sadie in a walk. "Let's go."

Miss Bess followed without having to be prodded, and Summer relaxed as they rode. They broke into a gallop for a while, and Summer was grateful she had left her hair loose today. It felt so good to have the wind blowing its fingers through it.

They passed the river and the rocks they had sat on during their picnics together. Beyond the river and around a large knoll was a breathtaking scene. From the main house, no one would ever imagine how beautiful the rest of the land was. It dipped and rose with shallow valleys full of trees of every kind. One could see where the river gently cut through the land.

The horses easily climbed up and down the low hills, and suddenly Summer wasn't very hungry. She would rather spend the day exploring this land with Christian. She knew it wasn't rational given his behavior toward her last night. But as they rode in peaceful silence, Summer could almost pretend nothing had gone awry.

Just then, Christian called back to her. "How about here?"

She reluctantly agreed, hoping to have the chance to come out here again some other time. It was a shame, really, that no one could see this vista from the house. She supposed that was what made it all the more special. She wondered if Mr. Wilson ever came out here to enjoy all that he owned.

Christian helped Summer dismount and they settled a blanket onto the grass. She unpacked her lunch while Christian sprawled out with his hands behind his head. He looked so comfortable that it made Summer feel more at ease. Maybe nothing was wrong after all. Last night could have been something entirely different than she had perceived it to be. Christian could have not been feeling well; perhaps it was something he ate at the restaurant. Or he could have been wrestling with something from his past or current situation. Summer really was just getting to know him, and certainly shouldn't assume she knew everything about the man. She should give him the benefit of the doubt.

One thing was for certain—Summer was here with him now and would treasure every moment they had together. For in just two weeks' time when she quit her position, she knew she may never see Christian Titus again.

Christian watched Summer toss her straight blonde hair over the curve of her delicate shoulders as she gazed out over the panoramic view they had from their picnic blanket. She looked peaceful and relaxed. They had chatted through lunch as though nothing out of the ordinary had taken place last night.

She had eaten her sack lunch with those sumptuous lips he had kissed not much more than twelve hours before. And now he was faced with telling her he could no longer pursue her. Of course, she would wonder why. And Christian knew he could not give her the answer. If he did in a moment of weakness, it would destroy any chance of him finding out her role in the counterfeit ring. No, he wouldn't be able to answer her questions. Nor would he be able to bear the look in her eyes when he told her the news. He would be strong, even though his own heart was breaking. He told himself that if he simply didn't look in her eyes, he could do it.

But first, he must try to garner any information he could. For certainly after he brushed her off, she would have nothing to do with him. This was his last chance.

"You had mentioned last night your parents weren't too happy about you being here in Waterford Cove," Christian began nonchalantly. He hoped by probing around on various topics that perhaps Summer would let something slip. "Have you considered writing to them frequently to keep their worries at bay? Or maybe you already do?"

Summer glanced at him, then continued her admiration of the view. "You're right, of course. I admit I have done a poor job at keeping in communication with them. Maybe if I was faithful to write, it would ease both their minds. I'm sure they wanted me home long ago. It's just that…" she trailed off.

"'Just that' what?" Christian prompted.

She looked him full in the face now, and Christian wanted nothing more than to kiss her lips again. "It's just that, well, I have a new freedom, you know? I was raised to marry well and live in finery. My husband was to be chosen by my father, and I didn't want that kind of confinement." She blushed suddenly, and Christian wondered why. "But lately, having a husband doesn't seem so confining after all. Not since I met you."

A bold one, wasn't she? Yes, but that was one of the things that set her apart. She was willing to follow would-be criminals into a darkened forest, to sneak into a mansion and steal confidential information, and now, cleverly disclose her feelings for a man in broad daylight. Yes, she was something.

But what were her motives? Could he be misreading her and she was actually on his team? No. He began to shake his head then caught himself. Impossible. He had seen firsthand that her actions proved she wanted a piece of the counterfeit pie. It was always about money, wasn't it? Always. Perhaps Summer saw a way out of her parents' tight and confining grasp if she was wealthy by her own doing. She might have reasoned if she could only get her own money, even by means of thievery, that she could be a free person. A criminal still, but perhaps one with better motives than most. But that didn't give Christian the right to want her. He was a professional and his job, his goal in life, was to bring down such people. People that would use illegal means to cheat the government and their fellow citizens. Mere liars, at best. And he was not about to attach himself to a liar. Those days were ten years behind him.

The time had come. It was now or never.

Summer jumped up and dusted off her white dress. "I suppose it is time to get back to work. Thank you, Christian, for a wonderful—"

He cut her off. He had to. "Summer, before we go—"

"I never noticed that before." Now it was Summer's turn to interrupt. "What am I looking at over there? It looks like some sort of cabin." She pointed. "Do you see it?"

Christian stood and followed her eyes to a spot on the far side of the valley. Nestled between two low hills sat a run-down log structure of some sort. It was well hidden by numerous trees and looked like it hadn't been touched for years.

"Yes, I see it there. I noticed it the other day when I was out riding." *Enough small talk,* he thought. *Just say it.*

Summer was folding the blanket now. "What do you suppose it is?"

"Probably a homesteader's cabin. This area was settled a long time ago. But Summer, there's something—"

"Wouldn't it be fun to go check it out sometime? I wonder if there is anything left inside: artifacts, old furniture. It would be interesting to see, don't you think?"

Enough! He grabbed the blanket, threw it to the ground and took Summer by the hands. "Summer. Stop." She looked up at him, confused. "There's something we need to talk about. Right now."

"All right, Christian. What is it?" Her brow furrowed, and Christian wanted to stroke away the confusion she felt.

"It's just this: I can't see you anymore. I have come to care for you deeply, but there is something I can't get past."

"Whatever it is, I'm sure we can work it out." She looked so scared and hopeful at the same time. Christian hated himself for it. How could he care so much for a girl who was so wrong for him?

"No, we can't. And I can't tell you what it is." She started to interrupt, but he stopped her by squeezing her hands. "You have no idea how much I wish I did not have to say these things to you. I think I'm in love with you, Summer." At that, he bent, and with a desire he longed to squelch, he kissed her deeply, knowing it would be their last.

She seemed confused at first, then responded to his kiss with such passion, it made Christian's head whirl. At last, they broke their embrace.

"I don't understand, Christian. Why are you doing this to me? Don't you know I care about you? I'm falling in love with you, too. Whatever it is, let's talk about it and make things work between us."

He shook his head and forced himself to back away from the woman he loved. He must be cursed or something to have fallen again for a lying, deceitful woman. Somehow, he knew he would go on loving her, even though he could never have her as his own.

He mounted Sadie and shook his head at her again. Tears streamed down her face as he rode away. He turned his head and watched her until he was out of sight around the bend.

SIXTEEN

Well, now, don't you look radiant this evening, my dear?" Uncle Dustin bent to kiss Summer's cheek as she came down the stairs in a gown she had shopped for after work. Going around town in a fancy carriage doing a bit of shopping was just what she needed to take her mind off of the disastrous picnic with Christian.

She smoothed down the golden folds of silk that matched her hair perfectly. The layers were edged with the finest beads and lace. Summer felt all grown up, like a real lady. Butterflies vied for attention in her stomach, and she pressed her hand against them to quiet them down.

Aunt Elizabeth glided into the room, looking much younger than Summer could ever remember. Summer reminded herself that Aunt Elizabeth really was still quite young. She could even get married and bear children at her age. Why, she was only in her mid to late thirties! Images of Uncle Dustin and Aunt Elizabeth married with a family of their own crowded out the nervousness Summer felt. She would have to begin praying for just such a thing to happen.

By the way Elizabeth was dressed, it appeared the two of them were having an evening out as well. "Do you two have big plans tonight?" Summer inquired with a twinkle in her eye.

"As a matter of fact, we have dinner reservations, but afterwards, we're wondering if you would mind us joining you at the ball? You see, your aunt is an acquaintance with the hosts, and they sent her an invitation this morning."

Summer was caught off guard momentarily, but quickly recovered. Her aunt and uncle were coming to the dance? Somehow, that made Summer a bit uncomfortable, like her independence was being infringed upon. But these weren't her parents, and they wouldn't be coming to check up on her. They had as much a right to be there as anyone else. "Oh, no. By all means, come. It is rumored to be quite the gala. At least, that is what George Wilson told me."

Elizabeth suddenly appeared quite pale. She swallowed hard and touched the jewels at her neck. "You mean, George Wilson will be there?"

"Yes, of course," Summer replied. "After all, he is my escort this evening."

Elizabeth turned white as a sheet and leaned heavily on Uncle Dustin. Perhaps Elizabeth should stay home this evening. She wasn't looking well. "Your," she croaked, "your escort?" Her voice rose on the last syllable.

What a strange reaction. Then a thought came to her as to why her aunt looked so aghast. "It's not what you think, Aunt Elizabeth. I understand Mr. Wilson is a married man. I assure you he has no ill intentions toward me. I am simply going as his guest. In fact, his wife Harriet will most likely be accompanying us." In Mr. Wilson's invitation over lunch, he had calmed her fears by saying his wife was usually in attendance at these society events.

Elizabeth waved her hand in the air, like she was trying to shoo away a pesky gnat. "Yes, yes, of course. I mean, no, no, I would never think such a thing about you, dear. I trust you implicitly." Now she used her hands to wave Summer out the door. "You just run along then and have a wonderful evening. I'm sure Matthew will drive you safely there and back. We'll look for you if we come. Bye now!"

Suddenly cheery, her aunt bade her farewell, and Summer found herself out on the step and walking toward the carriage. She had never seen her aunt act so peculiar. Never mind. Summer assured herself that all was well. Elizabeth's concern over her niece was simply that—concern.

The carriage rolled along through the August night, passing beautiful houses spilling out their warm lamplight onto the streets. Summer's stomach still fluttered at the thought of the evening before her. Was it foolish to hope the coming conversations would give her insight into the mystery surrounding George Wilson's late accountant? She knew the idea was far-fetched. Still, going to the gala was better than sitting at home, wishing something would happen that would free Laura's poor brother.

Doubts assailed her mind as she thought of Mr. Wilson. What if he had invited her there because he was interested in her romantically? She shuddered at the thought. Not that Mr. Wilson wasn't a handsome man, but he was married and certainly much older than she. Summer sent up a prayer asking that Harriet Wilson would indeed accompany her husband.

Matthew pulled the carriage up before a sweeping marble staircase that led to a sprawling mansion. She had been there one other time, shortly after she had arrived in Waterford Cove, for a ladies' luncheon. She fondly remembered that day, sitting with Justine Davidson and making a new friend.

Tonight, the home looked much different. Soft music and candle-light washed the steps with their elegant touch. Timidly, Summer ascended the staircase and was greeted by the host and hostess. Their words flowed like honey, practiced formalities that mixed like harmony with the string quartet playing in another part of the house.

She was directed through a stylish foyer and up two staircases that led to a massive ballroom. Ladies and gentlemen of all ages graced the parquet floor with expert dance steps and fashionable clothing. Men in black suits and polished shoes smiled demurely at their partners who were even more eye-catching in their bustled ensembles and bejeweled necks. Summer now knew she had no reason to be nervous there. This was all completely familiar to her. She may have never met anyone in attendance, but she had played the debutante game her entire life.

When she stepped into the room, heads turned and some nodded politely in her direction. She spied George Wilson by one of the balcony doors speaking with a man Summer thought looked familiar. His wispy hair and stance reminded her of someone. He faced Mr. Wilson, so Summer could not make out his features. No matter. It was probably someone she had seen around the estate. There were always different people coming and going.

A hand at her arm brought her out of her thoughts, and she turned to find Harriet Wilson at her side. A breath Summer didn't realize she was holding came whooshing out. Having Mrs. Wilson there somehow made everything all right. Now she could relax about Mr. Wilson and focus on asking questions that might lead to the answers she sought.

The matron was dressed in a muted silver ensemble with sparkling white diamonds at her neck and ears to complement her graying hair. The entire combination was quite beguiling. "I see you had the same idea I did tonight." When Summer looked confused, Harriet laughed lightly and gestured to Summer's dress. "Why, your dress and jewelry complement your hair and skin tone perfectly. Oh, do please forgive me. I don't believe we have ever officially met." Harriet's hand went to her diamond necklace, and she seemed to hesitate. "I'm Mrs. George Wilson. But you may call me Harriet."

Summer was taken aback by the woman's friendliness toward her, albeit she did seem a bit nervous and shy. Obviously, Harriet hadn't heard the rumors going around that Mr. Wilson was romantically interested in Summer and that was the only reason she had gotten the position in the politician's office. Summer demurely introduced herself to her employer's spouse.

"Have you been enjoying your time working for Mr. Wilson?" Harriet said while daintily sipping a bit of her drink.

"Oh, yes, Harriet. It has been most enjoyable. I find it a bit difficult to get to know anyone in the office, but the work itself suits me well." Summer hesitated. "I must confess to riding your land a bit earlier today. I went for a picnic and found the most beautiful valley just beyond a hill."

"Oh, I know where you mean. Just gorgeous back there, don't you think? It's a wonder George and I never take the time to explore like we used to. Seems as though we are always too caught up in going to balls or political functions of some sort or the other. Come to think of it, I don't think either of us have been back there in years."

Summer spotted Mr. Wilson making his way over to them. "We were just speaking of the valley beyond the hill on our land. Summer tells me she rode out there for a picnic."

"Oh, yes. Marvelous property. Only wish I could take the time to see it myself. Seems like a shame to own such a piece and not be able to enjoy it," Mr. Wilson said in his booming voice. He looked like a man in his prime tonight, with his silvering hair and air of authority.

"Miss Edwards, allow me to introduce you to a few fine folks. Then if you'll forgive me," he smiled lovingly at his wife, "I would like to take my bride around the dance floor a time or two."

Summer smiled at the way they were looking at each other. "Of course, Mr. Wilson. I understand perfectly."

Mr. Wilson was true to his word and made sure Summer had met several people before leading Harriet in her silver dress to the gleaming dance floor. Odd, how the two seemed so in love. As the rumors were apt to fly at the Wilson estate, it was said the married couple hadn't gotten along in years and shouting and objects being thrown were often heard in the home. Well, despite what may have happened in the past, Summer wished them all the best now.

The couple Summer had been speaking with turned to greet someone else, and she was left alone for the moment. She decided now was as good a time as any to strike up a conversation with someone new. One never knew when a tidbit of information would come in handy later on.

Putting on her most charming smile, she slipped in and out of the crowd. Everyone seemed to be engaged in their own conversations, but then a man caught her eye. He was a solemn looking man with a heavy beard, so unlike the stylish clean-shaven faces she was used to seeing at functions such as this. He had on thick glasses that distorted his brown eyes and looked like the kind of man you couldn't get a smile out of for all the world. How intriguing.

He looked the other way when Summer came near, then turned his back to her as he sidled up to the refreshment table. Summer would not be so easily ignored.

"What a lovely ball, would you not agree?" Summer decided small talk might cause the man to look her way as he filled a plate with hors d'oeuvres.

"Ja, ja," he said with a thick accent.

Oh, Summer thought. *He's just shy because he doesn't know much English.* Well, Summer would give him the grace he probably longed for. How hard it would be to attend such a function and not know how to communicate with anyone.

But perhaps he knew a few words. She should at least try to make him comfortable. "Have you met many people here tonight? I know when I came in, I didn't recognize more than two faces."

The man must be terribly shy, for he turned his back even more to her and answered softly with his heavy accent, "No, no, not many."

Summer felt at a loss as to what to say next. She bid him a quiet farewell and sipped her cup as she made her way to a wall. If she couldn't find anyone to talk to, perhaps she could observe them from afar. A few minutes passed and her eyes found the shy, Norwegian man she had tried to talk to. Surprisingly, he was engaged in a heated discussion with the same man who, upon entering tonight, had been in discussion with Mr. Wilson. They must know each other to be speaking so passionately. Then Summer realized the truth. She knew the other man too. Not the Norwegian, but the one who had the same build, the same glasses and the same brown mustache as the man from the racetrack. The man responsible for killing Nigel Fairbanks.

Summer gasped audibly, and a few curious looks came her way. This man was Andrew, the one who had visited George Wilson's office and who later had a heated meeting with Frederick Ellis in the woods. There could be no mistaking the wire-rim glasses shadowing pale, grey eyes and the high forehead under wispy, thin hair.

A chill ran up her spine as she realized she was staring across the room at a murderer. An innocent man had lost his life because this man had pulled a trigger. Summer knew money was the motive but disgust coursed through her veins as she thought of what people would do for wealth and prestige. She knew from experience such earthly trappings weren't all people hoped they would be. If handled properly, they could be used for good, but in the last few weeks, Summer had witnessed the dark of what greed could bring—death. And to think she ran away to Waterford Cove naïvely thinking her parents' money and status had nearly ruined her life.

The Norwegian man looked about ready to pop, his face was so red from anger. Summer stole through the crowd, trying to reach the men so she could hear what they were talking about. But before she could get within hearing range, the thin man grabbed the other by the arm and hauled him out onto the balcony, most likely to take their fight somewhere private. *All the better*, she thought as she made her way through another balcony door. She would hide in the shadows and listen to what they had to say.

The night was almost pitch black, with only snatches of moonlight peeking out now and then through the blowing clouds. The bearded man seemed to have lost his accent as he whispered threats to the other man.

"Listen, Shaw. This is my job, and no low-down snake is going to slither his way in here and take it from me."

"Oh, forgive me," Andrew said snidely. "I'll just run back and tell the boss man what a good job you are doing at the Wilson house. Hiding out as a stableman, seeing pretty young secretaries in your spare time." Andrew sneered. "You might as well just go on home with your tail between your legs, Titus, you good for nothing—"

The rest of the words were lost on Summer. The last name *Titus* flashed in front of her with the brightness of a thousand burning candles. The bearded man was Christian! Her Christian, her sweet Christian with the intense amber brown eyes and sweet kisses. Christian, the stable hand she had fallen in love with—in cahoots with this whole murder scheme! It was all too much to take in. No wonder he had broken off their relationship. He had a job to focus on, and according to the ledgers she had found, what was love compared to riches beyond his wildest dreams?

He had clearly made his choice. Even if he hadn't been the one to personally kill Nigel Fairbanks, he was involved somehow, and that was all that mattered.

Christian stalked quickly back into the ballroom and Summer followed instinctively. She didn't know what she would say to him, but she felt like giving him a piece of her mind. It would be wiser, however, to just forget Christian Titus ever existed. Summer knew now who he was deep in his heart and that all his words to her had been pure rubbish. But as she watched him get his coat and make ready to leave, Summer knew Christian's captivating eyes and easy smile would haunt her dreams for years to come.

SEVENTEEN

She was one of the most beautiful women he had ever laid eyes on. Andrew Shaw had observed her at the office one time and had thought of her many times since. From her flawless, honeyed skin to her thick, blonde mane, Ms. Edwards was a sight to behold. Andrew figured he may as well have a little fun while he was there.

He scoffed softly to himself as he crossed the room toward the secretary. *Let Titus go for tonight.* What a coward. He was probably halfway to the bunkhouse by now, ready to lick his wounds for the evening. Good riddance.

Christian Titus couldn't crack open this case, even though it was right under his nose. What a joke. So, Andrew would just play him until Christian was forced by the higher-ups to leave. No self-respecting Pinkerton boss would stand for one of his men to do so poorly on a job. Then Andrew would have the whole Wilson estate to himself, under the guise of being a Pinkerton. While he *worked*, Andrew would find a way to get rid of George Wilson and take over the whole counterfeit ring.

When Andrew had first heard of the operation, he had thought to take a portion as payoff for his silence. Artfully, he had won the confidence of both Nigel Fairbanks and Frederick Ellis. Over the course of a few months' time, Andrew had formulated a plan, a plan that ensured him an even larger percentage as payment for taking out Nigel Fair-

149

banks. Unfortunately, Andrew had mistakenly thought Ellis was smart enough to figure out how to handle the books and where the operation was located. Nigel never would give him that information, other than saying it was on the Wilson estate—somewhere.

Now all Frederick could offer him was ledger information saying how much money had been made. Andrew had yet to get his hands on any of it. This most frustrating situation had caused Andrew to have to step in and take matters into his own hands. He would find out where the money was made, oversee its production, ensure that Wilson was permanently out of the way, and be wealthier than he had ever imagined. And in the meantime, he would steal a few private moments with this young beauty of Titus's.

"Excuse me, miss." Andrew caught her arm to stop her pursuit of Titus. He could tell she wanted to follow Christian by the way she was scurrying across the room. No wonder Christian hadn't been able to discover and overturn the counterfeit ring; this girl would be a distraction to any man. "I'm sorry if I startled you, but I wanted to introduce myself before the evening ended."

She cleared her throat. "Um, yes. By all means." A flush crept up into her cheeks as she spoke. "I'm Miss Summer Edwards."

"Pleased to make your acquaintance. I'm Andrew Shaw, and you would make me the happiest man alive if I may have the pleasure of this dance." He bowed and gestured grandly towards the dance floor.

Her hand flew to her throat, and she stammered an unintelligible response.

"The night is about to end, Miss Edwards. Won't you do me just this one favor? It will give us a chance to get to know one another."

"All right, Mr. Shaw." She placed her hand tentatively in his. "To get to know one another."

Sadie had never been prodded so fast. Christian fairly flew over the ground on his way back to the bunkhouse. What a flop tonight had been. Summer had struck up a conversation with him, and he had almost been found out. He had nearly blown his entire cover by letting his temper get the best of him when Shaw showed up. Christian groaned in regret as he remembered their heated words in front of so many people. He should have been able to keep his temper in check until he and the other agent could talk in private. Of course, it was probably Shaw's plan all along to egg Christian on in front of the others. Anything to make Christian leave the Wilson case.

Blast it all! Christian was a good Pinkerton. He knew it. His track record proved it. If anyone could ferret out a criminal operation, it was Christian Titus. And here, headquarters had sent Shaw out to do his job for him.

As the horse slowed in approach to the Wilson's drive, Christian admitted defeat. Despite his skills, he had failed. An image crossed his mind, one of Summer's long blonde hair blowing in the breeze as they ate their picnic together. Her eyes a picture of trust and affection. Their lips as he embraced her for the last time. Christian knew then he had failed worse than he had ever imagined he could. He had spent the last ten years of his life building up his career only to throw it away on a beautiful face. Anger, fresh and new flashed hotly in his chest as he thought of being blindsided yet again by feminine wiles and the demure smile of a woman. And just like Tabitha, Summer had weaseled her way into his life, leading him to believe she was something she was not.

The anger diminished into a dull pain as he unsaddled his horse and headed to the bunkhouse. Christian figured he might as well pack up and leave in the morning. What good would it do to stay and fight a battle he had already lost? Andrew Shaw would happily take over, gloating as Christian left town. Christian had clearly not given this case the time and attention it needed, because he would rather have given his time and attention to something—no, someone else.

He settled on his lumpy mattress and pushed the image of Summer's shining green eyes out of his mind. He had not only lost the biggest case he had ever been assigned; he had lost what could have been the love of his life. He had no choice now but to leave and forget he ever met Miss Summer Edwards.

"I don't feel right about staying here anymore, Lizzy." Dustin stroked Elizabeth's hand lovingly as they sat side by side on the velvet-covered settee in her drawing room. "I came to Waterford Cove to check on Summer, you know that, but…" Dustin trailed off and gazed into Elizabeth's eyes like he was a thirsty man drinking from a deep, clean well.

And Elizabeth did feel clean. Clean and whole and new and restored. She knew Dustin and his love had been the reason for some of that. But she couldn't give him all the credit. The Lord had used Dustin in her life yet again. Dustin's love for her had opened her eyes to Jesus and His unconditional love. Elizabeth's heart soared even now, days after she had knelt before her Maker and confessed she was like a boat, adrift in a sea of lies and brokenness, and she needed her Savior once again.

The simplicity of that prayer had alarmed her with its ability to knock down the walls she had hidden behind all these years. The prayer had come from a place of longing deep in her heart she had tried so hard to keep buried. But from the moment Dustin Edwards had toppled under her that fine day, Elizabeth had known she'd never be the same.

Dustin drew her into an embrace, making Elizabeth glad they had decided to skip the gala. Time alone with Dustin was precious. He hesitantly pulled back from the hug. "I need to do the right thing by laying my head somewhere else while I am still in town." A handsome ruddiness came into his cheeks as his eyes caressed her lips. He reached out and gently pushed back a wisp of hair that had landed on her shoulder. "A woman of your character and beauty is a mighty tempting thing for a man." Dustin grinned and stood.

"I'll stay here tonight since it is so late. But tomorrow I'll find a room to rent. Good night, my sweet Elizabeth. I shall see you in the morning." And with that, he took the stairs two at a time in his fine cut tuxedo.

Elizabeth sighed and leaned back against the settee. It had been a wonderful evening. She couldn't remember when she had had a better time. The dinner at the restaurant was delicious, and their shared moments of tender looks and sweet embraces were priceless.

Elizabeth sipped the last of her after-dinner coffee and had to admit to herself she'd fallen head over heels in love with this amazing man named Dustin Edwards. Again. Tonight, she felt like the years they spent apart had simply melted away and their hearts were now beating as one. She giggled quietly to herself over her girlish thoughts. She felt like someone who was being courted for the first time.

"Sounds like you had a wonderful evening," a voice said from the door to the drawing room. Summer stood there looking like a vision. She was breathtaking. Elizabeth couldn't stop the tears that sprang to her eyes at the sight of her daughter.

"Are you all right, Aunt Elizabeth?"

Elizabeth laughed in spite of herself and brushed the tears quickly away. "Oh, yes. Yes, I am just fine. Just a lot of emotions running through me lately. I can go from laughing to crying and back again at the drop of a hat. Don't mind me," she said with a gesture of her delicate hand. "Please, have a seat." Elizabeth's heart started a new staccato rhythm as Summer sat in the chair across from her.

Now. She should tell her now. Tell Summer the story from beginning to end. Elizabeth felt her hands grow clammy and her stomach take a plunge. She always felt brave when she was with Dustin, but facing the truth alone was another story. No, she wasn't alone. The Lord was with her and would give her courage. The secrets she kept had nearly been her undoing. She wouldn't allow them to imprison her any longer. Freedom had come, but the last bar of restraint needed breaking down. And now was the time.

Now was as good a time as any. Summer knew after what she had witnessed and learned tonight at the ball that she needed help. Shivers wriggled up her spine as she thought of that nasty Andrew Shaw's hands on her shoulder and back as he whirled her around the dance floor. Never in a million years would she have chosen to dance with such a worm as he. But the lure to learn more about him and how she could use that information to bring him to justice spurred her to stoop to such a level.

One thing she'd found out for certain tonight—Shaw was an excellent actor. He played the part of a gentleman, knew all the right things to say, all the while never revealing much about himself. He smiled and tried to be charming, while Summer's skin had crawled until she didn't think she could take any more of the charade. As the first dance had ended, she persuaded him to go to a buffet table for refreshment.

Summer had probed and asked him where he was from, his line of work, and what had brought him to Waterford Cove. He told her some outlandish story about being a banker from North Carolina who had come to do some business with Mr. Wilson. Summer remembered seeing the two men conversing when she had first entered the ballroom that evening. Perhaps that part of his story was true. Nonetheless, Summer could not help but think he was a very good liar.

As he spoke, her mind continued to flash back to the day at the racetrack when she had spied from the office and listened to him and Frederick Ellis discuss the arranged murder of Nigel Fairbanks. She had seethed inside to think that anyone would consider another's life to be worth so little as to have it snuffed out for the sake of a few dollars. At one time, Summer had wondered how many dollars would bring someone to such an action. But the night she had found the ledgers, she knew just how much that murder had been worth.

Even though she had walked away with no new convicting information about Andrew Shaw, Summer remembered her promise to Elizabeth and Dustin the night she had told them what was happening. She had said if she ever got in over her head, she would go to them or the police immediately. After hearing Christian speaking to Shaw tonight and then dancing in the arms of a murderer, she figured she was officially swimming with sharks.

Summer sat down on the chair across from her aunt. They looked at each other and both started speaking at the same time. They laughed in unison and sat back on their cushions simultaneously.

"You go first," Summer said.

The smile that had been on Elizabeth's face when Summer had come in the room had vanished. In its place was a pale version of Elizabeth's normally pink lips. "There is something I need to talk to you about, Summer, but you may go first."

"All right." Summer took a deep breath. Deep and cleansing oxygen filled her lungs while she prayed her aunt would receive this news with grace and peace. "By the way, where's Uncle Dustin?"

Elizabeth glanced toward the stairs and smiled again faintly. "Oh, he decided to retire for the evening. We didn't end up coming to the ball. I hope you don't mind."

"No, that's completely all right. But something did happen there that I need to talk to you about." Summer paused and went on. "There was a man there named Andrew Shaw. I believe he is the one who killed Nigel Fairbanks, Mr. Wilson's former accountant." She waited while her aunt absorbed this information.

Elizabeth reached across the small coffee table and touched Summer's knee. The gesture comforted Summer, and she realized just how tense she had been these last couple of hours. "Are you certain it was him?"

"Yes. Quite." Summer briefly explained her reasoning.

"Is there any other evidence to prove he was the one to kill the man? If you went to court with this, it would be a young lady's word against a powerful accountant and his cohort. It seems to me you may need more than that to go by."

Summer felt sure in her heart she was right on all accounts, and was somewhat offended her aunt did not believe her. Then she considered what Elizabeth had said and realized the validity of it. It would be her word against Shaw's and Ellis's. Who would believe her? Her testimony may not even be considered reputable since she had hidden her true identity and basically lied to get the job in George Wilson's office.

"You're right, of course. It isn't enough to go by. I can't tell you how disappointed I am to realize that now. But there is something else. Something I don't even want to say, for then it makes it all the more true."

"Come sit with me, child," Aunt Elizabeth encouraged, and Summer wasted no time in taking a seat beside her beloved aunt on the settee. "You see," but Summer could not continue. Tears came to her eyes as she thought of Christian's involvement. Of how he had cast her aside for money. Even if he wasn't the one who had pulled the trigger, he might as well have. He was after the same money. They all were, and he wanted his cut. Summer had no idea how he was involved, but that didn't matter. He had never been honest with her, never truly revealed who he was. Yet, she had fallen in love with him anyway. Her heart, which had always run from the idea of marriage, had been ready to embrace it willingly.

"There, there," Elizabeth comforted as she laid Summer's head on her shoulder and let her have a few moments to collect herself. "Tell me all about it."

Summer could never remember her own mother ever having been so comforting to her in all her growing up years. Ruth Edwards was a Christian woman, but Summer had always felt at arm's length with her. To be held by someone who cared meant more than Summer could ever have imagined. She wiped her eyes with a lace-lined handkerchief and spoke tremulously. "Christian told me earlier today he could no longer see me and that we had no future together. I couldn't understand why he would act the way he did after dinner last night and how he could cut off our relationship when it had only begun to blossom." Summer sniffled, and Elizabeth took Summer's hand in her own. "I love him, Aunt Elizabeth."

Elizabeth squeezed Summer's hand gently, and Summer looked down at their entwined fingers. For a moment, she couldn't tell whose fingers were whose. She had never before noticed how alike their hands were. Same color, same fine bone structure, even the same small blue veins on the top of each hand throbbed faintly with each pulse. A strange feeling came over Summer just then. It was like a fine secret was just beyond her reach, but as her mind grasped for it, the mystery floated away like mist.

Summer mentally shook herself and continued. "Tonight, I overheard Christian talking with Andrew Shaw. They were on the balcony at the ball, and Christian was accusing Shaw of coming in to take over his job. Shaw mentioned a boss they both worked for, and—" Summer sniffled and let Elizabeth draw her own conclusions.

With her finely manicured finger, Elizabeth raised Summer's chin so their eyes met. "I know your heart is breaking right now, but if you want my advice, here it is. Send a note to Christian tomorrow and remind him of the invitation I extended to him for lunch on Sunday. Uncle Dustin and I will serve as your chaperones. When he's here, ask him to explain himself. There may be a good explanation for all of this, one that may allow the two of you to explore a future together. But if you let him go without knowing the truth, you will regret it for the rest of your life."

Something in the set of Elizabeth's mouth and the look in her eyes told Summer she was a woman who knew what she was talking about. What was Elizabeth's past and why did she live here in Virginia, so far from the rest of the family? All good questions, but there was no time for that now.

"Summer, I want you to know how much it means to me that you would come to me with all of this. I want to help you, and I know your Uncle Dustin will too. Let's have breakfast together in the morning and sort this all out. I think your uncle will have some good advice for you. On both accounts."

The two women rose and went to the foot of the stairs to say good night. But before Summer could place her dancing shoes on the first step, Elizabeth did something no one other than Uncle Dustin had ever done with her—Elizabeth bowed her head and with unseen steps to the heavenly realm, ran all the way to the throne of God to beseech Him on Summer's behalf.

EIGHTEEN

lizabeth laughed softly to herself for the second time that evening. She looked back at the last few days and barely recognized the woman she had been before Summer and Dustin had invaded her life. Before she had allowed God to be Lord again over her heart. Before the walls had come down with the sledgehammer of truth and forgiveness.

She had sat every day in this museum of a house, a lonely, fearful, condemned woman. Now, she was full of joy and obviously courage, for who would have thought she would ever lead her very own daughter in prayer?

She sent up another prayer, this one of pure thanksgiving as she made her way down the hall to her room. A praise to the God of her life, words that communicated just how thankful she was for the Lord's unfailing love toward her and for bringing these people she loved back into her life.

No, she hadn't told Summer about the past tonight, but in her heart, she knew it wasn't because she was a coward. Elizabeth had been waiting for and dreading this conversation for over two decades. Now she looked forward to it. But she would wait for the Lord's timing.

But lately, having a husband doesn't seem so confining after all. Not since I met you. Those words spoken by Summer only hours before taunted Christian. He punched his pillow for the countless time and got some resentful grunts from the other men. Quickly he got out of bed, self-hatred for what he was about to do propelling him out the door. The sun was barely skimming the horizon as he went through his morning chores at the stables. Not much was stirring at this time of the morning on the Wilson estate, and that suited him just fine. He needed to be moving in order to sort this all out and working with the horses allowed him to do that.

He had failed. That was the bottom line. He had failed not only his Pinkerton boss; he had failed himself. Rules that had gotten him by for ten successful years had been tossed aside. His mistakes would cost him. No, he wouldn't lose his job, but Christian knew he would lose a little reputation. And reputation was everything in this business. Getting distracted meant a man couldn't be trusted. What boss in his right mind would entrust an assignment to a man who had lost credibility?

He pitched and forked new hay into the stalls as he recalled that not all of his time in Waterford Cove had been wasted. He remembered the night when he ran toward the voice in his heart calling him home. A voice he had outpaced for many years. How good it felt to know he wasn't alone in this world. God was with him and that was a priceless realization. For the first time in many years, Christian looked forward to that still, small voice speaking direction and truth in every situation. He had gotten ahold of a Bible of his own and had spent more time in it over the last few days than he had in the last ten years combined.

Christian prayed for peace and forgiveness as he brushed down the racehorses and gave them clean water. He knew that no matter what circumstances dictated, he could rely on the Lord. If his boss never again gave him a high-profile assignment like this one, life would go on and he would find his happiness in the Lord. The matter of Summer may take a bit longer, but he prayed God would heal his heart, all in good time.

The self-loathing and memories Christian had woken up with faded as the morning went on, and he soon felt new direction and serenity. There were only three things to do now before he went home and left the Wilson case behind. The night he had spent at the orphanage had given him a healing he hadn't expected. He may never be able to hold his own child, but being with the kids there had been therapeutic for him. He wanted to go one last time before he left town.

He dreaded the next task on the list, but knew it must be done. He would go into town and pay to have a telegraph sent to Washington, letting his boss know he was handing over the job to Shaw.

But it was his last errand that would prove to be the hardest—confessing to Shaw that he was conceding. Shaw would get what he came for, and Christian would go home knowing the failure to perform on this job would follow him. He cringed as he pictured the triumphant look on Shaw's face that would surely be there when he told him the news. *Lord, see me through this.*

The telegraph would be a humbling task, but Christian wanted to avoid speaking with Shaw as long as he could. So, he saddled Sadie, and trotted toward town.

"Good morning, Uncle Dustin, Aunt Elizabeth." Summer nodded to each in turn as she took her place at breakfast. The table before her was spread with sweet-smelling bread, sliced fruit, and steaming mugs of hot coffee. Summer had always been a breakfast eater, but today her stomach did flip-flops, and she felt like she might be sick. Making small talk seemed the wiser of the two options. "I trust you both slept well last night?"

Dustin and Elizabeth exchanged a quick glance, and Dustin reached over and held Elizabeth's hand. "It's probably no secret to you, but Elizabeth and I have gotten quite serious since I came. We talked last night, and we feel it best that I find another place to rest my head." Dustin's eyes twinkled at Elizabeth, and they shared an intimate moment.

Summer could feel the love between the two of them and was overjoyed at the treasure they had found in each other. Questions about how well they knew each other before Dustin had come to Virginia surfaced often in Summer's mind, but it never seemed appropriate to ask. They would tell her their history when the time was right.

Summer's stomach rebelled against the few sips of coffee she had introduced to it, reminding her of what she had to do that day. "After praying about it most of the night, I feel it's best to go to the police this morning. With permission from the two of you, of course. I know I don't have enough evidence to prove it was Shaw who killed Fairbanks, but I feel it is my only recourse."

"But of course, dear. We had just been discussing it before you joined us for breakfast. We will all go down to the station together." Elizabeth sipped her coffee and delicately ate a piece of fruit, not looking a day older than thirty. She really was a young woman, a beautiful woman who would make Uncle Dustin very happy.

Summer cleared her throat and picked at a piece of bread. "Actually, I wondered if I could go alone." At the doubtful look on her aunt's face, she hurried on. "I won't be in any danger because I will be at the police station. And I just feel—" Summer trailed off and looked imploringly at her uncle. He would understand her. He always had.

Summer saw her uncle squeeze Aunt Elizabeth's hand, and her aunt nod slightly to Dustin. "We trust you completely. Shall Matthew give you a lift in the carriage?"

"Yes, I think that would suit me just fine. Thank you so much for understanding this is something I need to do on my own." Summer included both of them in her gaze. "I love you and am so grateful for the two of you in my life. What would I do without you?"

Summer stood. "Please tell Matthew I will be ready in fifteen minutes." She turned back quickly and said, "Don't forget tonight at seven is the fundraiser at the new location of the King's Castle."

She hurried to her room to quickly pin up her hair and choose her most professional-looking dress. She wanted to be taken seriously and feared she may be laughed at for trying to do a man's job. She looked in the mirror and tried out her fiercest look. It wasn't much and probably wouldn't get her far, but she would speak her piece and would insist on being heard until she said all she came to say.

As she walked to her writing desk to gather the notes she had made from Frederick Ellis's secret ledger, she caught a glimpse of the small calendar there. Saturday. It was Saturday. She hadn't taken that fact into consideration when she'd made the determination to go to the police and put an end to this whole charade.

Well, no matter. Someone would be working today at the station. After all, crime didn't stop just because it was the week's end. Summer grabbed her papers with an air of determination and marched out to meet Matthew at the carriage. Nothing could stop her now.

All right, so maybe Christian wasn't as brave as he first thought. The telegraph office came into view, but he let Sadie mosey on by as if it wasn't there. He figured he could very well send the telegraph to the agency about his failure after he stopped by the train station to buy a one-way ticket for him and his horse. He also figured he could visit the orphanage first. After all, what was the hurry? But after his ticket errand was done and he neared the orphanage, Christian knew it was just his pride talking. He would spend a few minutes with the boys and do what needed to be done. No matter how much it would hurt his ego.

Garrett Cole and his fiancé, Justine, had done marvels with the old factory-turned-orphanage. Christian had heard stories of how some of the children who now lived in this house of love had once eaten out of people's garbage and slept in the cold with no shelter over their heads. Boys as young as seven were in charge of the care of their younger siblings. The tragedy of it all struck Christian hard every time he thought of it.

Laughter could be heard above the clop, clop, clop of Sadie's hooves as he neared the building. A group of boys, clean and well dressed, were playing ball outside. "Mr. Titus!" One yelled, motioning to Christian. He was off Sadie in a flash and after securing her, joined the group of youngsters and their adult volunteer. After only about a minute, he found himself smiling as if he hadn't a care in the world. The game lasted until they were all panting, red in the cheeks and out of breath in the morning air.

Justine Davidson appeared at the door, her brown hair and kind eyes glimmering in the sunlight. "It's a big day around here, boys. Come on in, and after breakfast we can head on over to the property." The group of youngsters wasted no time obeying her and scampered into their home.

"A big day, huh?" Christian inquired as they stepped into the brightly lit building.

"Yes, Mr. Titus. Isn't it marvelous? The fundraiser is tonight, and it won't be long until we move the children into their new home." She looked at him questioningly as she picked up and cuddled a little girl in a bright green dress. "Oh, say you'll come and help us celebrate. Your presence here has meant so much to the boys."

Christian uneasily ran a hand across the back of his neck. He planned on hunkering down tonight, staying low and not stirring up any emotions or bad memories. But as he looked around the big room with its laughing children, scarfing down their breakfast, he knew he couldn't deny his desire to attend.

"Miss Davidson, I do thank you for the invitation. But there's something else. This is hard to say, but I am leaving town."

"Oh? I hope your trip doesn't take long."

"It's not a trip exactly. I won't be coming around anymore to visit the boys. I'm going back to my hometown. My work here in Waterford Cove has ended." Christian could feel his heart twisting in his chest as he spoke the reality of his situation out loud.

"What's this? Leaving so soon, Titus?" Garrett Cole joined their conversation. His eyes sparkled with life, and Christian found himself a bit jealous over the couple. Christian knew they had experienced some bumps along the way, but to look at them now, no one could deny they were in the center of God's will for their lives. Perhaps one day, Christian too would find God's place for him.

For now, though, he needed to move on. He gave them a hasty explanation and made his way out the door.

"See you tonight, Mr. Titus!" A boy of about eight called as he came in from carrying a water pail. The boy, Justin, flashed a grin at Christian and blended into the group of kids indoors.

Yes, perhaps you will, young Mr. Justin, Christian thought with a smile as he mounted Sadie. What could one more night hurt? *Perhaps you will.*

NINETEEN

ere goes nothing, Summer thought as Matthew pulled the carriage up to the station. Or perhaps more appropriately, here went everything. She was about to hand over what knowledge she had of the case. Once she did, the situation would no longer be in her hands. She was also about to hand over her freedom. Once this came out, her parents would insist she come home to North Carolina and rebuild her now fragile reputation. Her freedom to marry whom she chose was on the chopping block, a guillotine made of her own doing.

Summer felt foolish as she turned the knob of the door to go into the building. How silly to think she was capable of single-handedly uncovering a murder plot. Foolish indeed. And that's just what she was, a silly girl who would now be ruled by her parents' wishes once again. But she could always look back at her time in Waterford Cove with some contentment. She had relied on the Lord in the last few weeks more than she had in her entire life. Her relationship with her aunt had blossomed and they could continue to stay in touch. She had helped get the orphanage up and running, even though she hadn't been there as much as she had intended. And then there was Christian. His amber eyes flashed before her as she stepped up to a secretary's desk. Would she be bringing him down along with Andrew Shaw?

Aunt Elizabeth's words from last night rang in her ears. Yes, it was possible Summer was mistaken and there was an explanation as to what Christian and Andrew had been speaking of.

She could believe telling the police about Shaw would somehow clear Christian's name and bring his innocence to the light, but Summer couldn't lie to herself. She asked the secretary if she could speak with a police officer and was told to take a seat.

Summer sat stiffly in the hard, wooden chair, feeling like a criminal waiting for a death sentence. But it wasn't her life that was on the line now. It was Andrew Shaw's and the love she had once shared with Christian. She began to fill out a standard police form, feeling like a traitor as she wrote out her name, address, and other pertinent information.

"Miss Edwards?" A voice boomed from a nearby doorway. A tall, muscular man in his sixties stood in an office doorway, and Summer obeyed like a trained dog. The man introduced himself as second in command at the station, a Mr. Rudy. He had an imposing presence that made Summer want to sit down and say, "Yes, sir."

Mr. Rudy marched around the back of his well-kept desk and took a seat. Summer hesitated only a moment, knowing this was it. The truth was about to be laid out on the table.

"Mr. Rudy, thank you for seeing me today. I'm Miss Summer Edwards and I…." She trailed off as a lone piece of paper on the immaculate desk caught her eye. She did her best to maintain a straight face as the information from the paper registered. It read "Shaw 5:00" with tomorrow's date on it. The symbol in the corner was unmistakable. It was the same one on the paper Shaw had given Ellis when he'd set their meeting in the woods.

Realization the police officer was somehow involved shuddered up her spine and she stood quickly. "I'm sorry, Mr. Rudy. There has been a mistake. Please excuse me." Summer forced her feet to walk at a normal pace as she left the office. She wanted to run, to get far away from there, to a place she thought would be safe. A refuge in which she could unburden her load of secrets and be done with her quest. Instead she had come into another den of vipers, snakes grasping with their slithering tails to get at the money that was somehow connected with Mr. Wilson.

She burst out into the sunny morning, breathing heavily. What other explanation could there be but that the second in command at the police station was one of those snakes? Just one more in an ever-increasing pile of serpents wanting more, more, more. Summer clutched her stomach and tried to take another deep breath. She felt deep in her heart this was why the Lord had led her to go undercover at the Wilson estate rather than going straight to the police in the first place. If the police were crooked, who else could she turn to? Who else was there to trust?

Summer's eyes searched the street for Matthew and the carriage. Maybe she would tell him she wanted to walk a bit, in order to straighten out her thoughts. After that, she must get back home and talk this over with her aunt and uncle. They would know what to do.

As she scanned the street, rather than spotting Matthew, a familiar horse came to a halt before her. Summer's eyes had a will of their own and looked straight into the golden irises of Christian Titus. He looked down at her, and Summer did her best to remind herself that he too was a reptile in disguise. But as he spoke her name softly in surprise, she knew her hopeful heart would not listen to reason.

She was breathing heavily again, but not from terror and doubt this time. Christian dismounted and came to stand before her.

"Summer," he said again, and they stood there for some moments just looking at each other. Then slowly yet steadily, Summer's mind began to take over her senses. What right did Christian have to still hold her heart captive when he was clearly concealing his true self? It was time to set aside her emotions and tell this man his counterfeit character was about to be revealed.

"I heard you, Christian," Summer managed to say between clenched teeth. Her fists were knotted at her side and for the first time in her life, she felt like taking a swing at someone.

Christian had the audacity to look confused. "What do you mean, you heard me? Are you talking about our picnic when I told you I couldn't see you anymore?" Something lurked in his eyes as he spoke. Hurt, perhaps?

Well, let him feel all the hurt he can. Serves him right, the liar. "You know what I mean. I heard you at the ball with Shaw on the balcony. I can't believe you are involved in this whole thing. I was a fool to ever believe a thing you said, Christian Titus. That's probably not even your real name." Summer huffed and crossed her arms in front of her.

So, the little gal had overheard him? Now here she was trying to turn the spotlight on him. She had some nerve. Two could play at that game.

"I saw you, too."

"Of course, you did! I wasn't the one in disguise at the ball."

"That's not what I mean. I followed you into the woods that night when you were listening in on that private conversation. I saw you in Mr. Wilson's office and watched you open that secret drawer. Then I followed you to your fancy house on Lumière Square. You're just as low-down as the rest of them, wanting the money for yourself." Christian figured he would call her bluff and see if she denied it.

Summer stood there rigidly, turning from pink to red to white and back again. Then suddenly to Christian's surprise, her shoulders slumped, and she looked at her feet.

"You're right, of course." Her eyes met his and begged him silently to understand.

He would not yield, no matter how darling she looked with her lower lip trembling like that. She had all but just admitted she was guilty. Christian was glad their relationship had ended when it had. She was just like Tabitha, a liar from the beginning, and no amount of charm could weasel her out of this situation.

"I knew it!" Christian accused with an air of triumph. "I should have had you pegged from the beginning as an impostor." Summer had the audacity to look shocked. "I saw you that first morning, coming out from behind the rock at the Wilson's driveway entrance. Then I heard you apply for a position as a maid, even though your hands looked like they had never seen the inside of a wash basin. But Mr. Wilson was so charmed by your beauty, he couldn't help but fall all over himself. As it turns out, I was no better than he."

"I can explain —"

But Christian cut her off with a slice of his hand through the air. "No. No more lies. I can't take it. I know you are involved in the ring, Summer, but I don't have enough proof to incriminate you. I'm leaving town tomorrow, so I'll leave that job up to Shaw. He can find out your part in all of this."

"But Shaw—" Summer began but Christian ignored her and mounted Sadie. He left before she could lie to him again.

Summer stared after Christian's galloping horse. What in the world just happened? Her mind whirled and tried to replay every word of their conversation. All she could think of was Christian's eyes when he first saw her standing there, then the sudden accusation and hatred behind them. And he was leaving town tomorrow? The thought pierced straight through her.

She looked up and saw Matthew and the carriage rounding the corner. Summer flagged him down and took her seat on the leather upholstery. Matthew started the path home, and Summer stared out at the passing scenes. A merchant opening his shop door, a young girl skipping with her sunbonnet hanging down her back, a family walking in the park. But they were all lost on her as she tried to make sense out of it all.

Summer felt like her world had been flipped upside down. How could it be he was accusing her of the same thing she thought was true of him? Then she remembered he'd said he had seen her that night in Mr. Wilson's office and followed her home.

Oh, my goodness! thought Summer. *He followed me home.* She remembered with clarity how their romantic evening had turned sour when they pulled up to the house. He must have connected the dots that night and realized it was she who had broken into George Wilson's office to steal information. No wonder he broke off their relationship the next day. Christian must have been furious when he thought she was after his money.

169

Matthew pulled up to the front gate to let Summer out. She came into the house, intending on asking her aunt and uncle what step she should take next. But all that greeted her was silence and a note on the entryway table. Elizabeth wrote she and Uncle Dustin had walked into town for some shopping and lunch and were planning on making inquiries for a place for Dustin to stay. Her aunt mentioned they didn't expect to be back until it was time to get ready for the fundraiser that evening. The note ended in an encouragement for Summer to take a leisurely day to herself, now that the situation had been handed over to the police.

Frustration boiled up inside her. Not anger that her aunt and uncle were out having a nice time together, but a helplessness of what to do next.

Summer went to the kitchen and ate some of the fruit she had missed that morning and made herself a cup of hot tea. As she sipped, she prayed. Prayed the Lord would make things clear and she would know what to do next. It was Saturday, and she was not expected at work, but suddenly, it seemed the wisest thing to do would be to try and retrace her steps to Shaw and Ellis's meeting place. If Officer Rudy was to meet with one of them tomorrow night, it just might be in the same place.

TWENTY

Summer felt refreshed by her morning snack and prayer time and was soon mounting Miss Bess for her ride out to the Wilson estate. The late morning air was crisp and clean, and Summer felt confident as she rode up the long drive to the Wilson house. Let Christian Titus think what he wanted. She knew her innocence and only wished she could have helped Laura and Landon more than she had. As it stood, an innocent man was to be condemned for a crime he never committed. She asked the Lord to take over this mission she had tried to control, and a sweet peace filled her.

As Summer surveyed the general area where Shaw had met Ellis, she couldn't deceive herself any longer. The woods were thick and went on for acres and acres. It was doubtful she'd find the exact spot again.

Even so, she figured since she was already on her horse, she might as well ride the land for a bit and see if a landmark looked familiar. It was obvious the police officer had a meeting with Shaw tomorrow at 5:00. She supposed she could follow them tomorrow night, but that would be sneaking around again, and she had promised to be done with that. If she did follow them, she would take someone trusted with her, perhaps Uncle Dustin.

For a while, Summer let Miss Bess take the lead and go where she pleased. Summer didn't know which way to turn; she'd never had a great sense of direction. The acreage the Wilson's owned was vast and stretched far beyond the house in three directions. She and Christian had seen some of the western portions of the property when they had had their last picnic together. She knew that part of the land was beautiful, but since she had already been over there, she nudged Miss Bess toward the north to see if anything triggered her memory.

Summer explored a long while on horseback but in the end, came up emptyhanded. She was hungry and sweaty from riding so long, but she felt determined not to give up so easily.

The horse was winding its way south again, but instead of going back to the house, Summer thought to try and find the little rundown cabin she and Christian had seen. It was probably not worth her time, but nonetheless, she urged the horse in the direction she thought would bring her around to the back side of the cabin.

She remembered it lay in a valley with a stream running through it. They rounded a hill, and she congratulated herself as she saw the valley and the cabin before her. Maybe she had a better internal compass than she thought. She nudged the horse toward the stream for a drink.

Suddenly, voices filled the air, and Miss Bess started. Summer patted the horse's neck and changed directions, working to get them out of sight behind some trees.

"It's up and running now, Shaw. Told you I could do it."

A familiar voice spoke next, sharp and annoyed. "You cost us a day's work, boy. That's at least fifty grand. Don't think your stupidity will go unpunished."

Fifty grand for a day's work? What kind of operation were they running? Is this what Christian was wrapped up in?

Suddenly, Summer's horse nickered. She knew she had been found out when the men's voices stopped and a shout rang out. She turned Miss Bess around and high tailed it into the trees before she could be seen. But it proved a useless escape. She could already hear another rider closing in on her.

✦

Christian casually meandered into the bunkhouse to begin packing his things. The telegram to the home office had been sent, and tomorrow he would be on his way. In the morning he would tell Shaw the job was all his, but for now, he needed a break. He looked forward to going to the event tonight and was hopeful Summer would not be there. If she came, he was afraid he would grab her and demand to hear an explanation. And that was no way to expose liars. His entire career had been made out of bringing the truth to light. And there were right ways of doing it and wrong ways. Shaking a woman by her shoulders and demanding it was definitely the wrong way.

Most of the men were gone for the day, either on break for the week's end or doing odd jobs around the property. Christian laid out his suit for tonight but tucked the rest of his clothes in his bag.

A knock sounded at the bunkhouse door, and a groomsman entered before Christian had a chance to respond. "Two letters came for you this morning while you were in town, sir."

Christian thanked the man and opened the first. Feminine handwriting scrawled across the short note. Summer's written word, reminding him of her aunt's lunch invitation tomorrow. He stuffed it hastily into his trouser pocket and tore open the second envelope. It bore no return address, no marking that would give it away to an untrained eye. But Christian knew what was inside. His heart fell to his stomach as he sank down onto a chair to read the verdict of his future career.

Summer's heart was in her throat as she rode Miss Bess with everything in her. She had evidently stumbled on a conversation that no one was supposed to overhear and now the criminals were in hot pursuit.

She swung her horse east and a little south and was rewarded with the sight of a larger creek coming into view. Things began to look familiar, and then she recognized the place she and Christian had come for lunch so often. Spurred on by new hope, she urged Miss Bess into a faster gallop. She knew the house was not far ahead. If she could only get to the stables or in sight of the house, she would be safe.

Summer looked behind her and saw no one pursuing. Maybe she had lost the lone horseman or he had given up. The barn was in sight now, so she slowed Miss Bess to a trot and made her way into the stable with a sigh of relief. The horse was dripping with sweat, and she knew she had run the animal too hard after so much walking up and down the hills of the property.

The sound of a horse's hooves outside the barn startled her, and she dismounted quickly. She had no time to hide before a dirty man came in. She looked in every direction for a way to escape, someone to help.

He smiled to show teeth yellowed by years of tobacco stains. "Look what we have here."

Summer tried to be friendly and act nonchalant. "Hello, there. Nice day for a ride, isn't it?" As she talked, she edged closer to the door. If he tried something in the stables, no one would ever hear her scream.

"I'm not interested in the nice day, miss." He grabbed her roughly by the shoulders and threw her to the ground. "Git on over to the bed of hay there," he said, pointing to a stack in the middle of a stall.

Summer glanced around frantically, still trying to find a way out. There had to be a way.

He got on top of her and began unbuttoning the bodice of her dress. When that didn't go as fast as he wanted, he began to tear it off.

"Get your hands off of me!" Summer screamed and tried to pound his chest and bite his arm. The man would not be so easily deterred.

She prayed for a miracle to happen, and suddenly the man's dirty, sweaty body was off of hers, and she looked about, mouth agape as Christian pummeled the man with his fists.

"Don't ever lay a hand on her again!" Christian gave the man one final blow to the jaw.

The man regained his balance as he rubbed his jaw. "Fine by me. Just remember," he said, turning cold eyes on Summer. "Stay away or you'll be sorry."

Leaving drops of blood in the dirt, the man got on his horse and rode away.

All his training as a Pinkerton urged Christian to get to his horse as fast as he could. But never had he wanted so badly not to listen to reason. It only took him half a second to decide what to do. Before he gave chase, he went to Summer and helped her up off of the dirt. She stood, trembling as he gathered her in his arms for one sweet moment. Abundant relief coursed through him as he melded her against his chest. *She's all right.*

Sadie was still saddled from his ride to town earlier that day, so he had her out the stable door in a flash, hot on the trail of the lowlife who had almost taken Summer's virtue.

As he entered the blinding daylight, Christian could see the man was gone, leaving him only a small wisp of dust to follow. That was enough for Christian. He urged his horse on faster as he thought of what might have happened if he hadn't been out taking a walk. He shook the disturbing images away. *She's all right.*

But something niggled at the back of his mind as he rode. The man was threatening Summer to stay away. But stay away from what?

After a few minutes of following the man's trail, Christian admitted defeat. The ground was dry, covered in thick underbrush and remnants of last year's fall leaves, showing no signs of horse prints. He would make his way back to the barn to comfort Summer. If she wasn't there, he would find her at her home.

As Christian rode back to the stables, the letter from the home office seemed to burn a hole in his pocket. Its words were seared on his heart, words that brought more questions than answers.

Christian thought back to the night when he and Summer had walked in the park and shared their first kiss. A night when he began to think of a possible future together. Then everything came crashing down when he dropped her off at her aunt's home. He had known then that it was all a lie, their words to each other, their entire relationship. He knew Summer was not who she said she was, and he had wanted to prove it.

So, the next morning, he had gone to the telegraph office in Waterford Cove, sending an urgent message to his home office, requesting a thorough background check on Miss Summer Edwards. And today it had arrived. *Good work, boys.*

As he had sat in the bunkhouse and read the words before him, he could scarcely believe what he saw. *Adopted.* The words had stood out like they were written in red ink. Papers had been signed when Summer was only a few days old. But it was the signatures of the adoptive parents and the mother's name on the birth certificate that rocked Christian to his core.

What would she think if she was told? From the family history she had shared with him, it was obvious she didn't know. The stories she had relayed about her strict upbringing in North Carolina, the freedom she had found by visiting her aunt—all of it revealed she had no inkling whatsoever who her real parents were. It was clear the people she thought were her parents were really her aunt and uncle and that her Aunt Elizabeth was her mother. But the most shocking part of all was that although the letter did not state who Summer's father was, it did show Elizabeth's bank account statement, with staggering sums of money deposited monthly into her account. There were statements dating back to Summer's birth, and anyone with any sense could see Elizabeth Anton was being paid off to keep her little secret.

Christian could only conclude the father was someone of great wealth and had a reputation to uphold. Perhaps a prominent banker or lawyer in the community. Maybe even a judge or someone in the factory industry. Whoever he was, he did not want to be found out, so he continued to pay Elizabeth a handsome amount of money to buy her silence.

The barn was empty and Summer's horse gone when he arrived at the stables. He had to know if she was okay, unharmed. He would go to her house and pay her a visit. She couldn't refuse him after he had saved her from such a horrid event. Surely, she would open her door to him. After all, she had written to say the offer of lunch still stood. Maybe she wanted to accuse him in front of her aunt and uncle. No matter. He only wanted to speak with her for a moment to reassure himself that she was indeed fine and perhaps be bold enough to share the shocking news he had received today.

I still love her, he realized. *I love her enough to tell her the truth.* For as his past had taught him, withholding information was as bad as a lie.

TWENTY-ONE

Elizabeth and Dustin came home earlier than expected, with packages in hand and joy in their hearts. The day had been one to remember. Dustin had found a handsome apartment to rent not far from her home on the square. He would begin moving tomorrow after church.

The two had shopped and laughed and ate their way through the day, discovering the joy of being together again. Dustin had dropped a few hints about wedding rings and they had even peeked into a few shops to browse the beautiful sets. He had yet to propose formally to her, but she knew Dustin was in this for life. The thought of spending the next fifty or so years with this man made her want to dance in the streets.

Only one thing gave her pause—she needed to sit down with Summer and tell her she was her real mother. Ruth would be fit to be tied when she learned that Elizabeth was about to reveal the past without her knowledge and consent, but Elizabeth had never promised her sister she would keep this secret. It was time Summer knew the truth. Elizabeth's heart convicted her though, even as she tried to reason with herself. She really should ask Ruth and Marvin for permission first. Dustin had gently suggested this also, but Elizabeth hadn't wanted to hear it. It would stir up too much mud and surely cause a fight. Elizabeth did not want to lose any of her new found peace. But in her heart, she knew waiting until she could speak with Ruth and Marvin was the right thing to do.

As they came into the house and she turned to shut the door behind them, what she saw at the curb caused her heart to fall to her stomach. She gasped aloud with dismay. It appeared the peace and joy she had only recently rediscovered was about to be put to the ultimate test.

Summer used her best hankie to try and wipe the dirt and sweat from her face as Miss Bess made her way to the stable at the back of her aunt's house. She knew she looked a sight, with hay sticking out of her skirt and hair. She couldn't wait to take a hot bath and wash away the memory of that horrible man. She shuddered and thought for the hundredth time what would have happened if Christian hadn't come to her rescue when he did. It showed the depth of his character and re-affirmed to her heart he couldn't be involved in a murder-for-money-scheme. Tears smarted her eyes and she wiped them away, which only served to further smudge the dirt.

Hopefully her aunt and uncle weren't home yet from their day of er-rands. She needed some time to get cleaned up and make herself more presentable. They would never forgive themselves if they knew what had happened. But even as she had this thought, Summer knew she would tell them. She had to. She had stumbled upon a very important piece of this puzzle. No one threatened another person like that unless they were hiding something illegal. Then there was the conversation she had overheard. Fifty grand in a day? The numbers in the ledger were beginning to make more sense.

As Miss Bess made her way to her place in the stable, Summer thought she heard numerous voices in front of the house. She groaned inwardly, realizing two horrid things at once: her aunt and uncle were back from town, and they had company. Well, no matter. Summer would simply sneak up the servants' staircase and take a bath before anyone saw her.

Movement in the barn caught her eye and she realized it was too late for that. "Hello, there, Miss Summer." Matthew beamed at her as he took the reins and unbridled Miss Bess. His grin quickly faded as he took in her appearance.

"I'm all right, Matthew," Summer assured him. "Nothing to worry about."

"I knows you can take care of yerself, miss. I'd be more worried about what the company might think."

"Since when have you cared what others think?" Summer teased him, trying to get the attention off of herself.

"Since your parents showed up in that fancy buggy about two minutes ago."

Summer felt all the blood drain from her face and she quickly dismounted. *My parents?* This changed everything! If they knew what had happened today, they would drag her by the ear back to North Carolina quicker than she could blink. They were not known to be the most forgiving or patient of people and would garner no guff from anyone, especially her.

Well, there was nothing to do now but go and confront what she had rightfully coming to her. If she had only been able to solve Landon's case before they came. Now the boy stood no chance. No chance at all.

"Mother! Father!" Summer said in greeting.

Elizabeth could see Summer putting on her best face as she welcomed Ruth and Marvin.

"Summer! Just look at you." Ruth *tsked.* "Is this how you've been composing yourself while you've been away?" Ruth shook her head disapprovingly.

Anyone could see something serious had happened to Summer, and Ruth was only concerned with appearances? Elizabeth seethed inside. Ruth should be asking more after Summer's welfare.

Elizabeth gently touched Summer's arm. "Did you take a fall, dear?"

"As a matter of fact," Summer hesitated and looked to Ruth and Marvin, "no, I didn't take a fall. I was pushed down." Elizabeth noticed Summer was holding her blouse closed where buttons should have been.

Ruth gasped and Marvin was there to hold his wife up as the group made their way into the house.

Elizabeth led Summer over to a settee, insisted she lie down and covered her dirty, torn clothes with a blanket.

"Well, aren't we just a little mother hen?" Ruth jabbed Elizabeth with a piercing glare Elizabeth felt down to her toes. She wanted to shrink in response but was reminded that although Ruth and Marvin had raised Summer, Elizabeth had given the girl life and had come to love Summer as a person, not just because she was her daughter.

Dustin volunteered to make tea while Summer rested on the couch. Ruth buzzed about the room, verbalizing all of their questions. *How did this happen? Who did this to you?* And on and on without so much as a pause to allow an answer. Summer, however, just lay quiet, her pretty face pale and drawn.

Elizabeth could stand the suspense no longer. She asked softly, "Did Christian do this to you?"

Summer sat up and swallowed a bit of the tea Dustin had brought to her. "No, no," she reassured, but her parents were not so easily put off.

"A man you know did this to you?" Marvin Edwards roared. "I'll have his head! I'll have him locked up for the rest of his days for accosting my daughter."

"No, Father. It was no one I knew."

Ruth hung on his arm and fretted. "I knew we should never have let her come here, Marvin. Look what our foolish choice has brought to our poor Summer. I'm so glad we took it upon ourselves to come and rectify this situation."

Summer took another sip of tea while Dustin knelt next to her and held her hand. Summer looked so frail and young lying there, with her torn dress and dirt-streaked face. Ruth and Marvin may feel they had sent Summer away in error, but Elizabeth felt she herself was as much to blame. She and Dustin should have insisted they go with her this morning to the police station. What had happened between now and then that had endangered Summer's life?

Marvin turned on Elizabeth. "How could you have let her out of the house unsupervised, a girl of her upbringing? You know she can't handle herself. She's a child!"

"I'm a grown woman, Father. I can take care of myself."

"Obviously not!" Marvin laughed derisively.

Dustin, who had been quiet, spoke up in his gentle way. "Ruth, Marvin, there is much to be discussed and there are many things you need to be made privy to. But if I may, let's continue this conversation over some refreshments, say, in an hour or so. Summer looks like she may need some time alone to get cleaned up, and I am certain the two of you could use a few moments to collect yourselves after such a long train ride."

Ruth huffed and sent glares all around the room, her final one landing on Summer. "Fine. We will reconvene in an hour. I like my tea piping hot with fresh scones," Ruth said for the benefit of anyone listening. "Summer, you heard the man. Get up, and I will see to it myself that you come to tea looking like a presentable member of society."

Summer looked hesitant but obliged, and she and Ruth made their way up the stairs. Marvin went out to order the driver to bring in the luggage. Dustin drew Elizabeth to his side and gave her a squeeze. "It will be okay. Just wait and see," he encouraged.

But Elizabeth's faith was wavering. It seemed nothing would be okay ever again.

Christian put on his best black suit and tie and bent over to lace up his shiny black boots. He took time to trim his facial hair and did his best to look presentable. The small looking glass by the door of the bunkhouse showed somber golden eyes looking back at him. It was going to be a joyous event; he hated to go in such a mood.

Earlier, when Summer hadn't been in the barn at the Wilson's, he figured she must have headed home. She probably needed a good bath and a change of clothes. With a grateful heart she was okay, he had headed toward Elizabeth's house to see for himself. He fervently hoped when he arrived that he and Summer would have a chance to talk. A real talk where he could tell her about the information that had come to him. He didn't expect her to believe him, but he had to try anyway. He was leaving tomorrow, and he couldn't live with himself if he left town with this secret.

But as he had arrived at Lumière Square, someone else was there to greet Summer. A fancy carriage, obviously rented by those who were from out of town and wanted others to know their financial status, stood prim and proper in front of the gate, its horses huge and black, blinders on their eyes.

A well-to-do couple alighted from the carriage and looked around as if to see if anyone would bow to them. Christian stopped his horse and watched the scene unfold. Elizabeth and Dustin were just inside the door when they noticed the couple, and no one could miss the looks on their faces. Elizabeth had hidden what appeared to be both fear and embarrassment as she greeted the other woman. The two had embraced politely, and Christian at once saw the resemblance. In a moment, he knew who the couple was —Summer's adoptive mother and father.

Then Christian's heart had nearly beat out of his chest as he saw Summer hesitantly walking toward the group. Her face, although schooled in polite decorum, could not hide her obvious unease. She greeted the couple by their parental titles, solidifying Christian's suspicions.

If he couldn't talk to her face to face, seeing her surrounded by family would have to suffice. Now was not the time to go to her. He knew she needed to be with her parents. Elizabeth closed her front door, and Christian felt as if he had been shut out of Summer's life for good.

"Mother, you are welcome to sit down. I'm sure you are weary from your journey. I'll make this bath quick." Summer had been trying to calm her mother since they went upstairs, but nothing had worked. Perhaps if she could get the woman to rest, she would stop fretting. Summer wondered how she had endured twenty years under the same roof with her mother. One hour was enough to drive her mad. But perhaps she was being a bit too harsh in her thinking.

Ruth Edwards lived quite a sheltered life in her large home in North Carolina. Everything in her world was under her strict supervision, and Summer felt sure her mother liked it that way. Safe and in control. Having Summer out in the wide world for so long surely had taken its toll. Not to mention showing up just in time to see Summer at her absolute worst.

Summer sighed and got into the hot tub of soapy water. Yes, she should extend more patience to her mother and less sighing.

While Summer soaked, she could see Ruth flitting around the bedroom, laying out a clean dress for her. It appeared she had brought some new items from their personal seamstress in North Carolina. From her vantage point in the tub, she knew she did not recognize the day gown.

"There is much to tell you, Mother." Summer said from the bathroom.

Ruth simply raised a hand and waved her off as she continued to dart around the room. "Never you mind, child. I want your father in the room when you explain yourself. That way, you can get the reprimand you deserve. You know better than to go out alone without a chaperone. Why, you could have been killed today. Is that worth this precious freedom you seek so highly?"

Summer sighed and resigned again to be more respectful. Her mother and father had yet to see her as an adult, and Summer had no idea how to convince them otherwise. Her idea of proving herself by helping Laura clear her brother's name hadn't panned out. She mulled over the idea of telling her parents she had fallen in love since coming to Waterford Cove. She could argue she was a grown woman now. A woman who could make decisions for herself. But even thinking those words made her sound young and immature. No, she had no idea how to show her parents she wasn't a child any more.

Her mother continued to rant and fuss, but Summer tuned her out. As she rinsed away the last of the dirt, she prayed for patience and the ability to respect her parents. It was the only thing left to do.

TWENTY-TWO

"Tea is served." Elizabeth carried the tray to the parlor table. She tried to hide her shaking hands by pouring the cups with her back to her guests. Ruth and Marvin sat on either side of the fireplace, their faces sour.

Summer sat next to Dustin and appeared more at peace than Elizabeth would have expected. From Ruth and Marvin's earlier reaction to Summer, they were none too pleased at her unchaperoned escapade. If that had rattled them, she could only imagine what their response would be when they were informed of all that had taken place.

Elizabeth took a fortifying breath and delivered tea and scones to everyone in the room. She even served herself, though she doubted she could take a bite. But it was something to occupy her hands, and that seemed comforting to her right now. She seated herself in a chair by the window and waited.

Dustin, in his gracious way, began the conversation. "Marvin, Ruth," he looked them each in the eye, "quite a few things have happened lately that may come as a shock to you." He caught Elizabeth's eye and winked at her. "My heart tells me to give you the happiest news first." He stood and pulled Elizabeth up next to him. With his arm around her, he said proudly, "Elizabeth and I have found one another again, and I don't intend on letting this wonderful woman get away from me a second time."

Ruth gasped softly and Marvin chuckled. "Dusty, you old dog. I knew you still loved her after all these years. That's why you would never let us make a match for you in North Carolina. You were holding out for my dear Ruth's sister." He chuckled again and stood to slap Dustin on the back.

Elizabeth couldn't help but smile at her brother-in-law's reaction, but sobered as she looked at Ruth. Instead of the rebuke she thought would come, Ruth stood slowly and embraced Elizabeth.

Pulling back, Ruth smiled a smile that brought tears to Elizabeth's eyes. "I'm happy for you Elizabeth. You deserve much happiness after what you have been through."

Elizabeth couldn't believe what she was hearing. Her sister, a person whom she thought she would receive censure from, was welcoming her happiness? Elizabeth had lived for so long with thoughts of self-condemnation, she had learned to assume everyone else condemned her, too.

Even Marvin grinned at her as he took his seat again by the fireplace. Amazing. God's love and kindness to her were amazing.

"But what's this of Summer's being pushed down today? When we first saw you, dear, I feared for your life. You looked like you had been more than pushed down." Ruth leaned forward in her chair.

"Yes, that is true. The man who pushed me tried to force himself on me until a friend of mine, Christian Titus, came and pulled him off. Christian went after the man, but I left the stable before I knew if he caught him."

Elizabeth held her breath as everyone in the room realized the familiarity with which Summer referred to her friend.

"Christian, is it?" Ruth asked in an accusatory tone.

"I meant, Mr. Titus."

"And how is it that you have become so familiar with a man as to call him by his first name?" Marvin wanted to know and pinned Summer to the settee with a fierce look. Without giving her the chance to answer, Marvin turned on Elizabeth, all joy gone from his expression. "When we agreed to let her stay with you for a vacation, there were certain things we expected of you. While I am pleased with the news of you and Dustin, I have to ask if you were so distracted with one another that you could not properly care for my daughter?"

Dustin stepped in, and Elizabeth breathed a sigh of relief. He always knew the right thing to say. "Elizabeth and I agree Summer is a grown woman, able to make her own decisions. And she has made some very good ones during her stay here. She has volunteered at the orphanage and will be honored tonight at a special event at their new location." Dustin glanced at Summer, and she nodded to him slightly.

"She has also made a few mistakes, but has come to us for forgiveness and help. We honored her request to not inform you of the details. We felt it her place to let you share in her life."

"You don't trust us?" Ruth sobbed into her handkerchief. "I told you, Marvin. I told you the minute she got here, she would forget all about us." The sobbing stopped instantly and Ruth stood up. She towered in front of Elizabeth's chair and shook a condemning finger at her. "You told her, didn't you? I told you she would, Marvin. I tried to tell you." The wailing returned full force and Marvin lowered his wife into her chair once again.

Elizabeth dared a peek at Summer, sitting there sipping imported tea out of a one-of-a kind china cup, leaning back on an even more expensive couch, bought by Elizabeth's own silence. Oh, how she wanted to throw away all the grandeur of this loathsome home, take Summer in her arms and tell her she would love her no matter her actions, come what may.

But she remained silent, leaving Summer confused and alone as the older adults in the room danced a dance they had been mentally practicing for twenty years.

Words swirled in the air like a rare but deadly snowstorm hitting an unsuspecting North Carolina town. The clock whirled round and round, telling Summer with its chimes that she must begin getting ready for the fundraiser or she would be late.

You told her, didn't you? I told you she would, Marvin. She's but a child! She has proved she can't take care of herself. What would people think if they heard what you did? You should be ashamed. Oh, we are so happy the two of you found one another again. You were holding out all these years waiting for Elizabeth, weren't you?

Round and round the words circled like snowflakes that suddenly turned to buzzards flying overhead, threatening to attack her at any moment. Summer felt weak and helpless. She wanted nothing more than to run away and hide.

Suddenly, she was on her feet, headed away from the storm. She tried to run but time felt slow as her leaden legs made her way from the room. The worst part was, her parents had yet to hear the whole story. Soon they would learn she had been behaving like a child, sneaking around, thinking she knew what was best, trying to prove she was a responsible adult. The whole thing was blowing up in her face, and there wasn't a thing she could do about it.

No one followed her to her room, and for that, Summer was grateful. She didn't want to talk to anyone at the moment. The trouble with her parents had distracted her from the focus of her mission. She hoped it wasn't too late to help Landon, but in the pit of her stomach, she had a feeling it was.

It would probably be best to put all of that aside for the time being. Tonight was about the King's Castle and all that Garrett and Justine had accomplished for the children. Summer chose one of the new gowns her mother had brought from North Carolina and did her best to button up the back. She could almost reach all the way. Well, never mind. She would simply ask Aunt Elizabeth to help her when she went downstairs.

The gown was unlike any she had ever worn before. It was a new style, one she had seen in store windows recently, but it struck her as a bit buxom. Summer was more than surprised her mother would allow her to wear it. Perhaps she didn't know what it would look like once Summer had it on. But as she looked at her reflection in the full-length mirror, she liked what she saw.

The neckline of the deep rose-colored dress scooped slightly, revealing Summer's delicate Norwegian bone structure. A similarly colored amethyst necklace rested between her clavicles. The bodice was tightly fitted and came to a point where it met the very full skirt. Admittedly, Summer did feel a bit exposed, but she also felt very grown up. Her mother would no doubt request her to change when she saw her, but Summer decided if that happened, she would hold her ground.

What would Christian think of her in this dress? Would he approve or think it too brazen for a girl so young and unmarried? She would never know, for he didn't want to see her again.

But she wanted to see him. She'd known in the brief time he'd held her in his arms in the middle of the stall that he was no criminal. Shaw's arms the night before had been demanding, possessive. Christian's embrace was loving, strong. Summer had endured Shaw's clutching hands during their dance; she would welcome a lifetime being cradled by Christian's.

In the one brief instant she had been cocooned there, she knew. Knew that he and Shaw were more than just opposites. They weren't even two sides of the same coin. That would be putting them too close together. Shaw was a cold-blooded killer. The lowest of the low, playing with people's lives for his own personal gain. Christian was a tender-hearted man, seeking to know his heavenly Father once again. He was genuine, kind, and altogether worthy of her love. He couldn't be on Shaw's side. There had to be some other reason for his disguise at the ball and the fact that he and Shaw shared the same boss.

A small glimmer of hope lit inside her as she remembered Aunt Elizabeth's advice. Perhaps he would answer her invitation to come for lunch after church tomorrow. But now with her parents there, it would turn into a disaster, to be sure. Yet, she did hope he would come. She felt a burning need to assure him of her innocence.

With her hair secured in the back with a simple clip, Summer headed down the back staircase in hopes of seeing Elizabeth first so she could be buttoned up the rest of the way. She found her aunt in the kitchen alone, drinking tea and staring out the window as the sun sank lower in the sky.

"Would you mind buttoning me up?" Summer asked, presenting her back to her aunt. She could feel Elizabeth's fingers shaking as she worked to do the task. "Are you all right?" It seemed Summer wasn't the only one affected by that ghastly conversation an hour ago.

"All done," Elizabeth said, but Summer noted her aunt hadn't answered her question.

Summer turned to face Elizabeth and noted that she too had changed and wore a rose-colored dress and had her hair styled very similarly to Summer's. "We look like a mirror image of each other tonight, don't we?" Summer said.

"Yes. Yes, we do. Except you are much more lovely."

"I would guess that Uncle Dustin would disagree with you entirely."

"Summer," Elizabeth began, "we need to talk. But now is not the time, nor the place. At the very least, I must apologize for all of our behavior today in the parlor. It was atrocious. Will you ever forgive us?"

Summer was normally quick to forgive, but this afternoon was so upsetting and confusing, she wasn't sure what she was forgiving. "I don't know what all of you were talking about, so there's nothing to forgive. But I too need to apologize. Please forgive me for leaving the room so abruptly."

Elizabeth drew Summer into a hug, and Summer's heart softened as they embraced. She was confused and tired and a little scared of the unknown right now, but she could find peace in her Lord and in this newfound relationship.

"Of course you are forgiven," said Elizabeth. "It was an upsetting conversation. Let's all sit down tomorrow and talk things out, hmmm?"

Summer agreed, and they went to see if everyone else was ready to leave. The five of them headed out to the awaiting carriage, but Summer was dreading the inevitable —the moment she would have to climb into a different carriage that would begin her journey back to Charlotte.

TWENTY-THREE

Garrett Cole and Justine Davidson were in their element. They stood at the front of the four-storied structure, greeting guests. When it was complete, the King's Castle would be true to its name with turrets, numerous bedrooms, school rooms, and acres of fields to roam. For the moment, the frame of the building would serve to give the fundraiser guests a good idea of what kind of home the children could look forward to.

Christian couldn't help thinking as he was welcomed by the couple at the door that any child who got a chance to live there was quite lucky indeed. He stepped inside what would be the massive great room where local community members and high-society alike stood together, dressed in their very finest. Christian could already picture the children coming there in a few months' time, bringing with them their belongings, making this mansion their own.

Little towheaded girls and brown-haired boys would scamper up to their rooms and choose their beds with glee. Children who had spent years out in the rain, hungry and alone, would live with loving, godly people to watch over their care. It was enough to make a grown man cry. Christian wiped his eyes quickly.

"Attention, please!" Garrett called and conversations died down. "Thank you for coming tonight to show your support of the King's Castle." Garrett held up a hand to check the clapping. "We believe God has given us this land and this home to bless children who are without mother or father. The Bible says this in James chapter one, 'Pure religion and undefiled before God and the Father is this, To visit the fatherless and widows in their affliction, and to keep himself unspotted from the world.'

"We believe that caring for these children and giving them a home and food when they were homeless and hungry is our highest calling in life. We thank you for making this orphanage a possibility and welcome each and every one of you to lend a hand to its completion and then, of course, to visit anytime."

Justine said her thanks to all of the special volunteers who had helped with the first location of the orphanage. Christian knew Summer's name was on the list, so when Justine began to recognize certain people in the room, Christian held his breath as his eyes searched the crowd. And that's when he spotted her by the doorway with her aunt and uncle and parents. He had thought of little else this afternoon than her reaction should he get the opportunity to tell her the news.

She caught his eye as well, and rather than glower at him in distrust, Summer actually smiled. He surmised it was a smile of thanks for coming to her rescue. If that was the only gift she ever gave him, he would unwrap it again and again.

The thank-yous ended with clapping appreciation, and Christian began mingling with the crowd. He kept an eye on Summer, and every time he looked at her, she was looking at him. He didn't want to get mired down in her lies again, but something about her background check gave him pause. Other than the startling account of her parentage, there was nothing else in the report that would lead anyone to think she was a criminal. Maybe there was more to this than he was aware of.

Then a new thought crossed his mind. A ludicrous thought. Perhaps she worked for another agency. Not the Pinkertons; if she worked for them, he would know about it. But maybe a lesser-known outfit had hired her to go undercover, just like him. He dismissed the thought as soon as it came, but it kept tapping him on the shoulder all evening with its possibilities.

Summer made her way through the room on the arm of her father, Marvin Edwards, the man who had raised her from birth. She looked completely in her element, as if she had done this type of charity work a thousand times before. And she probably had. Her endeavors at the orphanage certainly didn't line up with her being a piece of a counterfeit ring. A thought he'd often pondered crossed his mind again – if he could find where the money was being printed, good would triumph over evil and at the same time, Summer's name might be cleared. If by a miracle that happened, it was still possible they could have a future together.

But then again, if he did find it and she was proven guilty, Summer would be brought to court and punished for her part. He wouldn't be there to see what transpired because within hours, he would be hitting the road and Shaw could work to find the printing press. It was out of Christian's hands.

Summer had looked for an opportunity all night to speak with Christian and personally invite him to dinner. If she didn't get the chance to convince him to come, the evening would end and that would be that.

Her father had stuck close to her side all night, and Summer itched for some freedom. Excusing herself to get some fresh air, she stepped out to the front lawn. Stars were beginning to wink overhead, and she breathed in the fresh air.

"Nice night, isn't it?" a voice said at her side.

Summer inhaled quickly and turned to see Christian's charming smile directed her way. "I want to thank you for saving me today, Christian," she said shyly. Looking up into his eyes, she felt time stand still. So maybe he was a thief. God forgave thieves, didn't He? She continued to swim in his magical gaze until Christian cleared his throat and broke eye contact.

"You're very welcome. I believe God sent me at exactly the right time. Although I regret to tell you I lost the scoundrel's trail."

"I know your presence there was providential." She shuddered. "I can't imagine what would have happened if you hadn't come exactly when you did."

Christian grinned at her and touched her upper arm. "Just consider me your guardian angel."

"Guardian angel, indeed," Summer repeated and couldn't help but giggle. It felt so good to talk to him like this that she never wanted it to end.

Summer caught movement out of the corner of her eye and saw her aunt approaching. Elizabeth greeted Christian in her gentle, friendly way and to the untrained eye, no one would be able to tell anything was amiss.

"I hear from good sources you went back to the orphanage after our little visit there together." Elizabeth took a sip of her coffee and looked at Christian with questioning eyes over the rim of her cup.

Summer watched in amazement as Christian flushed slightly in the twilight. "Yes, ma'am. I wanted to go back and spend some time with the older boys. They need a good influence in their lives. I hope I brought a bit of that to them. I will miss them when I leave town."

Elizabeth put her hand on his arm. "You're leaving town, Mr. Titus? Oh, we will miss you dreadfully. Do say you'll come to church with us in the morning and join us for lunch at my home. We go to Christ's Church on 5th Street. Service at nine o'clock. Maybe we'll even get a lively round of cards going after we eat. What do you say?" Elizabeth implored him with kind eyes.

Summer held her breath as she awaited his response.

"Of course, I will come, Miss Anton. I would be honored. Shall I meet you at church then and save you a pew?"

Summer felt invisible as the two made plans and Elizabeth asked him to be sure and save seats for Ruth and Marvin as well. Elizabeth left them with assurances that Mr. and Mrs. Edwards would be delighted to meet him. Summer wasn't so sure.

"There's to be dancing by candlelight on the back patio this evening. Would you care to join me, Miss Edwards?"

Summer tentatively linked her hand around his large arm. She turned to him and with a great deal of courage asked, "Would you mind meeting my parents first? They have heard of you and if we are to dance tonight, I don't want them to be worried about me."

Christian smiled at her. "What a thoughtful daughter they have." Instead of leading her around the back of the house to the patio, they entered through the front door and found her parents. They looked relieved when they saw her, and Summer was glad she had sought them out.

"Mother, Father, this is Mr. Christian Titus. We met recently, and he has been helping out at the orphanage with the older boys. Aunt Elizabeth invited him to go to church with us tomorrow and then back to her place for lunch." She hesitated at the look on her mother's face. "I hope you don't mind."

"Why would we mind?" Ruth Edwards said with a practiced smile Summer would recognize anywhere. And the storm that would ensue later because of it.

"Mr. and Mrs. Edwards, it is a pleasure." Christian impressed Summer by giving a gentleman's bow to her parents. "Tomorrow it will be a delight to better make your acquaintance. But as for tonight, I respectfully ask your permission to dance with your lovely daughter."

Summer could see her father vacillating on his decision before he finally gave in. She released the breath she had been holding as she and Christian bid them farewell and stepped out under the stars. A hundred votive candles and numerous candelabras lighted the enormous patio, the only part of the construction that was mostly finished, as a string quartet serenaded the couples.

The soft waltz that was playing was effortless to step into, and they made their way across the impromptu dance floor.

"It's marvelous to see all of this come together so well," Summer said. "I had my doubts when the orphanage first opened up at the factory. I was on the church committee that backed Justine until she and Garrett were able to garner enough funds to bring in more children."

Christian guided her in the steps as if this were second nature to him. Summer again wondered at his background. He seemed much too refined this evening in his finely cut black suit and gentlemanly ways to simply be a stable boy.

"I'm happy to see the children will have such a loving home to grow up in. I would imagine the King's Castle will see many children through their childhoods over the years." Christian looked wistfully at the home. "Makes me wish I could have grown up here."

"Christian, why would you say such a thing? Surely you had parents who loved you?"

Christian was silent a long while, and Summer didn't think he would respond. "No, Summer," he said softly. "I didn't. My mother loved me, that much I know, but not enough to stop the abuse from my dad. He neglected my mother and me in order to pursue his selfish way of living. I left home before I was even as tall as him and have been on my own ever since."

"Completely by yourself? Who took care of you? How did you make it?" Summer faltered in one of her steps, thinking of Christian as a home-less teenager, just a boy, alone in the world because of a self-centered father.

Christian regarded her with a look she couldn't quite read. "It wasn't always that way. For a very short time, there was someone."

The song ended and the couples around them laughed and clapped. Summer wanted to shush them and hurry the musicians into the next tune. Christian had been with someone before. It made sense. So, why did she feel as though she had been betrayed?

A new tune started and Christian twirled her around the dance floor once again. Summer braved the question, "Who was she?"

"My wife, Tabitha," Christian said honestly.

Summer waited for his explanation, wanting to know more about this man who had made her heart dance.

"We were married only a short time. I didn't really even know her. I later learned that after she left, she moved somewhat close to Water-ford Cove. Many months after she took off, I got a letter from a friend of hers. It said she had died. In childbirth. It was only then that some other things about her past began to surface. Before we met, she had worked with a gang of thieves."

"Oh, Christian." Summer drew him into an embrace. What a terrible ordeal this man had been through. "Was," Summer cleared her throat as they continued dancing, "was the baby yours?"

"Yes," Christian said softly. "At least, the timing was right. But I am sorry I never told you before. I was always so afraid you would reject me. I told myself I would never fall again for another woman, someone who could lie to me and then throw me away like Tabitha did."

Their gazes locked and Summer could read the questions in his eyes, the amber flickering in the light of the candles. He was asking a question she wanted, no, *needed* to answer: *Can I trust you?* He had accused her of being a liar. He had told her he'd seen her don a maid's uniform. Enter her employer's house without permission. Copy a ledger. Followed her home. He thought she was involved in—what did he call it? Oh, yes. A ring.

"Christian, what's a ring?"

He looked startled, and the song ended before he could answer. They clapped politely, and the quartet announced a short break. Christian took Summer by the elbow and led her into the grassiness beyond the candlelight. It was getting a bit colder and now that they weren't dancing, the evening's dampness seemed to go right through her. Maybe it was just an effect of their conversation turning to more serious things.

She repeated her question as he gazed out into the blackness behind the house. She thought he would offer his coat to her, but he seemed lost in thought. Suddenly he turned, taking her hands in his.

"Summer, I need you to be honest with me. And I need to be honest with you. There are a lot of things you don't know about—"

His words were left hanging in the air between them as she heard the voices of her parents calling her.

"I have to go. But—" Then with great boldness, Summer used the cover of darkness to gently kiss his sweet lips. "I'll see you in the morning. I hope we have a chance to talk after lunch."

The taste of his lips on her own lingered long after the carriage had taken them home and Summer had bid her family goodnight. It was a feeling she wanted to hang on to forever, no matter what tomorrow held.

TWENTY-FOUR

Wake up, sleepy head!" A friendly voice rang out as the clear morning sunlight streamed through Summer's window. "We have to leave for church in an hour," Aunt Elizabeth reminded her as she pulled back the rest of the curtains. "And if I'm not mistaken, you will want to look extra special today. Christian's going to be there."

What in the world had gotten into her aunt? Joy was bubbling out of Elizabeth and unabashedly spilling all over Summer. She smiled in spite of herself and stretched as she got out of bed. "How did you know?"

"A woman in love can easily spot another," Aunt Elizabeth replied saucily. "Now get scootin' and wear that beautiful light purple number you haven't worn for a while."

Elizabeth took her leave, and Summer stood in the middle of the room, giggling. "The purple one, huh?" she murmured softly to herself as she went to the wardrobe. "I just hope no one at church recognizes me from the race track. Because that's the last time I wore it!"

"What are you muttering to yourself about in here?" her mother wanted to know, showing her face at the door.

"Oh, just thinking of what I'm going to wear to church today."

"Do sit down for a moment, Summer. I have something to say."

Summer stiffly lowered herself to the edge of the bed, waiting to be berated for something. Her mother sat next to her. What could she have done wrong now?

"I have to apologize."

Summer could not have been more shocked.

"I was too hard on you yesterday." Her mother threw up her hands and they landed with a soft thump on her lap. "I guess seeing you torn to pieces when we arrived did a number on my nerves." She took Summer's hand in hers, something she had never done before. "I hope you will accept my apology and I hope we can move on from here. I realize there are more things that have happened since you have been staying at Elizabeth's house, and I want to hear about them. I wish we had time now, but we have to leave soon after breakfast. And I know we have company today. But I do hope we have the opportunity to talk soon."

Summer was speechless for a moment, but managed an intelligible response. Her mother had never been this soft and kind. Never. Maybe this was a sign Ruth Edwards was beginning to realize her daughter was indeed growing up.

Christian dug his second-best suit out of the bottom of his bag and tried to shake out the wrinkles. A whole day with Summer. He tried his best to believe he could say goodbye to her after lunch at Elizabeth's house. But his heart called him a liar as he continued the train of thought he'd been having for most of the night—ways he could have Summer as his own for the rest of his life.

Her kiss had been like a tonic to his aching heart. The only problem was, it was an addicting medicine that only made a man crave more.

He repacked his bag and left it on his bed, knowing he would have to come back this afternoon to get the rest of his things and tell the foreman he was leaving town. He would also have to face the music and tell Shaw he could have the job. He wanted to put that off until the last possible moment. In fact, he preferred to shout it over his shoulder while he and Sadie made a fast getaway. Anything to keep from seeing Shaw's look of smug triumph.

Christian felt nervous walking up the steps to the church. It had been years since he had attended a service. Since he had recommitted his life to Christ, he had spent afternoons in his bunk, studying the Scriptures on his own. But today, he was in a room full of people who loved God as much as he did, who desired to live their lives for Him. Maybe this wouldn't be so bad after all.

He found some empty seats and looked back at the door of the sanctuary. That's when he saw her. Summer walked in with her family, and he motioned them to join him. It was a relief to feel like he was part of their group and to know strangers were no longer looking his way questioningly as he sat alone with an entire empty pew beside him.

Since the organ had not started playing the opening hymn yet, Christian stood up and greeted each member of Summer's family by name. They seemed quite cordial this morning as they each found a seat on the long bench. Christian was disappointed when Elizabeth and Dustin sat beside him, with Summer safely cushioned between them and her parents on the other side.

When the service was done, Christian felt a renewed sense of purpose in his day. The pastor's sermon and the accompanying hymns centered on living life for Christ alone. For His glory and purpose. The words reemphasized to Christian the importance of following God's Word in what he did and said, his one aim to reflect Christ in his everyday life.

"You may follow us back to Elizabeth's house if you'd like, Mr. Titus," Ruth Edwards said to him in a friendly way as they left the sanctuary.

"Christian knows the way, don't you, son?" Dustin clapped him on the back and grinned broadly.

Summer smiled shyly at him as she entered the carriage, and his heart leapt with the prospect of spending time with her. But as he watched their horses pulling away, he realized he would be pulling away later today himself. And not just temporarily. No, it would be for good. He would never see Summer again unless he came back to Waterford Cove for a job, and that was a long-shot.

With resolve, he promised himself he would not leave town until Summer knew he still loved her. It was the least he could do. She may just be exactly what she appeared and nothing more. Or she may be a criminal, for all he knew. But before he told her how he felt, he would ask her the truth—why she had been working for Wilson and what she had been doing that night copying from the ledger book. Maybe she would even be willing to share with him what she found, and he could turn it in to Shaw to help the other agent break the ring.

But asking for the evidence meant Christian would have to come clean with Summer as well. If she wasn't guilty, he would expose himself as a Pinkerton. What could be the harm then? The worst that could happen would be Summer's rejection of him for his deceit, for allowing her to fall in love with a man who wasn't what he first seemed.

Christian laughed to himself as he and the carriage in front of him came to Lumière Square. He was assuming a lot of things. Maybe Summer wouldn't listen to a word he said and would throw him out on his ear if he tried to explain his way through this. Another thought slammed hard against his chest—she may also reject him when he told her the truth about her past.

"Why don't the two of you have a walk around the community garden before lunch is served?" Suggested Aunt Elizabeth when they arrived at the front gate.

Summer wanted to squeeze the woman. Bless her for knowing that she and Christian had a few things that needed sorting out. As much as their kiss from last night still lingered in her mind, Summer had sat through the service with a huge weight on her shoulders. She must find a way today to get Christian to hear her out about Shaw and the cabin she suspected had more to do with this whole mystery than anyone might imagine. Why else would Shaw send a thug after her to tell her never to come back to that area again? No matter what else happened today, Summer felt she needed to confess to Christian what she knew.

He would then know her innocence, and if he was involved like she had originally thought, well, she would know by his reaction. And that would be that.

The garden in the center of Lumière Square was the perfect place to take a slow walk or sit and enjoy summer's final blooms before autumn really set it. They strolled side by side, each looking down where their feet met the paving stones. It seemed there was so much to say, yet she didn't know where to start.

"Summer, there is something you need to know."

"I need to tell you some things, too, Christian."

They sat down on a bench, and Summer wondered if her face looked as serious as Christian's. She took a deep breath. Lord, help me be bold. "I am not who you think I am, Christian."

"I'm not either, Summer."

"I didn't think so, but I've decided to trust you anyway. You accused me the other day of being involved in a *ring*. I have no idea what that is, but no matter. There's something else that I believe—"

"It's a counterfeit ring. I'm a Pinkerton agent, sent here by my home office in Washington to find the printing press and bring down the mastermind behind it."

Summer knew Christian was gauging her reaction. "A Pinkerton agent? A counterfeit ring?" she repeated stupidly. It all made so much sense now. The outrageous numbers in the ledger, the cabin she was threatened never to come near again, Shaw murdering Fairbanks so Ellis could run the show and give Shaw his fair cut.

"Yes. Either you are a very good actress or you are involved in some other way. Because I saw you those times sneaking around. If you didn't know it was a counterfeit ring, what did you think was going on?" Christian asked incredulously.

Summer laughed in spite of herself. "I can see how you thought I was involved." Then she sobered. "I witnessed a murder, and I was trying to get to the bottom of it in order to free an innocent man."

Christian's shocked look quickly turned to a small smile. "You were trying to find clues that would free someone framed for murder? But who?"

"His name is Landon Moore. His sister is my lady's maid. He was framed for killing Nigel Fairbanks. Shaw killed Fairbanks so Ellis could take over as Mr. Wilson's accountant and get a handsome payout because of it. I had no idea it revolved around a counterfeiting scheme. No wonder Shaw demanded his share of the profits. They would have been enormous."

"Shaw." Christian set his jaw. "I should have known he didn't come here to take over my role as the lead on this job. He came to kick me out of the way." Christian rubbed a hand over the back of his neck and laughed softly. He looked at her sheepishly and admitted, "Oh, Summer. It seems like we both have some more explaining to do." He gathered her in his arms, and Summer melted there. "I want to explain everything, and I want to hear more about what you know. But just for now, for this moment…" He trailed off and pulled back to look into her eyes. "It's enough to know you are innocent of what I accused you of. Will you ever forgive me?"

Summer kissed him on the cheek and laughed with tears in her eyes. "I have more questions than answers, but of course I forgive you." She turned more serious again. "Will you forgive me for deceiving you, too?"

Christian kissed her hand and grinned down at her. "Yes, my lady."

Summer could hear Elizabeth calling them in for lunch. Suddenly, Summer recalled that the police officer had an appointment with Shaw tonight at five o'clock. Christian was a Pinkerton! He should know about the meeting and have the chance to follow Mr. Rudy. "Christian, are you up for a few rounds of parental disapproval? It's lunchtime and my family is waiting. But there's more to the story, and once you hear it, I think you'll agree with me that what I am about to tell you can't wait until later."

TWENTY-FIVE

Christian's heart thumped out a familiar rhythm as he and Summer took their places in the formal dining room. It was the beat that said he was close on a trail; he could smell the victory just ahead. Shaw. Christian should have followed his instincts on the man. He had suspected from the first time they had met many years before that Shaw was not an agent who could be trusted. Christian felt like a fool to have blindly taken Shaw's word that the home office had sent him to take over the case without first giving Christian a heads up on the matter.

But it wasn't over yet. Shaw had not won. He had not run Christian out of town with his lies. Shaw was the mastermind behind the counterfeit ring, not Wilson. Christian replayed the conversations he had overheard between Harriet and George Wilson. Harriet had accused her husband of being involved in something underhanded and Wilson had claimed his innocence. The only thing Wilson had admitted to his wife was that years ago, he had had an affair.

An affair. Christian took his seat at the table across from Elizabeth and Summer. The papers stuffed in his pocket suddenly seemed as though they weighed ten pounds. Food was passed and small talk ensued around the table, but Christian's detective mind began to whirl faster and faster. He felt dizzy as he put the pieces of the puzzle together. A wealthy man depositing funds into Elizabeth's bank account. Elizabeth and Wilson living in the same town all these years. Ruth and Marvin trying to keep Summer away from her aunt. George Wilson's immediate hiring of Summer for a position in his office even though she had come dressed as a maid with no work references. Wilson inviting Summer to have lunch with him and then to be his special guest at the ball.

The truth was suddenly crystal clear. George Wilson was Summer's father.

"Mr. Titus, where do you hail from?" Marvin Edwards was asking.

Christian would have to rein in his thoughts and join the present conversation and ruminate later. "Near our nation's capital."

"Mr. Titus is a Pinkerton agent, Father. He is here on assignment, working to bring down a counterfeit ring." Summer smiled triumphantly before she took a bite of her potatoes.

Ruth and Marvin sat speechless but Dustin piped up. "A Pinkerton, you say? Now that answers a lot of questions, doesn't it, Lizzy?"

Elizabeth swallowed. "Yes, it certainly does." She looked questioningly at Summer.

"Mother, Father, you need to know what's happening and what I have been doing since I came to Waterford Cove."

"You mean besides hanging around dangerous men?" Ruth Edwards flicked her eyes in Christian's direction.

"He's not dangerous. In fact," Summer reached across the table to squeeze his hand, "Christian saved my life yesterday. He's an honorable man in every way. I love him."

"Summer! Do refrain from speaking so boldly at the dinner table," Ruth reprimanded her daughter.

"Mother, I mean no disrespect. In fact, I feel it is more respectful to be honest and forthright, even if it may be uncomfortable for the moment." She smiled at Christian. "No more secrets."

Christian glanced at the other adults in the room to see how they would react to such a comment. Elizabeth was the only one looking down at her plate.

"You see, I befriended my lady's maid shortly after arriving. Laura asked me to do her a favor—go to a horse race and find out if indeed her brother was squandering their earnings in gambling." Summer paused. "Landon Moore was in fact doing just as his sister suspected. But I was in the wrong place at the wrong time and witnessed something I would not wish upon anyone."

Ruth Edwards's face was perfectly white as she whispered, "What, child? What did you see?"

"I saw a man named Nigel Fairbanks shot in the chest. It was a setup, with the murder being pinned on Landon Moore. Fairbanks was the accountant of George Wilson. Perhaps you recognize his name?"

Ruth nodded.

"Yes, we know who he is," said Marvin.

The older adults in the room exchanged knowing glances.

"I did not go straight to the police. Instead, after praying about it, I felt I should go undercover working for Mr. Wilson to try and get to the bottom of this so Landon would be absolved."

"You have been working for George Wilson?" Ruth Edwards squeaked out, each syllable higher pitched than the last. "Oh, Marvin, I told you we never should have let her come here."

"It's true, Mother," answered Summer. "And after a conversation I had with Christian just now in the garden, everything I have witnessed makes sense. You see, Shaw, the man who murdered Nigel Fairbanks, is the mastermind behind a counterfeit money scheme. He wanted a cut, I'm sure, of all the money that ran through the hands of the new accountant he's in cahoots with, a Mr. Frederick Ellis."

"Summer might not have put this together yet," Christian squeezed her hand, "but there's something else. Shaw is also a Pinkerton. Obviously a crooked one. He came to me announcing the home office had sent him to take over my job. In truth, he just wanted to ensure I was out of the way and he would get his money without getting caught."

Summer raised her eyebrows at him. "You don't say? Agent Titus, I think I just might know where the whole operation may be located."

Christian stood up suddenly, all food and other people in the room forgotten. "Where, Summer?" he demanded. "If we know the location, then we can bring Shaw down."

Summer's eyes looked into his and everything around him went perfectly still. "I think it's in the old cabin in the valley behind the house."

Christian slapped his palm on the table, causing everyone to jump. "I knew it was right under my nose! Summer, you are a genius! I love you!"

"I love you, too, Christian." Summer said seriously, but Christian's mind was already whirling with how to organize the takedown.

"You two should go to the police with this information. My little girl should be guarded at all times until these shenanigans are brought to a close. She could be in danger with all the information she is privy to." Marvin had a point.

But Summer was shaking her head. Would she insist she and Christian do this together? Christian had to admit it would hurt his pride to get the police involved, but he may need back up and couldn't do it without some manpower.

"No. No police," Summer said firmly.

Ruth and Marvin started to protest, but Dustin cut in. "What happened when you went to talk to them yesterday morning?"

So that's why Summer had been in town when Christian had accused her of being a liar. She was going to the police with her information.

Summer looked at her lap, then up at her uncle with somber eyes. "I met with a man, the second in command at the office. I'm convinced he's involved in this whole thing. I ran out before he knew why I had come." She shook her head again. "If he is part of this, I don't know who to trust."

If the police were out, how could he do this alone? Christian conceded he would just have to wait until he could contact the agency and request backup. That was standard protocol anyway when working with something of this magnitude. Local police were only involved on an as-needed basis.

"You're right, Summer. If the second in command is involved, we can't go to the police. I'll just have to telegraph Washington and ask for back up to come in the next couple of days."

"But you may not have a couple of days. Christian, if Shaw knows you were supposed to leave today, and you aren't gone by morning, he may suspect you are on to him. Your life may be in danger."

"Not to mention my daughter's life," added Marvin.

"He doesn't know yet," Christian said, shaking his head.

"But there's something else. The reason I know I can't trust the policeman I met is because I saw a note on his desk. It said *Shaw 5:00* with today's date and a symbol. The same symbol and time on the note I saw on Ellis's desk when he and Shaw met in the woods that afternoon I followed them. We know their meeting time, and if we can find where they intend to meet, we can bring down the police officer, Shaw, and the counterfeit ring all in one night."

"There is no *we* in this scenario," Marvin said firmly. He gave Christian a glowering look. "I'm glad you have the information you were looking for, Mr. Titus, but leave my baby girl out of this."

"Father, I am not an infant. I have been working undercover for some time now, and I can handle myself."

Christian let the two of them argue over Summer's adulthood while he began to formulate a plan. George Wilson came to mind. If he could confirm one final thing about the man before five o'clock, he felt positive this would all be over before the sun set that very night.

Summer, Ruth, and Elizabeth sat in the parlor sipping their afternoon tea, making small talk as though nothing was amiss.

Dustin, Christian, and Marvin were in the library just across the foyer. The door was closed, and Summer kept glancing at its heavy wooden frame, hoping to see the hinges turn and the door open.

She trusted Christian knew what he was doing. Had most likely been down similar roads in his career. He was a professional, probably very handy with a gun. She knew from reading newspaper articles that Pinkertons were especially trained in cracking down on counterfeiting. So, she shouldn't worry. But she did. She was in love with the man, and if anything happened to him tonight…

The worst part of all was Dustin was going with him. Marvin was to stay with the women. He wanted someone nearby for protection, just in case. That much she knew.

Summer glanced at her mother sitting silently in an antique rocking chair by the window. Elizabeth's face was drawn; her tea untouched.

This would never do. "Mother. Aunt Elizabeth," she addressed them. "We can't go on sitting here and worrying. We've got to take action. Do something to help the men we love in the other room."

"What can we do?" her mother wanted to know.

But Elizabeth was already a step ahead of her sister. She reached over to hold Summer's hand and bowed her head. Ruth slowly got out of her chair and joined the other two women.

After Summer and Elizabeth finished praying out loud that God would give them peace, protection, and wisdom, Ruth looked at her daughter with tears shining in her eyes. "I was wrong about you, Summer. You have indeed grown into a wonderful woman. A woman of God."

Christian came on the heels of Dustin and Marvin as they joined the women in the parlor. He was too keyed up to sit down. It was already two o'clock in the afternoon. If he was going to get out to the Wilson estate in order to do one last errand before going to the cabin, they would have to hustle.

Christian appreciated Dustin's unflappable manner. He needed someone with him who knew how to keep his head in an unpredictable situation. And Christian knew from experience this could go bad at any moment. Thankfully, Marvin had not asked to join them. He had readily volunteered to stay behind to watch over the girls. Christian truly didn't think Summer was in danger, but if it appeased Marvin, that was all right by him.

"Tell us what your plan is, Christian," Summer looked up at him with wide eyes.

A knock sounded at the door before Christian could respond, and Dustin went to answer it.

"Who was it?" Elizabeth inquired when Dustin reentered the parlor, carrying a sealed envelope.

Dustin shook his head and held out the missive for Summer. "There was no one there, just this letter left on the doorstep. It's addressed to you."

Summer opened the envelope with shaking hands. As she read, her face turned a sickening shade of grey and the paper fluttered to the floor. Christian snatched it up and read aloud.

To Miss Summer Edwards, Lumière Square

We know who you are and what you know. Now is the time to run and hide. If you ever set foot on the Wilson estate again, you will be killed. If you tell your beau, Christian Titus, any of the information you possess, he will die as well.

"They know," Summer said in a shaking voice.

"How can they?" Ruth Edwards demanded. "You haven't spoken with anyone!"

Christian had a sudden thought. "Summer, when you went to the police station yesterday, did you give them your name?"

"Yes. Yes, I did. It was on the paperwork I filled out, and I introduced myself to Officer Rudy."

"The blackguard. It must be from him. And Shaw must have told them I'm a Pinkerton. This only reaffirms what I need to do at the Wilsons' this afternoon."

"Why do you need to go out there, Christian?" asked Summer.

But he didn't answer. He was walking out of the room, calling out instructions over his shoulder. "Dustin, change of plans. Stay here and lock all the doors and windows. You and Marvin get Matthew and take turns guarding the door. I don't want to take any chances."

He saw Matthew in the stables and told him to go into the house with everyone else. Then Christian mounted Sadie and took back roads to the Wilson estate. The first order of business would be to retrieve the guns he had stored beneath his mattress.

TWENTY-SIX

Christian rode in from the north, well away from where the cabin was located. Clouds had moved in and it was beginning to drizzle; the skies overhead were a dark gray, making the hour seem later than it was. Christian was grateful for the weather, even though it caused Sadie's footing to be sloppy. At least the rain kept people on the estate from wanting to be outdoors, making it easier for Christian to do what needed to be done.

The bunkhouse was deserted, as it usually was on Sundays, and it didn't take long to change out of his church clothes and put a knife in his boot and two loaded guns on his hips. A large, dark brown overcoat concealed the weapons nicely, yet he left the jacket unbuttoned, so it would be easy enough to grab his pistols when needed.

Adrenaline rushed through his veins as he quickly looked out the window to see if anyone was around. He needed to make it to the atrium's secret door unseen. Knocking on the front door when he had hounds on his trail would not be the wisest thing he ever did. Better to go through the back.

Christian could feel everything coming to a head. He knew this was it. Reason told him to wait until he had backup, but seeing Shaw come to his just reward and cracking this case on the very night he had planned on leaving town were bonuses just too good to be true.

He could do it. Even if he had to do it by himself. There was one more man who might be able to help and Christian prayed Wilson had the fortitude he appeared to embody.

Just as Christian had hoped, Wilson was alone in his office. He looked up when Christian stood in the doorway. "May I help you?"

Taking off his hat, Christian stepped into the room and shut the door behind him. "Mr. Wilson, I'm Christian Titus."

"How do you do? I believe you're the young man who has been working in the stables these last few weeks."

"Yes, sir. That's correct. But I'm not a workhand by trade."

"No?" Mr. Wilson inquired and motioned for Christian to take a seat.

If Wilson was knee-deep in this, Christian needed to be ready for an altercation. If Christian's instincts were correct and Wilson was an honest man, the outcome would be entirely different. He decided to risk it all. "I'm a Pinkerton sent by the agency in Washington to investigate a potential counterfeit ring held somewhere on your property."

George Wilson's face went slack. "You don't say," he said as he sat back in his chair, clearly dumbfounded.

His boss's reaction was just the confirmation Christian had been hoping for. He plunged ahead. "I believe your former accountant was murdered by Andrew Shaw, a dirty agent. He set the whole thing up so Frederick Ellis could take over Fairbanks' job as accountant. I believe all dirty money passes through Ellis. Shaw, of course, gets a cut of everything."

"But that's impossible. I keep very close tabs on all the business finances."

"Someone found a secret ledger concealed in your accountant's desk. I believe that ledger holds the records for all the counterfeit money that is made here."

Sparks were bursting from George's pale green eyes. The eyes of Summer's father. "I haven't made my way to the election for Senate just to have my good name muddied by some greedy thugs."

"I thought you might feel that way. You should also know that the second in command at the police station, a Mr. Rudy, is also involved and has begun making threats to kill me and someone whom I love dearly."

216

"They are threatening your family, as well?"

"No, Mr. Wilson. They are threatening your family. Your daughter, in fact."

George rested his frame on his elbows and buried his face in his hands. "Summer. How did you know? How is she involved in this?"

"It's a long story. She witnessed the murder and began working here to uncover why someone would have Fairbanks killed. She was trying to help clear the name of a friend of hers, a boy who is taking the murder rap."

George looked up, anguish in his eyes. He rubbed a hand across his broad forehead. "What have I done? I never should have hired her! But when she came that first day, I knew right away who she was. I just wanted to be close to her, to get to know her."

"Yes, sir. She had the very same effect on me."

"You mean…?"

"I'm falling in love with your daughter, sir. But tonight, I need your help. Summer is at Elizabeth Anton's house with her parents and her uncle from North Carolina. They will protect her, but I can't do what needs to be done on my own. The police cannot be trusted. The short of it is, Mr. Wilson, I need your help."

Every noise outside caused Summer to jump as she worked to make a batch of cookies. It seemed like a good idea to keep her hands busy and her mind occupied while they all waited for some sort of news from Christian. It had begun to rain in the last hour, and Summer feared the weather would not be on Christian's side. Oh, how she wished he would have stayed so she could talk some sense into him. How in the world did he think he could go up against who knew how many men at that cabin? Shaw was a trained Pinkerton, and Officer Rudy most likely hadn't gotten to this place in his career by being a bad shot. Even if Christian had two guns, he couldn't defend himself against so many enemies.

Summer's mother had never encouraged her to be in the kitchen back home in Charlotte, but their head cook had always invited Summer in to watch and help with whatever she was working on. It was a relaxing distraction so she went on the hunt for a cookbook. Spying one on a shelf in her aunt's kitchen, Summer found a recipe she thought looked easy enough and went to work. When the first batch was in the oven, she took off her apron and joined her family in the parlor.

A faint sound could barely be heard above the now pounding rain. Summer sat up straighter in her chair and tilted her head to one side. There it was again. "I think someone's at the door."

"Don't answer it, for goodness sake," said Summer's mother.

"Hello?" came a muffled inquiry. "Anyone home?"

Summer at once recognized the voice. "It's Laura!" she said and ran to the door. Summer threw it open without thinking, then quickly pulled her lady's maid inside and slammed the door behind her.

Laura stood there dripping wet, carrying a satchel in each hand. "What in the world is going on? The only lights I could see from outside are the kitchen and the parlor."

Summer's parents stood gaping at the young woman, while Matthew silently took Laura's bags and headed up to the servants' quarters on the top floor of the house.

"Miss Moore, these are my parents, just in from North Carolina. Mr. and Mrs. Edwards. You may remember them from last year when we visited briefly."

Laura curtsied as she had been trained and welcomed them to the area.

"Laura, why don't you take a few moments to change into dry clothing, then come and join us for cookies in the parlor?" Summer invited.

Her friend looked both amazed and frightened that she would be invited to join them as a guest. Summer couldn't wait to tell Laura all that had transpired since she'd been gone visiting her grandmother. As the girl collected herself and went upstairs, Summer prayed both for Christian's safety and grace that Laura would receive the latest developments with patience and courage.

George Wilson was proving to be a wonderful asset. He had changed out of his business suit and had on his hunting clothes. Harriet was out visiting friends for the afternoon, so no excuses for his absence had to be made.

Wilson was a strong man, and his anger that someone would dare sully his reputation and try to pull off a counterfeit ring right under his nose made him a formidable foe. Christian was glad Wilson was on his side. The man also claimed he had been a hunter in his younger days and produced a rifle from his chambers, loaded and ready to fire. Christian hoped it wasn't needed but he doubted the validity of that thought.

The rain had pounded for a while then turned to drizzle again so the ground was soft and muddy as he and Wilson rode their horses along the south side of the property and then further to the west. Christian knew he was taking a chance in assuming Shaw and Rudy would come to the cabin. But since the printing press may be located there, Christian figured their meeting place couldn't be far away.

The two men tied their horses to some trees a good three hundred yards away from where they planned on hunkering down in the mud to wait and watch. The sun was completely hidden by low, dark clouds, the perfect cover for Christian and Wilson. The pair ran low against the ground, then shimmied through the mud on their stomachs to a cluster of bushes, keeping their guns sheltered from the rain yet prepared to shoot.

"It's about fifteen till the top of the hour," Christian informed Wilson in low tones. "Rudy and Shaw should show up somewhere around here. Keep a lookout in all directions, not just the cabin. We need to be ready at any time."

"Got it," Wilson affirmed, his green eyes flashing, taking in their surroundings.

The minutes crept by, but Christian did not lose his focus. He prayed under his breath for wisdom and safety. He thanked the Lord for Summer's willingness to give him another chance, allowing her to share the information she had garnered. If not for that, he wouldn't be here now, geared up to bring down the biggest crook he had ever known.

As his eyes scanned the area, Christian thought of his father. The lies and selfishness that had left him and his mother in dire straits. Christian thought of Tabitha and her lies. How they still had the power to cut him all these years later. Then he thought of the sermon he'd heard that morning, and the verse that said, "This then is the message which we have heard of him, and declare unto you, that God is light, and in him is no darkness at all."

Maybe that was the real reason behind his drive as a Pinkerton. God loved truth. God was Truth. And when Christian could be a part of that, could shed light on a dark situation, he felt good. He knew he was doing the right thing. God was just and God forgave. Christian realized in that cold wet moment that both justice and forgiveness brought light. And they could both only come from his heavenly Father. He could trust God for justice and he could emulate his Lord by forgiving. He silently prayed for the fortitude to do both.

Movement out of the corner of his eye caught his attention and he elbowed Wilson. Wilson was already looking that way and nodded to Christian. A man on horseback came riding up to the opposite side of the cabin from where Christian and Wilson were. They would have to walk around the back of the building if they wanted to see what the fellow was up to.

Christian and George kept a good distance away and slunk as low as possible to get to the other side. As they passed the back of the cabin, Christian could see candlelight pouring out from a window. A man in a soiled apron moved about quickly in the space and Christian would have bet his life there was a printing press in that structure. If there was only one man inside and Shaw and Rudy to contend with on the outside, this may be easier than Christian could have hoped for.

Christian and George had to crawl on their bellies and elbows the rest of the way. It was hard going, but as they got closer, Christian could see it was Shaw who had arrived. Rudy would not be far behind.

A man Christian assumed was Rudy came in from the east and dismounted his horse. Shaw and Rudy shook hands, and Christian tried to memorize their conversation to be used as evidence later on.

"The Edwards girl shouldn't be much of a problem anymore," Rudy laughed. "I had a nice little letter delivered to her house earlier today that ought to scare the bejeebers out of her. She won't be setting foot on this land anytime soon. I also gave her fair warning about Titus. Just to be safe."

"Smart man," Shaw praised and slapped him on the back. "Glad you could join our little operation out here. You won't be sorry you got in when you did. The cut you'll receive will be well worth your silence at the station. If you get anyone sniffing around for information about our business out here, you just point them in the other direction."

"You have my word," Rudy agreed, and the two men shook hands again.

Christian elbowed Wilson and whispered, "That's all I need to hear. Let's move."

The two muddy men stood up at the same time and cocked their guns at Rudy and Shaw. "Hands above your heads where I can see them," Christian demanded. Rudy looked surprised, but Shaw looked angry and began to move. Christian knew the other agent was quick and a trained marksman so he jumped behind a tree for protection and pointed his gun at Shaw. But the other Pinkerton had already drawn his weapon and a bullet whizzed by only an inch from Christian's head.

Christian retaliated by aiming for Shaw's shoulder and got him right where he wanted him. The man fell to the ground, and Rudy threw up his hands, begging them not to shoot. Christian disarmed Shaw and tied his good arm to a tree. He wasn't going anywhere. Wilson kept his gun trained on Rudy while Christian quickly went to the cabin's front door.

He burst in just as a young man grabbed a ring in the floor, revealing steps down to a basement. The smell of clean paper and fresh ink filled the one-room cabin, but there was no printing press in sight. Christian pointed his gun at the boy and demanded information.

He simply stood there pointing to the steps leading down to a base-ment. The boy gave a shout of warning and before Christian knew it, what seemed like hundreds of feet pounded up the steps. Christian felt a searing bullet go straight into his stomach, and he knew all in one instant that even though he had winged Shaw, the enemy had won.

TWENTY-SEVEN

Part of the group sat in the parlor, feet swinging idly to tuneless songs. Ruth wrung her hands together until they turned red. Marvin guarded the front door while he read the newspaper, and Matthew was at the back door, keeping it secure.

Elizabeth stared at the fire, her lips moving in silent prayer from time to time. Laura had taken in all of the new information about her brother's name possibly being cleared, claimed a headache and headed to bed. And Summer tried to pray as she paced and nibbled on a cookie.

Dustin was the only one who seemed to be in his right mind. He made notes about the situation on a piece of paper and seemed to be going over every detail. He was a very wise man, Summer knew, and she prayed he would be able to figure something out. He tapped on his paper with his pencil and made an announcement.

"I'm going next door. Back in a flash. Summer, while I am gone, draw me a map from here to the Wilson's house, then from the Wilson's house to the cabin you were telling us about." He put on his coat and hat and headed out into the late afternoon.

True to his word, only five minutes passed before Uncle Dustin came through the front door with two men at his heels. "Everyone, these fine young men are employed with Elizabeth's neighbors, the Johnsons. They have agreed to help keep you safe until Titus returns with news."

"Here's your map, Uncle Dustin." Summer couldn't help but think about her uncle's lack of a gun. She appreciated him going out to help Christian, but what good could he do unarmed?

His eyes twinkled at Summer, then at Elizabeth. "I'll be back." And with that, he was gone.

Christian lay on the hard floor of the cabin, pain searing through his middle. He knew he wouldn't have much chance of making it unless Wilson came to the rescue. And how could he? There must be fifteen men in the room. Christian moaned as boots began to kick his face and stomach. Blessed blackness began to overtake him, and one final blow to his bullet wound snuffed out the last of the light.

Dustin followed Summer's crude map, trying to read it clearly in the dim light. It took longer than expected to reach the estate, but he had made it. Fresh hoof prints could be seen in the driveway, with very little rain pooled in them. Dustin knew they had been made recently and hurried toward the house.

A group of men on horseback were gathered in the yard by the bunkhouse. "What goes there?" Dustin called, and they all turned his way, guns cocked.

Dustin lifted his hands above his head and wondered what in the world he had gotten himself into. "Who are you gentlemen?" They were a clean-cut group of men who almost resembled policemen with finely cut coats and matching guns.

"We could ask the same of you."

"Dustin Edwards," he went on boldly. He could be digging his own grave right now for all he knew. "I came to help my friend, Christian Titus. He is out here right now trying to uncover some criminal activity."

One of the men leaned over to whisper to another, and Dustin felt as though his life hung in the balance. If these men were part of the counterfeit ring, he may only have a few minutes left in this world. If they were some sort of policemen like he suspected, then maybe they were there to do the same thing as Christian.

"We're Pinkertons, sent from the home office on account of a telegram we got from Mr. Titus. When we got word Agent Shaw was here, we smelled trouble afoot," a tall, well-built man said as he sat on his horse.

Dustin breathed a sigh of relief and couldn't help smiling. "Then what are we waiting for? I have a map to where Titus thinks the whole operation is being held. It's about half a mile from here."

The group moved as one, following Dustin along a stream bed, over a large hill and down through a valley. As they neared the cabin, Dustin could see the door was open and there was a commotion inside. A Pinkerton told him to stay back, and he watched them surround the place, their guns at the ready. Dustin got himself out of the way and waited with baited breath to see what would happen.

Two men who were tied to a tree caught Dustin's eye. He hoped they were Shaw and Officer Rudy. The guard standing over him greeted Dustin with a nod.

"George Wilson," the man introduced himself while he kept an eye on his charge. "Am I glad to see you guys. I think Titus has been shot and I couldn't go up against all those men. They must have come from the basement of the cabin because when Titus and I went past the lone window earlier, we only saw one person inside."

Dustin looked at Wilson standing there in the darkening night. He had wondered a hundred times since Elizabeth had told him who Summer's father was what he would say if he ever got the chance to meet the man. Wilson had single-handedly shaped so many futures and had helped to steel away Dustin and Elizabeth's opportunity at happiness. But now that Wilson stood in front of him, Dustin felt no anger or retaliation.

For he had Elizabeth again. And Elizabeth had brought Summer into all their lives. And that was enough. Yes, Dustin wished he could go back, that he and Elizabeth would have had the last twenty years together, but he wouldn't change the fact that Summer had been born. He would not dwell on the former things, but instead to look to the new things God was doing.

Dustin dismounted his horse and came to stand before Wilson. Dustin extended his hand with his head held high. "Dustin Edwards, a friend of Christian Titus."

Wilson firmly returned the handshake. "Nice to meet you." Wilson asked hesitantly, "Are you of any relation to Summer Edwards?"

The two men turned their attention back to the cabin as gunshots and shouts rang out in the dusky air. Dustin and Wilson both got on the ground and watched in amazement as the Pinkerton men expertly fought the impromptu battle until every last member of the counterfeiting band was either shot or detained.

Dustin and Wilson left the man tied to the tree and went to see if Christian was all right. Dustin's fears were realized as he saw Titus being carried out by two agents, his belly wrapped in a makeshift bandage. It was stained with bright red blood.

One of the agents approached him and Wilson and said, "You two, take Titus here to the nearest hospital." He showed the men where his horse was tied and Dustin quickly mounted then Wilson and the other agent helped put Titus on in front of him, facing backward.

Wilson's leadership skills seemed to kick in. "Take him to the first barn you see as you head toward the house, Edwards. There's a wagon hitched up there already, and it will be easier to transport him to town that way. I'll meet you there and we'll take him in together. And you agents probably recognize Shaw there." He jabbed a thumb in the direction of the remaining criminal.

Christian was unconscious and bleeding badly as they finally neared the barn. Dustin and Wilson did their best to carefully lift him from the horse and into the back of the flatbed wagon. Christian was out cold and didn't even flinch as they moved him. Dustin "Hi-upped" to the horses, and they trotted briskly toward town. He felt helpless, knowing Christian may not make the rough ride to the hospital, knowing he might miss his chance at true love in this world.

Summer was losing hope. A rock of uneasiness had settled in the pit of her stomach but it wasn't from fear of losing her own life. She had a feeling something else was desperately wrong. The clock in the room struck seven, then eight o'clock. She couldn't take it any longer.

"Please, you've got to let me go check on them. They could be in danger. What if they need help?" But it was useless to ask, she knew. Neither her parents nor Elizabeth would let her go.

Footsteps at the door caused everyone in the room to turn in that direction, and Summer ran to see who was there. Marvin peeked out to make sure it was safe, then opened the door wide to let Uncle Dustin in. He was pale and disheveled and a large amount of blood covered the front of his coat.

"Dusty!" Elizabeth shouted as she ran toward him. She started to put her arms around him, then noticed the blood. "You're injured!" she exclaimed. "Someone, quick! Go for the doctor!"

Uncle Dustin began to remove his coat, and Summer could see the shirt underneath was also soaked with blood. "No, no. I'm all right. I'm not hurt. But—" he trailed off and looked at Summer.

"No!" she cried and buried her head in her hands. She couldn't bring herself to ask if Christian was alive or dead. The room began to spin, and someone put their arm around her shoulders and led her to a chair. She looked up to see Uncle Dustin kneeling before her.

"Summer, I'm sorry to have to tell you that Christian has been shot. We got him to the hospital, but there was nothing the doctor could do."

"No!" Then, "Is he—"

Dustin took her hand in his and said, "You might want to get down there as soon as you can. He was unconscious when Wilson and I transported him, but he may already be gone. I'm so sorry."

Summer cried softly but began to move right away. She grabbed her coat and without a word, went out into the night. Uncle Dustin was right behind her, his blood-stained clothes speaking volumes about Christian's condition. She prayed Christian would live and that they would be able to share a life together. But the rock in her stomach only grew heavier as her uncle drove her to the hospital in the same wagon that had transported Christian's body.

It was the longest night of Summer's life as she sat in the hospital waiting for news of Christian. He was under the care of a very young physician, so young Summer had her doubts of his abilities. Christian had lost so much blood in the time it took to get him to the hospital that no one believed he would live.

Her parents came with Elizabeth shortly after she and Dustin had arrived. Then two Pinkerton agents came in, and there were countless forms to fill out in order to pay witness to their knowledge of the situation.

Finally, around dawn, the doctor came out smiling, his clothes covered in blood. "Well, I'm happy to report Mr. Titus is still with us, and I do believe he will make a full recovery."

Summer was glad she was sitting. She felt like she might faint from relief.

"No offense," said Marvin, "but you look like you are straight out of medical school."

"I am," said the young man confidently. "I believe that's what saved this man's life. In recent years, a new school of thought has emerged in the medical community. Whereas a veteran doctor may have bled Mr. Titus, believing that would give him the most benefit, a new technique has been proven more effective. It is called a transfusion. You see, after I removed the bullet and stitched up Mr. Titus's wounds, I infused blood back into his system to replenish what he had lost. He is on the mend and should be able to go home sometime next week."

The doctor took his leave and while Summer sat trying to absorb this startling news, there were hugs all around. Just then, Mr. Wilson came in. Elizabeth inhaled sharply and everyone but Summer and Dustin looked aghast. Maybe they were uncomfortable being this close to someone so well-known in politics.

"Good morning, all." Mr. Wilson greeted everyone soberly. He looked at Elizabeth and then at Summer with the oddest expression on his face. Then he smiled. "Do we have news on our man Titus?"

Uncle Dustin piped in, "We just had word he is doing well and is expected to make a full recovery."

"Splendid. Glad to hear it." He came to stand in front of Summer, and she had a strange sense everyone in the room knew something she didn't.

"Miss Edwards, you must be very relieved. I understand you and Mr. Titus have formed an attachment?"

Summer felt herself blush but nodded. "We have. Thank you for coming down to the hospital to see how he is doing. That was very kind of you."

"Mrs. Wilson also sends her regards. I would have come earlier, but I had to fill out some reports for the agency. I assume they found you as well?"

Summer nodded again.

Mr. Wilson and Uncle Dustin struck up a conversation, giving Summer the chance to ask a nurse if she could see Christian. She told her that he wasn't awake, but that she could peek in the room for a minute. Summer happily accepted and went to pray over Christian and whisper words of encouragement to his unconscious mind.

When she came back to the waiting room, her parents, Aunt Elizabeth, Uncle Dustin and Mr. Wilson were all standing in a half-circle and every eye became fixed upon her.

Aunt Elizabeth spoke first. "Summer, there's something we need to tell you."

Her mother chimed in, "Yes, dear, something you should have known long ago."

Alarm bells went off in her head, and she felt her heart fall to her stomach.

Uncle Dustin reassured her everything was going to be all right, and her father put his arm around her and led her to a chair.

Mr. Wilson surprised her by speaking next. "Elizabeth, why don't you begin?" When Mr. Wilson called her aunt by her first name, Summer suddenly knew the next words spoken would change her life forever.

EPILOGUE

You look beautiful, Summer," her mother said as she helped button her up the back.

"A fitting bride for your handsome groom," agreed Elizabeth as she straightened Summer's veil.

"You are truly a woman of God, and you make all of us proud," Ruth added and the three ladies turned together toward the full-length mirror in the finished turret room of the King's Castle.

Laura straightened Summer's train and stepped to the side. Summer turned and smiled at her friend, remembering all they had been through. Landon's name had been cleared of all charges and his weeks in jail had been the perfect catalyst for reformed behavior. He had taken over Christian's stable job, and George Wilson was proving to be an excellent influence in the young man's life.

As she gazed back into the mirror, Summer thought of other details God had put to rights. The men involved in the counterfeit ring had been tried for their crimes and would not be hurting anyone else anytime soon. Summer also not only now knew about the circumstances of her birth, but George Wilson had stepped into her life with all the gusto of a loving father. She felt that the Lord had blessed her with four loving parents. God was so good.

Summer's eyes misted as she gave her mother a hug and told her how much she loved and appreciated her. Ruth hugged her back and murmured words of endearment to her daughter. It felt so good to be trusted and nurtured at the same time.

Elizabeth hugged her next, and Summer told her how proud she was that they were family. After the truth came out, Summer had watched in amazement as Elizabeth seemed to blossom into a joyful woman, growing and expanding her horizons day by day.

But one of the most amazing parts of the confession was that Ruth and Marvin had allowed it. So had George Wilson, with his wife's blessing. While Summer had gone to Christian's hospital room to spend a few moments at his bedside, the five adults in the waiting room had agreed that the secret had been kept for too long. It was the first time all five of them had ever been in the same room together, and it was as if God had orchestrated each of their hearts to come into agreement in that one moment.

The truth hadn't been easy to hear. Summer had been shocked, hurt, and excited all at once. But over time and through the course of many hours spent in Scripture and prayer, she had come to learn that the God of all creation loved her so much He had ordained for her life to look exactly as He intended it to be.

Summer was then left with the question of how she would respond to such a revelation. And she chose to see it in the light of God's redemption of all man-kind. They were all sinners. They all needed a Savior. And that Savior was powerful enough to work a miracle in each of their hearts, when they chose to let Him.

It had been tempting to harbor bitter feelings or judgment of each person involved. But if she did that, she would be saying that what Jesus did on the cross wasn't good enough— wasn't powerful enough. But Summer knew firsthand that it was. The Lord had revealed her roots and was fortifying them to produce lasting fruit.

"I am especially happy for you and Uncle Dustin," Summer said to Elizabeth. "You have come such a long way, and now that you are married, well, it's just too good to be true."

Elizabeth and Dustin had made vows they intended to keep as soon as Christian was well enough to attend the wedding last December. Elizabeth had been a radiant Christmas bride, and Dustin's joy was evident to all. The couple went on a three-month honeymoon, exploring together many of the places Elizabeth had only dreamed of through the pictures on her walls.

Her aunt and uncle truly were a perfect couple, though Summer had wondered about all the money George Wilson had deposited into Elizabeth's bank account over the years. Was the money tainted by the counterfeit ring? No one knew for sure, but Elizabeth didn't feel right about keeping the home or the possessions in it. She had said her silence about Summer had bought everything she owned and she wanted to make a clean break of it.

So, after the wedding, Garrett and Justine had invited Dustin and Elizabeth to become the resident grandparents of the King's Castle. Elizabeth laughed at the title since she was still young enough to have children of her own, but she and Dustin had immediately accepted.

Summer's eyes met the gazes of her two mothers in the mirror. God had worked miracles in each heart that had been in the hospital waiting room on that fateful day.

And now, it was Summer's wedding day. After the three ladies had a few moments of tears together, they made their way down to the great room of the mansion. Her mother and Elizabeth kissed her cheeks and made their way to the front to take their seats.

Summer's heart fluttered as her father and George Wilson each took an arm and walked her to the aisle that would bring her to her husband-to-be. She turned to each of these special men in her life, who trusted Christian Titus enough to take care of her the rest of her days. She kissed them each on the cheek and told them both privately that she loved them. Her father had tears in his eyes, and George looked like he had just been given a beautiful gift.

The wedding march began, and the next half an hour flew by with words of love spoken happily between her and Christian. He looked like a dream come true, standing next to an altar he had built with the older boys of the orphanage. She was so proud of this man whose name she would share. Christian had moved to Waterford Cove and was building a little cottage just in front of the King's Castle; a house where they could live as man and wife. Officer Rudy had gone to prison, and Christian had been offered his position as second in command at the station. Their future was taking shape right before Summer's eyes.

But what made her heart swell with love for this man was the investment he made in the children at the King's Castle. He was a common face around the orphanage and many of the children ran to greet him whenever he entered the home.

And now those same children, including young Amber who loved on the babies in the old orphanage's nursery, threw flowers as Summer and Christian, with rings on their fingers, ran down the aisle, laughing. Violin music began to play, and people made their way out to the lawn to mingle while they waited for refreshments to be served.

Tables had been set up under a large pergola, and sunlight and shadow danced through the flowers and vines covering it. Summer and Christian stepped into the privacy of the flower garden for a moment, away from prying eyes.

"Summer," Christian said huskily as he lowered his lips to hers. She giggled when he broke the kiss. "What's so funny?" he asked, poking her in the ribs. "Is my beard tickling you again?"

"Yes, but I like it," Summer said, smiling.

"Good, because there's plenty more where that came from." Christian claimed her mouth once more as Summer sent up her thousandth prayer of thanksgiving for bringing the freedom in her heart she'd always longed for.

DISCUSSION QUESTIONS

1. After Summer witnesses the murder and realizes she may lose her freedom if her parents find out, she feels a small but noticeable prick in her heart. Galatians 5 depicts the battle that wages in our hearts between the flesh and the Spirit—what our sinful natures want versus how the Spirit of God would guide us.
   - Name a time this week when you felt that pull between the flesh and the Spirit. How did you react?
   - Are you at a place in your relationship with the Lord where you are sensitive enough to hear His voice and respond with humble obedience?
   - Pray, asking God to help you to hear His voice and follow the Spirit's leading.
2. Summer's parents hid the truth from her. Both Christian and Summer don disguises to ferret out the truth.
   - What does God's Word say about truth? According to God's Word, is withholding the truth the same as lying? Do you think Summer's parents' lies protected or harmed her? Do you think God would have provided a way through for both Summer and Christian if they hadn't lied about their identities?
3. Elizabeth has convinced herself she should be penalized for her sin. She holds her secret sin so close it isolates her yet she wants so badly to

be free of it. Her story reminds me of Psalm 32:3–5 (NIV).

"When I kept silent, my bones wasted away through my groaning all day long. For day and night your hand was heavy on me; my strength was sapped as in the heat of summer. Then I acknowledged my sin to you and did not cover up my iniquity. I said, 'I will confess my transgressions to the Lord.' And You forgave the guilt of my sin."

- God gives us an amazing promise in 1 John 1:9. If we confess our sins, He is faithful and just and will forgive us our sins and purify us from all unrighteousness.
- What was Elizabeth's turning point with the Lord and how did that affect her relationship with others?

4. When Summer tries to fall asleep the night of the murder, her racing thoughts keep her awake. When Scripture comes to her mind, she realizes her restlessness comes from a lack of trusting the Lord.

- What do you do when racing thoughts won't seem to leave you alone? What does God's Word say about worrying and trusting?

5. Sometimes Elizabeth reads the Bible, letting God's message of grace and mercy penetrate her dark fortress of guilt. But the lies that she isn't good enough and that she deserves her lonely fate are easier to believe.

- Revelation 12:10 calls our enemy, Satan, the "accuser" and John 8:44 calls him the "father of lies."
- Jesus Christ is the Truth and speaks only what is true (John 14:6). His Word—the Bible—is truth (John 17:17).
- What we believe, whether lies or truth, drives our words and behavior (Luke 6:45), so take a moment to ask God to show you what lies you are believing. Then replace them with truth from God's Word.
- Take it one step further and write out a few verses from God's Word on index cards and post them in prominent places in your home to combat the lies Satan will try to throw at you in the future.

6. When Elizabeth goes to the beach to watch the waves and the sunrise and feels the wind and the sand, her perspective starts to change. Why do you think she's able to look into the future and forget the past when she's away from her home?

- When do you find it's easiest to hear from God? How does He speak to you during these times? In what ways have you found it effective to maintain that close communion with Him when you have to go back to "reality"?

7. James 5:16 says to confess our sins to one another so we may be healed. God is the only one who can forgive our sin, but—like Elizabeth—have you experienced healing when you've asked for someone's forgiveness or learned how freeing it can be to bring what our enemy would want to keep in the darkness out into the light?

- Maybe right now, there is a sin you need to confess first to your heavenly Father then to someone else to receive the forgiveness and healing you've been looking for. If so, don't delay. Come out into the light.

8. When Dustin looks at Elizabeth, she imagines that's how Jesus would look at her—with an absence of condemnation, with an assurance of grace and love.

- It's been said that what you think about God is the most important thing you'll ever think about. I'd like to propose that what you think God thinks about you is the second most important thing you'll ever think about.
- If Jesus stood before you right now and looked into your eyes, what would you read in His? How do you think He feels about you?

9. Christian realizes he can trust God for justice and he can emulate his Lord by forgiving—and that both of these things bring light.

- In what area is God asking you to trust Him for justice and emulate Him by forgiving?

DEAR READER

I could read and write love stories all day long. How about you? Sometimes I wonder why we never get tired of them, then I realize maybe it's because we picture ourselves in the story. We want to be the one who is loved and treasured, secure in the safe arms of someone who will love us unconditionally.

There's a repeated theme from Genesis to Revelation: God wants you and will go to any length to draw you close to Himself. Relationship existed in the Trinity from before time began and because of Jesus, we will have eternal relationship with our God. There's no doubt about it—God is the author of relationship and it's His gift to us—with each other and with Himself. What a generous God we serve.

But if you are married, it probably didn't take long for you to realize you married a sinner—and so did they. Most of us live within our marriage relationship with a contract mentality rather than a covenant commitment. You do your part, I'll do mine. You broke your end of the agreement which gives me license to break mine. Our God is the original Covenant Maker and the only Covenant Keeper, and He asks us and inspires us to treat our marriage like the covenant it is.

When our husband-wife relationships don't go the way we originally thought they would, we tend to want to hide. But what if, in full view of the sin that exists between us, we stepped forward and shouted loud about a covenant God? What if others saw God's covenant love for us lived out in this one challenging yet freeing act of commitment: I will love my spouse the most when they deserve it the least. Try it and see what God will do.

No matter where you and your spouse have been, you can come out from the shadows of shame that have been cast by a contract marriage and step into the light of the Gospel of Jesus Christ being lived out in your home with this theme resonating daily within your heart: "Marriage is a covenant *to God* that says, "Lord, I will give *Your* best to this person, I will serve them, I will love them, I will be *Your* hands and feet in their world, even when they break their promise."

The Vows Written in Permanent Ink Contest is an opportunity to share how God's covenant love to *you* has affected your covenant to your spouse. The two couples who won the contest for *Roots Revealed* not only got the opportunity to have their first names as the characters in the story, they wanted to share a bit of their marriage testimony with you as well.

It is my pleasure to introduce to you the real-life Summer and Christian, Elizabeth and Dustin. It is their hope that their stories would give you hope for your own marriage and reveal glimpses of our covenant God's faithfulness.

Summer and Christian's Testimony

Christian and I have been married for five years so far, and though we are in no way perfect at it, we have both tried to follow God's teachings throughout our lives together. It's helped us to build a relationship based on love, respect, honesty, communication, forgiveness, and withholding blame. Allowing God to help us in our marriage has also made it possible for us to overcome difficult challenges. Through prayer and seeking God's guidance, He has led us to solutions that never would have occurred to us otherwise, causing certain issues that used to be really serious and frequent to become fewer and farther between. As Christian and I have sought God's help through our various struggles—financial, psychological, familial, etc.—God has helped us learn the right way to deal with them so they diffuse instead of build up without getting resolved.

One of the many things we have learned throughout our journey together so far is that when one or both of us are feeling overly stressed or unhealthy in some way, we are more likely to be irritable, unkind, or lose our tempers. However, we have learned through the years how damaging it is to cast blame on each other when difficult things happen or when we're feeling overwhelmed (even when it is very tempting to do just that) because it only ever turns us against each other and makes things worse. Learning that the true enemy is never each other, but rather something else, has helped us immensely. It is so important for us to always consider ourselves as being on the same team against whatever it is we're struggling with, be it excessive stress from work, lack of sleep, anxiety about finances or the future. We try to always choose love over anger or blame, especially in the moments when it is most difficult—not just when it is easy to do so. After all, Jesus loves us all the time, not just when we are "well-behaved" or having a good day. He loves us when we are at our weakest, when we mess up, even when we are struggling to be patient with others or ourselves, and He wants us to be united.

We've also learned that unkindness usually stems from feeling angry with ourselves, guilty, unworthy, or hopeless. But in our darkest moments, that is when God wants us to reach out to Him the most so He can help us. Likewise, when a spouse is experiencing one of their darkest moments, that is when God hopes we will reach out to them, too, especially if they are struggling to find the strength to reach out to Him themselves. "Charity never faileth" (1 Corinthians 13:8) is a scripture that we have come to learn is absolutely true—charity is love, and God is love (1 John 4:8). So when we try to love each other unselfishly the way God does, it invites God to work miracles in our lives. That's because love—the unselfish, pure kind that originates from God—has the power to bring out the best in us (1 Cor. 13:4–7). I have seen it time and again in my own marriage. When I decide to show kindness and love instead of reacting negatively to problems, it brings out the best in Christian and myself, which helps things to diffuse and allows us to talk to each other about solving problems rather than fight about them. After all, "a soft answer turneth away wrath" (Proverbs 15:1). The same thing happens when Christian is kind and understanding with me when I am being difficult, allowing us to work together to discuss and resolve issues instead of harbor grudges that prevent us from moving forward together. Sometimes it is hard to be the one to show love first, especially if we are not feeling well or the person we are trying to love is in a state of stress, but we have learned that it is always the right response, opening up an opportunity for God to work miracles in our relationship.

Just like a lot of things in life, marriage comes with a lot of difficulties, but with God's help, those difficulties can help us to grow into the best versions of ourselves, which I know is what God wants for all of us. Remembering the commitment we made to God and each other when we were married—to always look to God for guidance, support each other, and stay loyal to one another no matter what—has helped our relationship to grow stronger rather than weaker through life's challenges and build our relationship into something even more beautiful and rewarding than it was in the beginning. We are so grateful for what God has done for us in our marriage, and we know He wants every one of us to have deeply fulfilling relationships in our lives. He's provided us the means for us to achieve that if we reach out to Him for the guidance and strength to apply His teachings little by little, especially regarding the ways we view and treat one another.

Elizabeth and Dustin's Testimony

Marriage, something we often consider just another partnership, but what truly is partnership? I have been married to my wonderful husband going on eight years. The journey has not always been easy. In fact, it's been a roller coaster of arguments, bitterness, anger, and grudges. Good days reigned for a while and then a trail of bad days followed and we repeated this cycle. I thought this was normal and that was how it was supposed to be—I was living in the worldly view of marriage.

I never considered the fact that God had so much more for us than just "getting through another day." We know Christ as our Savior, but we live in a fallen world, and I fell for the temptation and lies of the enemy. I was not strong, I didn't know how to apply God's Word to everything like I know now. I knew that God was able to heal and change everything, but I was so hardened in my heart, I was lost, and held in bondage —I was a slave to sin.

As years went on, we became more distant because we simply were not unified in anything—this mainly fell on my part. I was selfish and we had a scoreboard marriage, not a grace-based marriage. My decisions were mine, his were his, there was not any communication.

We swept every offense and issue under a rug, but that didn't make them disappear, it just put a bandage on it until the blistering wound grew and eventually got worse. We didn't know we had roots deep within our hearts that were spreading like wildfire and allowing the enemy to use our marriage as a playground. The enemy is sneaky and has a plan, and it is well laid out so that we slowly fall into that trap without even realizing it. We think it's normal and it's just "chemical imbalances."

The enemy seeks those weaknesses to plant wedges, and I had a lot of weaknesses. I didn't realize I was being deceived and lied to. I began to isolate myself because I was comfortable there, *but* it only made me more vulnerable and this is where I heard the lies even louder and I believed them even more. I was in a spot *right* where the enemy wanted me, I was *numb*. In my isolation, I began to seek other things and people that I thought I needed or wanted. This included me thinking of what it would be like to be with someone else, how my life would be better if I just left my marriage. These lies and deception led to infidelity on my part. The Lord says "you will not be tempted more than you can handle, but in this temptation I will provide a way out." I was given many ways out, but I chose not to take them. I chose the dangerous way, which was catastrophic.

There came a day in October of 2020 that God spoke so loudly to me that I had to react. God left the ninety-nine to find the one (Matthew 18:10–14).

I reached out to a dear friend of mine and low and behold, God was already there. God was already working what was meant for evil into something *beautiful*. In all my sin and despair, He never stopped pursuing me! I wasn't a lost cause after all! Although I was terrified that I would lose my marriage over this, I knew deep down that God was in control and I trusted God, that in my obedience to confessing that He would be faithful. Jeremiah 29:11 says "'For I know the plans I have for you,' declares the LORD, 'plans to prosper you and not to harm you, plans to give you a future and a hope'" (NIV).

On October 29, 2020, I revealed all of my sins to my husband. An immediate rush of the Holy Spirit guided each of us into a journey we will never forget. We began counseling that night with David and Tracy from Vows to Keep.

God is merciful, gracious, loving and is in the business of restoring and redeeming what is broken. God took all of our broken and hopeless pieces and began putting them back together, this time, the right way, with the Word of God. Matthew 19:6 NIV says "So they are no longer two, but one flesh. What God has joined together, let no man separate." God uprooted our roots of deception, pride, anger, lust, and bitterness and replaced them with His Word and His Spirit. He rewired and rerouted our marriage. The chains that once held us captive in a "self centered marriage" have been broken, and we now live a Christ-centered marriage where freedom and forgiveness reign. We love harder, put each other first, but most important of all, we now genuinely show Christ's love to the world through our marriage because God's one and only purpose for marriage is just that. We love because Christ first loved us. We forgive because Christ has forgiven us. Our entire home structure is different because we see through the lens of Christ and not the world.

God is faithful. We trust Him even when we cannot track Him.

Isaiah 55:9 NIV says "As the Heavens are higher than the earth so are my ways higher than your ways and my thoughts higher than your thoughts."

A last note from the author:

When I read these testimonies, I hear the theme song of hope being played. No matter where your marriage is today, our God provides hope. Who or what are you putting your hope in today? Place it in our covenant God who can teach you to love the most when your spouse deserves it the least. Lean in when you feel like pulling away. Pour out even when the only one pouring into you is God. You will see the fruit of your obedience to God's Word and you will be blessed.

"The steadfast love of the LORD never ceases, his mercies never come to an end; they are new every morning; great is *your* faithfulness. 'The LORD is my portion,' says my soul, 'therefore I will hope in *him*'" (Lamentations 3:22–24 ESV, emphasis added).

For more encouragement and truth for your marriage, visit vowstokeep.com where you will grow closer to your spouse and closer to the heart of God's design for your marriage.

Going shoulder-to-shoulder with you for biblically healthy marriages,

Tracy Michelle Sellars

ONE MORE THING...

Thank you so much for reading Roots Revealed. We hope it inspired you to grow in your faith.

If you have a minute, would you consider leaving an honest review of *Roots Revealed* on your favorite book-buying platform? Every review helps others learn about this book and others we have published. You can also help spread the word about Roots Revealed by...

- Mentioning the book on social media or your blog.
- Recommending it to friends, family, your small group, book club, or co-workers.
- Picking up a copy for someone would be encouraged by this message.

And if you'd like to discover more great Christian authors, visit CrossRiverMedia.com and sign up for our weekly emails. They are full of encouragement, sneak peeks of new books and interviews with all of our great authors.

If you loved *Roots Revealed,* book 2 of the Roots Run Deep series, be sure to read *Roots Reawakened* (book 1), and coming soon, book 3 *Roots Redeemed.*

ABOUT THE AUTHOR

Tracy Sellars was born to speak the truth of God's Word to your heart. She and her husband of twenty years live in the rolling hills of Ohio with their three teenagers. Tracy can usually be found on her front porch with her computer or in the recording studio with a microphone, teaching the body of Christ how to passionately pursue both their spouse and their Savior.

She is from the beautiful Black Hills of South Dakota but has moved twenty-eight times (and she's enjoyed every one). The shortest stay was three months. The house she lives in now is the longest—eight years!

Tracy and David have owned and restored almost 100 wrecked and classic vehicles. Currently, as a family they are working on a 1941 Buick Sedanette, a 1983 Mercury Capri, a 1983 Mustang, and a 1960 VW Bug.

If Tracy could write a novel in the bathtub, she'd be one happy camper. Pick up Tracy's new historical romantic suspense novels and learn how to grow closer to your spouse and closer to the heart of God's design for your marriage at vowstokeep.com.

Discover more great fiction at
CrossRiverMedia.com

ROAD TO DEER RUN
Elaine Marie Cooper

The year is 1777 and the war has already broken the heart of nine-teen-year-old Mary Thomsen. Her brother was killed by the King's army, so when she stumbles across a wounded British soldier, she isn't sure if she should she help him or let him die, cold and alone. Severely wounded, Daniel Lowe wonders if the young woman looking down at him is an angel or the enemy. Need and compassion bring them together, but will the bitterness of war keep them apart?

SWEPT INTO DESTINY
Catherine Ulrich Brakefield

Maggie Gatlan may be a Southern belle on the outside, but is a rebel on the inside. Ben McConnell is enchanted by Maggie's beauty and fiery spirit, but for him the South represents the injustice and deprivation he left be-hind in Ireland. As the country divides and Ben joins the Union, Maggie and Ben are forced to call each other enemies. Will their love survive or die on the battlefield of South against North?

SURVIVING CARMELITA
Susan Miura

It was Josie's hands on the wheel, her foot on the pedal. Her fault. Now, sweet Carmelita will never see her fifth birthday. Where do you run when the world implodes and you can't function? Josie leaves her Chicago suburban home to stay with a cousin in Key West, unaware her journey is guided by an unseen hand. Unaware that a trailer park pastor, a battered horse, a pregnant teen, and a mysterious beachcomber might just set her on the path toward an inconceiv-able hope and redemption.

CLAIMING HER INHERITANCE
Debra L. Butterfield

A shooting, a stampede, a snakebite... Sally Clark has received an inheritance of a lifetime, but first she has to survive living on the ranch in Montana. Chase Reynolds is astounded that his father has willed one-third of their ranch to a total stranger. Who is this woman and what hold did she have over his dad? What Sally and Chase discover is beyond their imagination and wields far greater consequences than the inheritance.

Lottie's Gift

Memories,
once allowed,
are difficult
to forget.

Books that ignite your faith.

Made in the USA
Middletown, DE
30 January 2022

60007748R00139